I0823648

UNCANNY IRELAND

UNCANNY IRELAND

Otherworldly Tales of the Strange and Sublime

Edited by

MARIA GIAKANIKI

THE BRITISH LIBRARY

This collection first published in 2024 by
The British Library
96 Euston Road
London NW1 2DB

Cataloguing in Publication Data
A catalogue record for this publication is available from the British Library

ISBN 978 0 7123 5520 9

Frontispiece illustration from Henry S. Crawford, *Handbook of Carved Ornament*, Dublin: Royal Society of Antiquaries of Ireland.

Cover design by Mauricio Villamayor with illustration by Mag Ruhig. Original interior ornaments by Mag Ruhig.
Text design and typesetting by Tetragon, London
Printed in Scotland by Bell and Bain

CONTENTS

INTRODUCTION

Ireland has always stimulated the popular imagination due to its rich cultural heritage and its distinct natural landscape, but also its tumultuous past of subjugation and rebellion. Despite being at the periphery of Europe, and becoming a free state only a century ago, in 1922, Ireland has had its own unique cultural impact on the western world. It is considered a land full of myths, visions, dreams and legends that have their origins in medieval sagas and an enchanting history of paganism lost in the depths of time. Ireland fascinates contemporary readers with its unearthly tales of fairies, changelings, banshees and other folklore entities; but it is also a place that was marked by continuous political and religious conflict for centuries. Ireland's historical and cultural past, rich in its complexities, is a space where the boundaries of imagination and reality are sometimes blurred and where fantastical and real horrors merge. Yet, at the end of the day, the oral tradition and literature is that which sheds light on things that might otherwise remain less visible—if not unseen.

Pagan mythology and folktales survived in Ireland through the centuries, despite the domination of Christianity and Catholicism as well as the severe blows on Gaelic culture by the British rule since medieval times, mainly thanks to the oral tradition that remained alive: the tales and stories told among the common people, which were transferred from one generation to the next, were an important cultural thread connecting the past to the present. In mid-nineteenth-century Ireland the idea of cultural nationalism had also gained ground due to the growing need for national independence from the British; while at the turn of the century, the Celtic Revival or Celtic Twilight—a renaissance of Gaelic culture in various countries—allowed this tendency to take a more solid form. The most substantial of the Celtic Twilight movements is considered the

Irish Literary Revival, which involved not only writers promoting the idea of a distinct Irish identity but also festivals that celebrated all things Irish, such as history, music and language. This intricate web of cultural activities naturally remained inextricably linked to the wish for national sovereignty.

From the mid nineteenth century to the early 1900s, Irish intellectuals and important literary figures such as William Butler Yeats turned their attention to Irish cultural heritage. Writers such as Lady Jane Wilde and later Lady Augusta Gregory collected folktales directly from the primary source, the Irish countryside, in an effort to restore the ancient spirit of tradition.* However, apart from the collection and retellings of folktales, which were closely intertwined with the realm of phantoms, spirits and superstitious beliefs of the common people, Irish authors penned new supernatural tales, often being inspired by mythology and folklore, thus contributing to the development of the ghost story genre; a genre which already flourished in Great Britain following the line of a great tradition of Gothic literature that blended magnificently the idea of the sublime with the darkness of the human psyche.

Ireland had of course its own authors of the Gothic, with the most prominent being Charles Maturin, mainly known for the emblematic novel *Melmoth the Wanderer* (1820). A few years later other Irish writers such as Joseph Sheridan Le Fanu, who was often inspired by folklore, also employed the Gothic conventions in either urban or rural Irish settings in order to produce certain enthralling tales of mystery and the supernatural.† Yet, it seems that nineteenth-century Irish authors of weird and uncanny stories drew inspiration mainly from the countryside and life in rural areas; moreover they often focused on common people rather than

---

* Their folktales were collected in particular from the rural parts of the west where the Irish language was still spoken (and partly is still spoken today).

† The British Library has published an anthology of these stories, *The Gothic Tales of Sheridan Le Fanu*, in the same series as this volume.

the upper classes in order to write an effective spooky story that might entertain readers during a cold evening at home. Also, the supernatural horrors depicted in tales reflected, in some cases, the difficulties in real life; the Great Famine or the Great Hunger (1845–52) in Ireland was succeeded by smaller scale famines in the following decades, bringing poverty and depopulation of rural areas, further enhancing the harsh living conditions of Irish peasantry in a country that remained mostly agricultural with low living standards. In this context, the supernatural tales of the latter half of the nineteenth and the first decades of the twentieth century often portrayed an engaging blend of the invisible world and the rough reality of the common people, while at the same time they depicted ancient Irish customs and beliefs connected to the folktale tradition.

Nevertheless, in the twentieth century, Irish tales of the strange and the uncanny were further evolved and modernised; authors such as Elizabeth Bowen explored, among others, themes concerned with Anglo-Irish identity, while writers such as Dorothy Macardle employed the supernatural in order to express political anxieties during the tumultuous years of rebellion and the war of Irish Independence in the 1910s and the 1920s. From the post-war years onwards, Irish ghost stories were infused with concerns that involved the lower and middle classes and their daily lives in urban settings, thus offering new perspectives that kept up with contemporary readers.

The degree to which Irish women writers were engaged in the development of uncanny tales is given particular attention in this anthology. Whereas Charlotte Riddell, Rosa Mulholland and Elizabeth Bowen have been frequently included in genre anthologies and their own short story collections have been reprinted, *Uncanny Ireland* presents the reader with an enticing variety of texts by Irish women, from Lady Jane Wilde and Lady Augusta Gregory's mesmerising folklore retellings to eerie narratives by the lesser known Anna Maria Hall, and the poets Dora Sigerson Shorter and Katharine Tynan, whose supernatural tales have only recently been featured in anthologies of fantastic literature.

In this context, the present collection has the purpose to demonstrate a wide range of Irish tales of the Gothic and the supernatural, both chronologically and thematically. The contents are divided in different "categories" mainly for the sake of highlighting the diversity of motifs; however, this classification does not have very distinct dividing lines and there is naturally a degree of overlapping. Furthermore, the main bulk of this volume consists of tales that explore uncanny territories with the living being haunted by the dead; but there are also tales where the living are haunted by fear, love, memories and their own self, their own weaknesses and vices; tales in which even history itself becomes a ghost that cannot be escaped.

In Ireland so much can be retrieved from the depths of time, thus creating a space for new retellings and reinterpretations of myths and legends. The remnants of a pagan past combined with Catholic faith and political conflict have rendered Ireland a bewitching land for those who wish to be initiated to its mysteries, marvels, wonders and horrors; moreover, looking beyond the unworldly creatures and arcane entities, in the tales of this book we see Irish authors showing that the complexities of the human psyche, and life itself, can be a haunting source of the strange and the uncanny.

MARIA GIAKANIKI is an independent scholar and editor based in Athens, with a particular research interest in the Irish ghost story and uncanny tales by women writers. She is the co-editor of the short story anthology *Bending to Earth: Strange Stories by Irish Women*, published by Swan River Press in 2021, and the manager of the Gothic fiction publishing house Ars Nocturna.

ACKNOWLEDGEMENTS

Many thanks to Jonny Davidson for the continuous help and feedback throughout the whole process of putting this book together; and to Brian Showers for the valuable advice and access to sources and texts.

A NOTE FROM THE PUBLISHER

The original short stories reprinted in the British Library classic fiction series were written and published in a period ranging across the nineteenth and twentieth centuries. There are many elements of these stories which continue to entertain modern readers; however, in some cases there are also uses of language, instances of stereotyping and some attitudes expressed by narrators or characters which may not be endorsed by the publishing standards of today. We acknowledge therefore that some elements in the stories selected for reprinting may continue to make uncomfortable reading for some of our audience. With this series British Library Publishing aims to offer a new readership a chance to read some of the rare material of the British Library's collections in an affordable format, to enjoy their merits and to look back into the worlds of the past two centuries as portrayed by their writers. It is not possible to separate these stories from the history of their writing and as such the following stories are presented as they were originally published with minor edits only made for consistency of style and sense. We welcome feedback from our readers, which can be sent to the following address:

British Library Publishing
The British Library
96 Euston Road
London, NW1 2DB
United Kingdom

UNCANNY IRELAND

Folktales and Folk Beliefs

1887

THE EVIL EYE

Lady Jane Wilde

Lady Jane Wilde was born in 1821 in Dublin or, according to some sources, in Wexford. She was a folklorist and poet and she used the pen name "Speranza"; she was also a nationalist, advocate for women's rights and mother of Oscar Wilde (1854–1900). In her forties, she was part of a wide Dublin literary circle and hosted a renowned literary salon. Jane and her husband, Sir William Wilde (1815–1876), a surgeon and folklorist, used to collect material on Irish myths and legends. Based on their first-hand research on the oral tradition of western Ireland, Jane Wilde compiled *Ancient Legends, Mystic Charms and Superstitions of Ireland* (1887) and *Ancient Cures, Charms and Usages of Ireland* (1890), attempting to record and convey the spirit of the Irish oral tradition. After the death of her husband, she lived the latter part of her life in London where she died in 1896.

Ancient Legends, Mystic Charms and Superstitions of Ireland is Lady Jane Wilde's seminal collection of Irish folk tales adapted for the reading audience of her time. This was a common practice adopted by many late nineteenth century authors in the context of the renewed interest in Irish culture and lore brought forth by the Celtic Revival. Wilde's collection was hailed by critics as a significant and delightful piece of work on Irish oral tradition, a series of supernatural folk tales derived directly from their primary source: the Irish peasantry. The author explains in her preface that in the process of setting down those strange and eerie glimpses of lore, she even tried to maintain the exact vocabulary used by the original narrators. In this respect, "The Evil Eye" is an impressive array of different cases associated with a grim superstition that has appeared in various cultures and traditions throughout the world, with the author enhancing her primary material through her witty commentary and lively descriptions.

THERE is nothing more dreaded by the people, nor considered more deadly in its effects, than the Evil Eye.

It may strike at any moment unless the greatest precautions are taken, and even then there is no true help possible unless the fairy doctor is at once summoned to pronounce the mystic charm that can alone destroy the evil and fatal influence.

There are several modes in which the Evil Eye can act, some much more deadly than others. If certain persons are met the first thing in the morning, you will be unlucky for the whole of that day in all you do. If the evil-eyed comes in to rest, and looks fixedly on anything, on cattle or on a child, there is doom in the glance; a fatality which cannot be evaded except by a powerful counter-charm. But if the evil-eyed mutters a verse over a sleeping child, that child will assuredly die, for the incantation is of the devil, and no charm has power to resist it or turn away the evil. Sometimes the process of bewitching is effected by looking fixedly at the object, through nine fingers; especially is the magic fatal if the victim is seated by the fire in the evening when the moon is full. Therefore, to avoid being suspected of having the Evil Eye, it is necessary at once, when looking at a child, to say "God bless it." And when passing a farmyard where the cows are collected for milking, to say, "The blessing of God be on you and on all your labours." If this form is omitted, the worst results may be apprehended, and the people would be filled with terror and alarm, unless a counter-charm were not instantly employed.

The singular malific influence of a glance has been felt by most persons in life; an influence that seems to paralyse intellect and speech, simply by the mere presence in the room of some one who is mystically antipathetic to our nature. For the soul is like a fine-toned harp that vibrates to the slightest external force or movement, and the presence and glance of some persons can radiate around us a divine joy, while others may kill the soul with a sneer or a frown. We call these subtle influences mysteries, but the early races believed them to be produced by spirits, good or evil, as they acted on the nerves or the intellect.

Some years ago an old woman was living in Kerry, and it was thought so unlucky to meet her in the morning, that all the girls used to go out after sunset to bring in water for the following day, that so they might avoid her evil glance; for whatever she looked on came to loss and grief.

There was a man, also, equally dreaded on account of the strange, fatal power of his glance; and so many accidents and misfortunes were traced to his presence that finally the neighbours insisted that he should wear a black patch over the Evil Eye, not to be removed unless by request; for learned gentlemen, curious in such things, sometimes came to him to ask for a proof of his power, and he would try it for a wager while drinking with his friends.

One day, near an old ruin of a castle, he met a boy weeping in great grief for his pet pigeon, which had got up to the very top of the ruin, and could not be coaxed down.

"What will you give me," asked the man, "if I bring it down for you?"

"I have nothing to give," said the boy, "but I will pray to God for you. Only get me back my pigeon, and I shall be happy."

Then the man took off the black patch and looked up steadfastly at the bird; when all of a sudden it fell to the ground and lay motionless, as if stunned; but there was no harm done to it, and the boy took it up and went his way, rejoicing.

A woman in the County Galway had a beautiful child, so handsome, that all the neighbours were very careful to say "God bless it" when they saw him, for they knew the fairies would desire to steal the child, and carry it off to the hills.

But one day it chanced that an old woman, a stranger, came in. "Let me rest," she said, "for I am weary." And she sat down and looked at the child, but never said "God bless it." And when she had rested, she rose up, looked again at the child fixedly, in silence, and then went her way.

All that night the child cried and would not sleep. And all next day it moaned as if in pain. So the mother told the priest, but he would do nothing for fear of the fairies. And just as the poor mother was in despair, she saw a strange woman going by the door. "Who knows," she said to her husband, "but this woman would help us." So they asked her to come in and rest. And when she looked at the child she said "God bless it," instantly, and spat three times at it, and then sat down.

"Now, what will you give me," she said, "if I tell you what ails the child?"

"I will cross your hand with silver," said the mother, "as much as you want, only speak," and she laid the money on the woman's hand. "Now tell me the truth, for the sake and in the name of Mary, and the good Angels."

"Well," said the stranger, "the fairies have had your child these two days in the hills, and this is a changeling they have left in its place. But so many blessings were said on your child that the fairies can do it no harm. For there was only one blessing wanting, and only one person gave the Evil Eye. Now, you must watch for this woman, carry her into the house and secretly cut off a piece of her cloak. Then burn the piece close to the child, till the smoke as it rises makes him sneeze; and when this happens the spell is broken, and your own child will come back to you safe and sound, in place of the changeling."

Then the stranger rose up and went her way.

All that evening the mother watched for the old woman, and at last she spied her on the road.

"Come in," she cried, "come in, good woman, and rest, for the cakes are hot on the griddle, and supper is ready."

So the woman came in, but never said "God bless you kindly," to man or mortal, only scowled at the child, who cried worse than ever.

Now the mother had told her eldest girl to cut off a piece of the old woman's cloak, secretly, when she sat down to eat. And the girl did as she was desired, and handed the piece to her mother, unknown to any one. But, to their surprise, this was no sooner done than the woman rose up and went out without uttering a word; and they saw her no more.

Then the father carried the child outside, and burned the piece of cloth before the door, and held the boy over the smoke till he sneezed three times violently: after which he gave the child back to the mother, who laid him in his bed, where he slept peacefully, with a smile on his face, and cried no more with the cry of pain. And when he woke up the mother knew that she had got her own darling child back from the fairies, and no evil thing happened to him any more.

The influence of the mysterious and malign power of the Evil Eye has at all times been as much dreaded in Ireland as it is in Egypt, Greece, or Italy at the present day. Everything young, beautiful, or perfect after its kind, and which naturally attracts attention and admiration, is peculiarly liable to the fatal blight that follows the glance of the Evil Eye. It is therefore an invariable habit amongst the peasantry never to praise anything without instantly adding, "God bless it;" for were this formula omitted, the worst consequences would befall the object praised.

The superstition must be of great antiquity in Ireland, for Balor, the Fomorian giant and hero, is spoken of in an ancient manuscript as able to petrify his enemies by a glance; and how he became possessed of the power is thus narrated:—

One day as the Druids were busy at their incantations, while boiling a magical spell or charm, young Balor passed by, and curious to see their work, looked in at an open window. At that moment the Druids happened to raise the lid of the caldron, and the vapour, escaping, passed under one of Balor's eyes, carrying with it all the venom of the incantation. This caused his brow to grow to such a size that it required four men to raise it whenever he wanted to exert the power of his venomed glance over his enemies. He was slain at last in single combat, according to the ancient legend, at the great battle of Magh-Tura* (the plain of the towers), fought between the Firbolgs and the Tuatha-de-Danaanns for the possession of Ireland several centuries before the Christian era; for before Balor's brow could be lifted so that he could transfix his enemy and strike him dead with the terrible power of his glance, his adversary flung a stone with such violence that it went right through the Evil Eye, and pierced the skull, and the mighty magician fell to rise no more.

An interesting account of this battle, with a remarkable confirmation of the legends respecting it still current in the district, is given by Sir William Wilde, in his work, "Lough Corrib; its Shores and Islands." In the ancient manuscript, it is recorded that a young hero having been slain while bravely defending his king, the Firbolg army erected a mound over him, each man carrying a stone, and the monument was henceforth known as the *Carn-in-en-Fhir* (the cairn of the one man). Having examined the locality with a transcript of this manuscript in his hand, Sir William fixed on the particular mound, amongst the many stone tumuli scattered over the plain, which seemed to agree best with the description, and had it opened carefully under his own superintendence.

A large flag-stone was first discovered, laid horizontally; then another beneath it, covering a small square chamber formed of stones, within which was *a single urn* of baked clay, graceful and delicate in form and ornamentation, containing incinerated human bones, the remains, there can be no reason to doubt, of the Firbolg youth who was honoured for his loyalty by the erection over him of the *Carn-in-en-Fhir* on the historic plains of Mayo.

After Balor, the only other ancient instance of the fatal effects of the malific Eye is narrated of St Silan, who had a poisonous hair in his eye-brow that killed whoever looked first on him in the morning. All persons,

* Now called Moytura

therefore, who from long sickness, or sorrow, or the weariness that comes with years, were tired of life, used to try and come in the saint's way, that so their sufferings might be ended by a quick and easy death. But another saint, the holy Molaise, hearing that St Silan was coming to visit his church, resolved that no more deaths should happen by means of the poisoned hair. So he arose early in the morning, before any one was up, and went forth alone to meet St Silan, and when he saw him coming along the path, he went boldly up and plucked out the fatal hair from his eyebrow, but in doing so he himself was struck by the venom, and immediately after fell down dead.

The power of the Evil Eye was recognised by the Brehon laws, and severe measures were ordained against the users of the malign influence. "If a person is in the habit of injuring things through neglect, or of will, whether he has blessed, or whether he has not blessed, full penalty be upon him, or restitution in kind." So ran the ancient law.

The gift comes by nature and is born with one, though it may not be called into exercise unless circumstances arise to excite the power. Then it seems to act like a spirit of bitter and malicious envy that radiates a poisonous atmosphere which chills and blights everything within its reach. Without being superstitious every one has felt that there is such a power and succumbed to its influence in a helpless, passive way, as if all self-trust and self-reliant energy were utterly paralysed by its influence.

Suspected persons are held in great dread by the peasantry, and they recognise them at once by certain signs. Men and women with dark lowering eyebrows are especially feared, and the handsome children are kept out of their path lest they might be overlooked by them.

Red hair is supposed to have a most malign influence, and it has even passed into a proverb: "Let not the eye of a red-haired woman rest on you."

Many persons are quite unconscious that their glance or frown has this evil power until some calamity results, and then they strive not to look at any one full in the face, but to avert their eyes when speaking, lest misfortune might fall upon the person addressed.*

The saving invocation, "God bless it!" is universally used when praise is bestowed, to prevent danger, and should a child fall sick some one is immediately suspected of having omitted the usual phrase out of malice and ill-will. Nothing is more dreaded by the peasantry than the full, fixed, direct glance of one suspected of the Evil Eye, and should it fall upon them, or on any of their household, a terrible fear and trembling of heart takes possession of them, which often ends in sickness or sometimes even in death.

Some years ago a woman living in Kerry declared that she was "overlooked" by the Evil Eye. She had no pleasure in her life and no comfort, and she wasted away because of the fear that was on her, caused by the following singular circumstance:—

Every time that she happened to leave home alone, and that no one was within call, she was met by a woman totally unknown to her, who, fixing her eyes on her in silence, with a terrible expression, cast her to the ground and proceeded to beat and pinch her till she was nearly senseless; after which her tormentor disappeared.

Having experienced this treatment several times, the poor woman finally abstained altogether from leaving the house, unless protected by a servant or companion; and this precaution she observed for several years, during which time she never was molested. So at last she began to believe that the spell was broken, and that her strange enemy had departed for ever.

In consequence she grew less careful about the usual precaution, and one day stepped down alone to a little stream that ran by the house to wash some clothes.

Stooping down over her work, she never thought of any danger, and began to sing as she used to do in the light-hearted days before the spell

* There is a strange idea current in Europe at the present time that one of the most remarkable potentates now living has this fatal gift and power of the Evil Eye.

was on her, when suddenly a dark shadow fell across the water, and looking up, she beheld to her horror the strange woman on the opposite side of the little stream, with her terrible eyes intently fixed on her, as hard and still as if she were of stone.

Springing up with a scream of terror, she flung down her work, and ran towards the house; but soon she heard footsteps behind her, and in an instant she was seized, thrown down to the ground, and her tormentor began to beat her even worse than before, till she lost all consciousness; and in this state she was found by her husband, lying on her face and speechless. She was at once carried to the house, and all the care that affection and rural skill could bestow were lavished on her, but in vain. She, however, regained sufficient consciousness to tell them of the terrible encounter she had gone through, but died before the night had passed away.

It was believed that the power of fascination by the glance, which is not necessarily an evil power like the Evil Eye, was possessed in a remarkable degree by learned and wise people, especially poets, so that they could make themselves loved and followed by any girl they liked, simply by the influence of the glance. About the year 1790, a young man resided in the County Limerick, who had this power in a singular and unusual degree. He was a clever, witty rhymer in the Irish language; and, probably, had the deep poet eyes that characterise warm and passionate poet-natures—eyes that even without necromancy have been known to exercise a powerful magnetic influence over female minds.

One day, while travelling far from home, he came upon a bright, pleasant-looking farmhouse, and feeling weary, he stopped and requested a drink of milk and leave to rest. The farmer's daughter, a young, handsome girl, not liking to admit a stranger, as all the maids were churning, and she was alone in the house, refused him admittance.

The young poet fixed his eyes earnestly on her face for some time in silence, then slowly turning round left the house, and walked towards a small grove of trees just opposite. There he stood for a few moments resting against a tree, and facing the house as if to take one last vengeful or admiring glance, then went his way without once turning round.

The young girl had been watching him from the windows, and the moment he moved she passed out of the door like one in a dream, and followed him slowly, step by step, down the avenue. The maids grew alarmed, and called to her father, who ran out and shouted loudly for her to stop, but she never turned or seemed to heed. The young man, however, looked round, and seeing the whole family in pursuit, quickened his pace, first glancing fixedly at the girl for a moment. Immediately she sprang towards him, and they were both almost out of sight, when one of the maids espied a piece of paper tied to a branch of the tree where the poet had rested. From curiosity she took it down, and the moment the knot was untied, the farmer's daughter suddenly stopped, became quite still, and when her father came up she allowed him to lead her back to the house without resistance.

When questioned, she said that she felt herself drawn by an invisible force to follow the young stranger wherever he might lead, and that she would have followed him through the world, for her life seemed to be bound up in his; she had no will to resist, and was conscious of nothing else but his presence. Suddenly, however, the spell was broken, and then she heard her father's voice, and knew how strangely she had acted. At the same time the power of the young man over her vanished, and the impulse to follow him was no longer in her heart.

The paper, on being opened, was found to contain five mysterious words written in blood, and in this order—

SATOR
AREPO
TENET
OPERA
ROTAS

These letters are so arranged that read in any way, right to left, left to right, up or down, the same words are produced; and when written in blood with a pen made of an eagle's feather, they form a charm which no woman (it is said) can resist; but the incredulous reader can easily test the truth of this assertion for himself.

1920

THE UNQUIET DEAD

Lady Augusta Gregory

Lady Augusta Gregory (1852–1932) was a dramatist, folklorist and dominant figure of the Celtic Revival. She was descended from an aristocratic Anglo-Irish family but in her later life she distanced herself from the British rule by becoming a fervent Irish nationalist. After her husband's death in 1892, she took an interest in the enthralling world of Irish myths and legends by collecting all the bits and pieces of oral tradition she could discover and writing them down for an urban readership. William Butler Yeats's collection *The Celtic Twilight* published in 1893 may have inspired her to further explore the folk tradition that shaped the distinct features of Irish culture. Moreover it was with Yeats that she co-founded the Abbey, Ireland's national theatre; her plays staged there were often infused with the invisible and the hereafter, the fairy realm and the phantom worlds of Irish lore.

While Lady Gregory's early volumes *Gods and Fighting Men* (1904) and *A Book of Saints and Wonders* (1906) focused on Irish mythology as well as legends associated with the lives of saints, in *Visions and Beliefs in the West of Ireland* (1920) she attempted to depict the wonderful strangeness of superstitious beliefs and pagan remnants of the rural population of Ireland's west. "The Unquiet Dead" consists of a series of first person narratives of common people about their own spectral encounters and macabre experiences, exposing a wide spectrum of metaphysical perceptions about the afterlife. In her short preface to "The Unquiet Dead", Lady Gregory highlights the pre-Christian notions about life and death that still lingered within the Irish, thus showcasing their perpetual connection to ancient myths and legends. At the same time this fragmented yet fascinating narrative is distinguished by a sense of authenticity and intended lack of refinement, implying that its primary material remained mostly "unpolished" and unadulterated by the author.

A GOOD many years ago when I was but beginning my study of the folklore of belief, I wrote somewhere that if by an impossible miracle every trace and memory of Christianity could be swept out of the world, it would not shake or destroy at all the belief of the people of Ireland in the invisible world, the cloud of witnesses, in immortality and the life to come. For them the veil between things seen and unseen has hardly thickened since those early days of the world when the sons of God mated with the daughters of men; when angels spoke with Abraham in Hebron or with Columcille in the oakwoods of Derry, or when as an old man at my own gate told me they came and visited the Fianna, the old heroes of Ireland, "because they were so nice and so respectable." Ireland has through the centuries kept continuity of vision, the vision it is likely all nations possessed in the early days of faith. Here in Connacht there is no doubt as to the continuance of life after death. The spirit wanders for a while in that intermediate region to which mystics and theologians have given various names, and should it return and become visible those who loved it will not be afraid, but will, as I have already told, put a light in the window to guide the mother home to her child, or go out into the barley gardens in the hope of meeting a son. And if the message brought seems hardly worth the hearing, we may call to mind what Frederic Myers wrote of more instructed ghosts:

"If it was absurd to listen to Kepler because he bade the planets move in no perfect circles but in undignified ellipses, because he hastened and slackened from hour to hour what ought to be a heavenly body's ideal and unwavering speed; is it not absurder still to refuse to listen to these voices from afar, because they come stammering and wandering as in a dream confusedly instead of with a trumpet's call? Because spirits that bending to earth may undergo perhaps an earthly bewilderment and suffer unknown limitations, and half remember and half forget?"

And should they give the message more clearly who knows if it would be welcome? For the old Scotch story goes that when S. Columcille's brother Dobhran rose up from his grave and said, "Hell is not so bad as people say," the Saint cried out, "Clay, clay on Dobhran!" before he could tell any more.

I was told by Mrs Dennehy:

Those that mind the teaching of the clergy say the dead go to Limbo first and then to Purgatory and then to hell or to heaven. Hell is always burning and if you go there you never get out; but those that mind the old people don't believe, and I don't believe, that there is any hell. I don't believe God Almighty would make Christians to put them into hell afterwards.

It is what the old people say, that after death the shadow goes wandering, and the soul is weak, and the body is taking a rest. The shadow wanders for a while and it pays the debts it had to pay, and when it is free it puts out wings and flies to Heaven.

An Aran Man:

There was an old man died, and after three days he appeared in the cradle as a baby; they knew him by an old look in his face, and his face being long and other things. An old woman that came into the house saw him, and she said, "He won't be with you long, he had three deaths to die, and this is the second," and sure enough he died at the end of six years.

Mrs Martin:

There was a man beyond when I lived at Ballybron, and it was said of him that he was taken away—up before God Almighty. But the blessed Mother asked for grace for him for a year and a day. So he got it. I seen him myself, and many seen him, and at the end of the year and a day he died. And that man ought to be happy now anyway. When my own poor little girl was drowned in the well, I never could sleep but fretting, fretting, fretting. But one day when one of my little boys was taking his turn to serve the Mass he stopped on his knees without getting up. And Father Boyle asked him what did he see and he looking up. And he told him that he could see his little sister in the presence of God, and she shining like the sun. Sure enough that was a vision He had sent to comfort us. So from that day I never cried nor fretted any more.

A Herd:

Do you believe Roland Joyce was seen? Well, he was. A man I know told me he saw him the night of his death, in Esserkelly where he had a farm, and a man along with him going through the stock. And all of a sudden a train came into the field, and brought them both away like a blast of wind.

And as for old Parsons Persse of Castleboy, there's thousands of people has seen him hunting at night with his horses and his hounds and his bugle blowing. There's no mistake at all about him being there.

An Aran Woman:

There was a girl in the middle island had died, and when she was being washed, and a priest in the house, there flew by the window the whitest bird that ever was seen. And the priest said to the father: "Do not lament, unless what you like, your child's happy for ever!"

Mrs Casey:

Near the strand there were two little girls went out to gather cow-dung. And they sat down beside a bush to rest themselves, and there they heard a groan coming from under the ground. So they ran home as fast as they could. And they were told when they went again to bring a man with them.

So the next time they went they brought a man with them, and they hadn't been sitting there long when they heard the saddest groan that ever you heard. So the man bent down and asked what was it. And a voice from below said, "Let some one shave me and get me out of this, for I was never shaved after dying." So the man went away, and the next day he brought soap and all that was needful and there he found a body lying laid out on the grass. So he shaved it, and with that wings came and carried it up to high heaven.

A Chimney-sweep:

I don't believe in all I hear, or I'd believe in ghosts and faeries, with all the old people telling you stories about them and the priests believing in them too. Surely the priests believe in ghosts, and tell you that they are souls that died in trouble. But I have been about the country night and day, and I remember when I used to have to put my hand out at the top of every chimney in Coole House; and I seen or felt nothing to frighten me, except one night two rats caught in a trap at Roxborough; and the old butler came down and beat me with a belt for the scream I gave at that. But if I believed in any one coming back, it would be in what you often hear, of a mother coming back to care for her child.

And there's many would tell you that every time you see a tree shaking there's a ghost in it.

Old Lambert of Dangan was a terror for telling stories; he told me long ago how he was near the Piper's gap on Ballybrit race-course, and he saw one riding to meet him, and it was old Michael Lynch of Ballybrista, that was dead long before, and he never would go on the race-course again. And he had heard the car with headless horses driving through Loughrea. From every part they are said to drive, and the place they are all going to is Benmore, near Loughrea, where there is a ruined dwelling-house and an old forth. And at Mount Mahon a herd told me the other day he often saw old Andrew Mahon riding about at night. But if I was a herd and saw that I'd hold my tongue about it.

Mrs Casey:

At the graveyard of Drumacoo often spirits do be seen. Old George Fitzgerald is seen by many. And when they go up to the stone he's sitting on, he'll be sitting somewhere else.

There was a man walking in the wood near there, and he met a woman, a stranger, and he said "Is there anything I can do for you?" For he thought she was some country-woman gone astray. "There is," says she. "Then come home with me," says he, "and tell me about it." "I can't do that," says she, "but what you can do is this, go tell my friends I'm in great trouble, for twenty times in my life I missed going to church, and they must say twenty Masses for me now to deliver me, but they seem to have forgotten me. And another thing is," says she, "there's some small debts I left and they're not paid, and those are helping to keep me in trouble." Well, the man went on and he didn't know what in the world to do, for he couldn't know who she was, for they are not permitted to tell their name. But going about visiting at country houses he used to tell the story, and at last it came out she was one of the Shannons. For at a house he was telling it at they remembered that an old woman they had, died a year ago, and that she used to be running up little debts unknown to them.

So they made inquiry at Findlater's and at another shop that's done away with now, and they found that sure enough she had left some small debts, not more than ten shillings in each, and when she died no more had been said about it. So they paid these and said the Masses, and shortly after she appeared to the man again. "God bless you now," she said, "for what you did for me, for now I'm at peace."

A Tinker's Daughter:

I heard of what happened to a family in the town. One night a thing that looked like a goose came in. And when they said nothing to it, it went away up the stairs with a noise like lead. Surely if they had questioned it, they'd have found it to be some soul in trouble.

And there was another soul came back that was in trouble because of a ha'porth of salt it owed.

And there was a priest was in trouble and appeared after death, and they had to say Masses for him, because he had done some sort of a crime on a widow.

Mrs Farley:

One time myself I was at Killinan, at a house of the Clancys' where the father and mother had died, but it was well known they often come to look after the children. I was walking with another girl through the fields there one evening and I looked up and saw a tall woman dressed all in black, with a mantle of some sort, a wide one, over her head, and the waves of the wind were blowing it off her, so that I could hear the noise of it. All her clothes were black, and had the appearance of being new. And I asked the other girl did she see her, and she said she did not. For two that are together can never see such things, but only one of them. So when I heard she saw nothing I ran as if for my life, and the woman seemed to be coming after me, till I crossed a running stream and she had no power to cross that. And one time my brother was stopping in the same house, and one night about twelve o'clock there came a smell in the house like as if all the dead people were there. And one of the girls whose father and mother had died got up out of her bed, and began to put her clothes on, and they had to lock the doors to stop her from going away out of the house.

There was a woman I knew of that after her death was kept for seven years in a tree in Kinadyfe, and for seven years after that she was kept under the arch of the little bridge beyond Kilchriest, with the water running under her. And whether there was frost or snow she had no shelter from it, not so much as the size of a leaf.

At the end of the second seven years she came to her husband, and he passing the bridge on the way home from Loughrea, and when he felt her near him he was afraid, and he didn't stop to question her, but hurried on.

So then she came in the evening to the house of her own little girl. But she was afraid when she saw her, and fell down in a faint. And the woman's sister's child was in the house, and when the little girl told her what she saw, she said "You must surely question her when she comes again." So she came again that night, but the little girl was afraid again when she saw her and said nothing. But the third night when she came the sister's child, seeing her own little girl was afraid, said "God bless you, God bless you." And with that the woman spoke and said "God bless you for saying that." And then she told her all that had happened her and where she had been all the fourteen years. And she took out of her dress a black silk handkerchief and said: "I took that from my husband's neck the day I met him on the road from Loughrea, and this very night I would have killed him, because he hurried away and would not stop to help me, but now that you have helped me I'll not harm him. But bring with you to Kilmacduagh, to the graveyard, three cross sticks with wool on them, and three glasses full of salt, and have three Masses said for me; and I'll appear to you when I am at rest." And so she did; and it was for no great thing she had done that trouble had been put upon her.

John Cloran:

That house with no roof was made a hospital of in the famine, and many died there. And one night my father was passing by and he saw some one standing all in white, and two men beside him, and he thought he knew one of the men and spoke to him and said "Is that you, Martin?" but he never spoke nor moved. And as to the thing in white, he could not say was it man or woman, but my father never went by that place again at night.

The last person buried in a graveyard has the care of all the other souls until another is to be buried, and then the soul can go and shift for itself. It may be a week or a month or a year, but watch the place it must till another soul comes.

There was a man used to be giving short measure, not giving the full yard, and one time after his death there was a man passing the river and the horse he had would not go into it. And he heard the voice of the tailor saying from the river he had a message to send to his wife, and to tell her not to be giving short measure, or she would be sent to the same place as himself. There was a hymn made about that.

There was a woman lived in Rathkane, alone in the house, and she told me that one night something came and lay over the bed and gave three great moans. That was all ever she heard in the house.

The shadows of the dead gather round at Samhain time to see is there any one among their friends saying a few Masses for them.

An Islander:

Down there near the point, on the 6th of March, 1883, there was a curragh upset and five boys were drowned. And a man from County Clare told me that he was on the coast that day, and that he saw them walking towards him on the Atlantic.

There is a house down there near the sea, and one day the woman of it was sitting by the fire, and a little girl came in at the door, and a red cloak about her, and she sat down by the fire. And the woman asked her where did she come from, and she said that she had just come from Connemara. And then she went out, and when she was going out the door she made herself known to her sister that was standing in it, and she called out to the mother. And when the mother knew it was the child she had lost near a year before, she ran out to call her, for she wouldn't for all the world to have not known her when she was there. But she was gone and she never came again.

There was this boy's father took a second wife, and he was walking home one evening, and his wife behind him, and there was a great wind blowing, and he kept his head stooped down because of the seaweed coming blowing into his eyes. And she was about twenty paces behind, and she saw his first wife come and walk close beside him, and he never saw her, having his head down, but she kept with him near all the way. And when they got home, she told the husband who was with him, and with the fright she got she was bad in her bed for two or three days—do you remember that, Martin? She died after, and he has a third wife taken now.

I believe all that die are brought among them, except maybe an odd old person.

A Kildare Woman:

There was a woman I knew sent into the Rotunda Hospital for an operation. And when she was going she cried when she was saying goodbye to her cousin that was a friend of mine, for she felt in her that she would not come back again. And she put her two arms about her going away and said, "If the dead can do any good thing for the living, I'll do it for you." And she never recovered, but died in the hospital. And within a few weeks something came on her cousin, my friend, and they said it was her side that was paralysed, and she died. And many said it was no common illness, but that it was the dead woman that had kept to her word.

A Connemara Man:

There was a boy in New York was killed by rowdies, they killed him standing against a lamppost and he was frozen to it, and stood there till morning. And it is often since that time he was seen in the room and the passages of the house where he used to be living.

And in the house beyond a woman died, and some other family came to live in it; but every night she came back and stripped the clothes off them, so at last they went away.

When some one goes that owes money, the weight of the soul is more than the weight of the body, and it can't get away and keeps wandering till some one has courage to question it.

Mrs Casey:

My grandmother told my mother that in her time at Cloughballymore, there was a woman used to appear in the churchyard of Rathkeale, and that many boys and girls and children died with the fright they got when they saw her.

So there was a gentleman living near was very sorry for all the children dying, and he went to an old woman to ask her was there any way to do away with the spirit that appeared. So she said if any one would have courage to go and to question it, he could do away with it. So the gentleman went at midnight and waited at the churchyard, and he on his horse, and had a sword with him. So presently the shape appeared and he called to it and said, "Tell me what you are?" And it came over to him, and when he saw the face he got such a fright that he turned the horse's head and galloped away as hard as he could. But after galloping a long time he looked down and what did he see beside him but the woman running and her hand on the horse. So he took his sword and gave a slash at her, and cut through her arm, so that she gave a groan and vanished, and he went on home.

And when he got to the stable and had the lantern lighted, you may think what a start he got when he saw the hand still holding on to the horse, and no power could lift it off. So he went into the house and said his prayers to Almighty God to take it off. And all night long, he could hear moaning and crying about the house. And in the morning when he went out the hand was gone, but all the stable was splashed with blood. But the woman was never seen in those parts again.

A Seaside Man:

And many see the faeries at Knock and there was a carpenter died, and he could be heard all night in his shed making coffins and carts and all sorts of things, and the people are afraid to go near it. There were four boys from Knock drowned five years ago, and often now they are seen walking on the strand and in the fields and about the village.

There was a man used to go out fowling, and one day his sister said to him, "Whatever you do don't go out tonight and don't shoot any wild-duck or any birds you see flying—for tonight they are all poor souls travelling."

An Old Man in Galway Workhouse:

Burke of Carpark's son died, but he used often to be seen going about afterwards. And one time a herd of his father's met with him and he said, "Come tonight and help us against the hurlers from the north, for they have us beat twice, and if they beat us a third time, it will be a bad year for Ireland."

It was in the daytime they had the hurling match through the streets of Galway. No one could see them, and no one could go outside the door while it lasted, for there went such a whirlwind through the town that you could not look through the window.

And he sent a message to his father that he would find some paper he was looking for a few days before, behind a certain desk, between it and the wall, and the father found it there. He would not have believed it was his son the herd met only for that.

A Munster Woman:

I have only seen them myself like dark shadows, but there's many can see them as they are. Surely they bring away the dead among them.

There was a woman in County Limerick that died after her baby being born. And all the people were in the house when the funeral was to be, crying for her. And the cars and the horses were out on the road. And there was seen among them a carriage full of ladies, and with them the woman was sitting that they were crying for, and the baby with her, and it dressed.

And there was another woman I knew of died, and left a family, and often after, the people saw her in their dreams, and always in rich clothes, though all the clothes she had were given away after she died, for the good of her soul, except maybe her shawl. And her husband married a serving girl after that, and she was hard to the children, and one night the woman came back to her, and had like to throw her out of the window in her nightdress, till she gave a promise to treat the children well, and she was afraid not to treat them well after that.

There was a farmer died and he had done some man out of a saddle, and he came back after to a friend, and gave him no rest till he gave a new saddle to the man he had cheated.

Mrs Casey:

There was a woman my brother told me about and she had a daughter that was red-haired. And the girl got married when she was under twenty, for the mother had no man to tend the land, so she thought best to let her go. And after her baby being born, she never got strong but stopped in the bed, and a great many doctors saw her but did her no good.

And one day the mother was at Mass at the chapel and she got a start, for she thought she saw her daughter come in to the chapel with the same shawl and clothes on her that she had before she took to the bed, but when they came out from the chapel, she wasn't there. So she went to the house, and asked was she after going out, and what they told her was as if she got a blow, for they said the girl hadn't ten minutes to live, and she was dead before ten minutes were out. And she appears now sometimes; they see her drawing water from the well at night and bringing it into the house, but they find nothing there in the morning.

A Connemara Man:

There was a man had come back from Boston, and one day he was out in the bay, going towards Aran with £3 worth of cable he was after getting from McDonagh's store in Galway. And he was steering the boat, and there were two turf-boats along with him, and all in a minute they saw he was gone, swept off the boat with a wave and it a dead calm.

And they saw him come up once, straight up as if he was pushed, and then he was brought down again and rose no more.

And it was some time after that a friend of his in Boston, and that was coming home to this place, was in a crowd of people out there. And he saw him coming to him and he said, "I heard that you were drowned," and the man said, "I am not dead, but I was brought here, and when you go home, bring these three guineas to McDonagh in Galway for it's owed him for the cable I got from him." And he put the three guineas in his hand and vanished away.

An Old Army Man:

I have seen hell myself. I had a sight of it one time in a vision. It had a very high wall around it, all of metal, and an archway in the wall, and a straight walk into it, just like what would be leading into a gentleman's orchard, but the edges were not trimmed with box but with red-hot metal. And inside the wall there were cross walks, and I'm not sure what there was to the right, but to the left there was five great furnaces and they full of souls kept there with great chains. So I turned short and went away; and in turning I looked again at the wall and I could see no end to it.

And another time I saw purgatory. It seemed to be in a level place and no walls around it, but it all one bright blaze, and the souls standing in it.

And they suffer near as much as in hell, only there are no devils with them there, and they have the hope of heaven.

And I heard a call to me from there "Help me to come out of this!" And when I looked it was a man I used to know in the army, an Irishman and from this country, and I believe him to be a descendant of King O'Connor of Athenry. So I stretched out my hand first but then I called out "I'd be burned in the flames before I could get within three yards of you." So then he said, "Well, help me with your prayers," and so I do.

Myths and Legends Reimagined

1897

THE CURSE OF THE FIRES AND OF THE SHADOWS

William Butler Yeats

William Butler Yeats (1865–1939), who won the Nobel Prize for Literature in 1923, is regarded as one of the great pillars of Irish literature mainly due to his illustrious poetical works. He was one of the leading voices of the Irish Literary Revival and the Celtic Twilight, and wishing to give prominence to Celtic culture, he founded with the like-minded the Irish Literary Society in London and the National Literary Society in Dublin.

Born in an artistic family, he was educated in both England and Ireland. His interest in occultism and esotericism incited him to associate initially with Dublin's Theosophical Society and the Hermetic Order of the Golden Dawn in London in the 1890's, while in 1911 he joined the Ghost Club, a paranormal research society that held séances and investigated "haunted houses". His perspective on life and literature was inextricably linked to the invisible and the unearthly world and his poetry and theatrical plays often drew on the entrancing realm of Irish folklore. He edited *Fairy and Folk Tales of the Irish Peasantry* (1888) and *Irish Fairy Tales* (1892), popular volumes of folk tales and legends, while his collection of short tales and fables *Celtic Twilight* (1893) and the uncanny mystical stories of *The Secret Rose* (1897) are among his most significant literary endeavours into the fantastic and the supernatural.

In "The Curse of the Fires and of the Shadows" included in *The Secret Rose,* Yeats features the "sidhe", an entity in Irish mythology similar to elves and fairies, and brings into being a bleak narrative of death and despair during the Irish Confederate Wars of the seventeenth century. This ominous tale of otherworldly atmosphere and unparalleled imagery is an alluring amalgam of ancient myth and history.

ONE summer night, when there was peace, a score of Puritan troopers under the pious Sir Frederick Hamilton, broke through the door of the Abbey of the White Friars which stood over the Gara Lough at Sligo. As the door fell with a crash they saw a little knot of friars, gathered about the altar, their white habits glimmering in the steady light of the holy candles. All the monks were kneeling except the abbot, who stood upon the altar steps with a great brazen crucifix in his hand. "Shoot them!" cried Sir Frederick Hamilton, but none stirred, for all were new converts, and feared the crucifix and the holy candles. The white lights from the altar threw the shadows of the troopers up on to roof and wall. As the troopers moved about, the shadows began a fantastic dance among the corbels and the memorial tablets. For a little while all was silent, and then five troopers who were the body-guard of Sir Frederick Hamilton lifted their muskets, and shot down five of the friars. The noise and the smoke drove away the mystery of the pale altar lights, and the other troopers took courage and began to strike. In a moment the friars lay about the altar steps, their white habits stained with blood. "Set fire to the house!" cried Sir Frederick Hamilton, and at his word one went out, and came in again carrying a heap of dry straw, and piled it against the western wall, and, having done this, fell back, for the fear of the crucifix and of the holy candles was still in his heart. Seeing this, the five troopers who were Sir Frederick Hamilton's body-guard darted forward, and taking each a holy candle set the straw in a blaze. The red tongues of fire rushed up and flickered from corbel to corbel and from tablet to tablet, and crept along the floor, setting in a blaze the seats and benches. The dance of the shadows passed away, and the dance of the fires began.

The troopers fell back towards the door in the southern wall, and watched those yellow dancers springing hither and thither.

For a time the altar stood safe and apart in the midst of its white light; the eyes of the troopers turned upon it. The abbot whom they had thought dead had risen to his feet and now stood before it with the crucifix lifted in both hands high above his head. Suddenly he cried with a loud voice, "Woe unto all who smite those who dwell within the Light of the Lord, for they shall wander among the ungovernable shadows, and follow the ungovernable fires!" And having so cried he fell on his face dead, and the brazen crucifix rolled down the steps of the altar. The smoke had now grown very thick, so that it drove the troopers out into the open air. Before them were burning houses. Behind them shone the painted windows of the Abbey filled with saints and martyrs, awakened, as from a sacred trance, into an angry and animated life. The eyes of the troopers were dazzled, and for a while could see nothing but the flaming faces of saints and martyrs. Presently, however, they saw a man covered with dust who came running towards them. "Two messengers," he cried, "have been sent by the defeated Irish to raise against you the whole country about Manor Hamilton, and if you do not stop them you will be overpowered in the woods before you reach home again! They ride north-east between Ben Bulben and Cashel-na-Gael."

Sir Frederick Hamilton called to him the five troopers who had first fired upon the monks and said, "Mount quickly, and ride through the woods towards the mountain, and get before these men, and kill them."

In a moment the troopers were gone, and before many moments they had splashed across the river at what is now called Buckley's Ford, and plunged into the woods. They followed a beaten track that wound along the northern bank of the river. The boughs of the birch and quicken trees mingled above, and hid the cloudy moonlight, leaving the pathway in almost complete darkness. They rode at a rapid trot, now chatting together, now watching some stray weasel or rabbit scuttling away in the darkness. Gradually, as the gloom and silence of the woods oppressed them, they drew closer together, and began to talk rapidly; they were old comrades and knew each other's lives. One was married, and told how glad his wife would be to see him return safe from this harebrained expedition against the White Friars, and to hear how fortune had made amends for rashness. The oldest of the five, whose wife was dead, spoke of a flagon of wine which awaited him upon an upper shelf; while a third, who was the youngest, had a sweetheart watching for his return, and he rode a little way before the others, not talking at all. Suddenly the young man stopped, and they saw that his horse was trembling. "I saw something," he said, "and yet I do not know but it may have been one of the shadows. It looked like a great worm with a silver crown upon his head." One of the five put his hand up to his forehead as if about to cross himself, but remembering that he had changed his religion he put it down, and said: "I am certain it was but a shadow, for there are a great many about us, and of very strange kinds." Then they rode on in silence. It had been raining in the earlier part of the day, and the drops fell from the branches, wetting their hair and their shoulders. In a little they began to talk again. They had been in many battles against many a rebel together, and now told each other over again the story of their wounds, and so awakened in their hearts the strongest of all fellowships, the fellowship of the sword, and half forgot the terrible solitude of the woods.

Suddenly the first two horses neighed, and then stood still, and would go no further. Before them was a glint of water, and they knew by the rushing sound that it was a river. They dismounted, and after much tugging and coaxing brought the horses to the river-side. In the midst of the water stood a tall old woman with grey hair flowing over a grey dress. She stood up to her knees in the water, and stooped from time to time as though washing. Presently they could see that she was washing something that half floated. The moon cast a flickering light upon it, and they saw that it was the dead body of a man, and, while they were looking at it, an eddy of the river turned the face towards them, and each of the five troopers recognised at the same moment his own face. While they stood dumb and motionless with horror, the woman began to speak, saying slowly and loudly: "Did you see my son? He has a crown of silver on his head, and there are rubies in the crown." Then the oldest of the troopers, he who had been most often wounded, drew his sword and cried: "I have fought for the truth of my God, and need not fear the shadows of Satan," and with that rushed into the water. In a moment he returned. The woman had vanished, and though he had thrust his sword into air and water he had found nothing.

The five troopers remounted, and set their horses at the ford, but all to no purpose. They tried again and again, and went plunging hither and thither, the horses foaming and rearing. "Let us," said the old trooper, "ride back a little into the wood, and strike the river higher up." They rode in under the boughs, the ground-ivy crackling under the hoofs, and the branches striking against their steel caps. After about twenty minutes' riding they came out again upon the river, and after another ten minutes found a place where it was possible to cross without sinking below the stirrups. The wood upon the other side was very thin, and broke the moonlight into long streams. The wind had arisen, and had begun to drive the clouds rapidly across the face of the moon, so that thin streams of light seemed to be dancing a grotesque dance among the scattered bushes and small fir-trees. The tops of the trees began also to moan, and the sound of it was like the voice of the dead in the wind; and the troopers remembered the belief that tells how the dead in purgatory are spitted upon the points of the trees and upon the points of the rocks. They turned a little to the south, in the hope that they might strike the beaten path again, but they could find no trace of it.

Meanwhile, the moaning grew louder and louder, and the dance of the white moon-fires more and more rapid. Gradually they began to be aware of a sound of distant music. It was the sound of a bagpipe, and they rode towards it with great joy. It came from the bottom of a deep, cup-like hollow. In the midst of the hollow was an old man with a red cap and withered face. He sat beside a fire of sticks, and had a burning torch thrust into the earth at his feet, and played an old bagpipe furiously. His red hair dripped over his face like the iron rust upon a rock. "Did you see my wife?" he cried, looking up a moment; "she was washing! she was washing!" "I am afraid of him," said the young trooper, "I fear he is one of the Sidhe." "No," said the old trooper, "he is a man, for I can see the sun-freckles upon his face. We will compel him to be our guide"; and at that he drew his sword, and the others did the same. They stood in a ring round the piper, and pointed their swords at him, and the old trooper then told him that they must kill two rebels, who had taken the road between Ben Bulben and the great mountain spur that is called Cashel-na-Gael, and that he must get up before one of them and be their guide, for they had lost their way. The piper turned, and pointed to a neighbouring tree, and they saw an old white horse ready bitted, bridled, and saddled. He slung the pipe across his back, and, taking the torch in his hand, got upon the horse, and started off before them, as hard as he could go.

The wood grew thinner and thinner, and the ground began to slope up toward the mountain. The moon had already set, and the little white flames of the stars had come out everywhere. The ground sloped more and more until at last they rode far above the woods upon the wide top of the mountain. The woods lay spread out mile after mile below, and away to the south shot up the red glare of the burning town. But before and above them were the little white flames. The guide drew rein suddenly, and pointing upwards with the hand that did not hold the torch, shrieked out, "Look; look at the holy candles!" and then plunged forward at a gallop, waving the torch hither and thither. "Do you hear the hoofs of the messengers?" cried the guide. "Quick, quick! or they will be gone out of your hands!" and he laughed as with delight of the chase. The troopers thought they could hear far off, and as if below them, rattle of hoofs; but now the ground began to slope more and more, and the speed grew more headlong moment by moment. They tried to pull up, but in vain, for the horses seemed to have gone mad. The guide had thrown the reins on to the neck of the old white horse, and was waving his arms and singing a wild Gaelic song. Suddenly they saw the thin gleam of a river, at an immense distance below, and knew that they were upon the brink of the abyss that is now called Lug-na-Gael, or in English the Stranger's Leap. The six horses sprang forward, and five screams went up into the air, a moment later five men and horses fell with a dull crash upon the green slopes at the foot of the rocks.

1852

A LEGEND OF BARLAGH CAVE

Fitz James O'Brien

Fitz James O'Brien (1828–1862) was born in Co. Cork but lived a considerable portion of his life in the United States. His body of literary work is comprised of fiction, poetry, essays and plays displaying an innate talent; he is often seen as a progenitor of modern horror and science fiction. Among his influences are E. T. A. Hoffmann and Edgar Allan Poe, while his tales of the fantastic have received praise not only from his contemporaries but also later authors such as H. P. Lovecraft, who wrote in his seminal *Supernatural Horror in Literature* (1927) that "O'Brien's early death undoubtedly deprived us of some masterful tales of strangeness and terror". His short stories "What Was it?" (1859) and "The Diamond Lens" (1858) are two of his most memorable and original pieces of writing and have been frequently included in twentieth century anthologies. Although his name is not as recognisable as Le Fanu's or Stoker's, he is highly regarded by many horror scholars as an innovative and influential Irish author of the weird and the uncanny.

"A Legend of Barlagh Cave" was part of O'Brien's *Phantom Light: A Christmas Story*, a novella which was serialised in *The Home Companion* in 1852. This short yet effective episode is actually a piece of fiction presented as a scrap of lore, albeit one imbued with Celtic mythology. It is also an archetypical tale of unrequited love, in which nature itself becomes a reflection of impending doom.

A HUNDRED years ago there lived upon the shores of this lake a young maiden named Aileen. She was beautiful, and of noble and generous disposition. Nigh to her father's home resided a youth called Connor, handsome as Apollo, and brave as Achilles. Aileen loved this youth, but was not loved in return; his affections were cast upon another maiden, worthy of love certainly, but not possessing one-half the charms of Aileen. The latter pined on in secret grief. Each day that she saw Connor go down to his boat and sail out to sea, a tide of blood would rush from her heart, and leave her almost fainting with excess of passion. She watched him when he sought the hills with his gun upon his shoulder, and her eyes traced him up the steep mountain paths with a sick yet loving gaze. But, oh! what untold agony that maiden suffered when, in the glorious summer evenings, as the sun was sinking in a golden sea, and the grey twilight was creeping like a fox from the hills, she beheld Connor and his betrothed wandering along the fragrant beach, with twining arms and touching cheeks. Then the gorgeous clouds that floated in the western sky, those airy unsubstantial shapes of splendour, seemed to her distempered fancy to change into faces that stared at her with fierce mockery, while the azure heavens glowered upon her with myriads of sneering eyes. The low wind, as it wandered along the beach, sounded in her ear like derisive laughter. The very sea-birds that whirled above the calm surface of the lake seemed to shriek wildly to her tales of anguish and despair. As time wore on, so much the deeper did her vain love eat into her soul and inflame her brain. Connor knew not this. He knew not that the hollow eyes and pale cheek which now never deserted Aileen, were all the fruits of love for him. When he met her, he was kind and gentle to the suffering girl—never dreaming that each soft word he uttered planted a fresh arrow in her torn bosom. Nay, once even he saved her from an imminent danger, and bore her in his arms to her father's cottage, when, if he had but known the despair that racked her heart, he would have left her to perish rather than restore her to a life which was nothing but one long calendar of anguish. At last, the passion that burned within her became too great to be concealed. She determined to make known to Connor her devouring secret. Before doing so, however, she thought she would consult the Spirit of the Hill, who dwelt in a vast breezy cave, on the summit of Cunna Conma, and endeavoured to discover from him some means of winning Connor to her side. One starry night, when the summer dews were falling like a gentle rain, and nought living was on foot save the fox and the wild cat, Aileen left her restless bed, and stealing softly from the house, took the wild and rugged path that led to the summit of the mountain. As she trod that broken and uncertain footway, strange fancies haunted her. The tall dark pines that fringed the narrow path seemed instinct with a sombre life, and nodded and whispered to each other gloomily. Indistinct and shadowy shapes rushed wildly through the thick brushwood, and chuckling laughter echoed through the trees. There was not an old grey stone that raised itself from out the coppice, which did not take the form and aspect of some terrible and unearthly thing; Aileen walked, surrounded by a mist of horrors. At length she reached the summit of the mountain, and wended her steps to the cave where dwelt the Spirit of the Hill. Large grey clouds continually veiled the entrance of this solemn place, and within, the plaintive winds chanted all night and day their mountain hymns. Aileen stood upon the rocky threshold, and with a bold and fearless voice, called upon the Spirit. A long, hollow moan, that sounded like the voice of some vanished year, replied to her summons.

"Spirit of the Hill!" she cried, "I summon thee to answer me. How shall I attain either happiness or death? Tell me, thou unseen being, how to win Connor or to die!"

A moment's pause, and then the answer came from the depths of the cave in tones like those of the tempest in a forest.

"Seek the cave of Barlagh tomorrow eve," said the hollow voice of the Spirit, "and there wilt thou find rest."

"Thanks, thanks!" cried Aileen, as the murmurs died away along the hill. "Tomorrow, then, I shall perhaps rest in Connor's arms."

She trod the downward path that night with a lighter step than she had known for months; and, happy in the belief that Heaven had at last taken pity on her hopeless love, she sought her bed, and sank lightly into slumber.

The evening sun was sinking into an amber sea, when Aileen, full of hope, sought this cave of Barlagh. As she urged her little boat through the rapids with a steady hand, her heart beat wildly in her bosom, and delightful visions full of bliss and love floated between her and the gorgeous sky. That destiny would lead Connor to the cave, and that there, through the intervention of the Spirit of the Hill, he would reward her attachment by a return of the passion, Aileen felt quite assured. No shadow of misfortune clouded her soul. No forbidding angel stood between her and the paradise of her imagination. The foaming waves of the rapids soon brought her little skiff abreast of the cavern's mouth, and sweeping round the rocky corner, she was about to enter, when a blue pigeon flew wildly out and almost skimmed her face. She started, and had scarcely time to utter an ejaculation of surprise, when a loud report rang through the echoing chambers of the cavern, and she fell back in the stern-sheets, with her life-blood welling from her bosom. Another second, and a boat shot out rapidly from the dusky cave, and Connor, who stood in the prow with his gun still smoking in his hand, beheld with horror the form of the bleeding girl. He jumped wildly into her boat, and lifting her in his arms, tried in vain to arrest the flight of her ebbing soul. Then there, with that solemn cave-temple rising grandly above her head, and none to look upon her agony save *Him* and the golden sun—there, in that hour of mortal trial, with the last energies of life quivering and flickering upon her lips, did

Aileen pour into Connor's ear the history of her despairing love. She told him of her long days of misery and sorrow, of her sleepless nights, of her sick and wretched soul. She told him how deep, how ungovernable, was her love for him, and how she strove in vain to conquer it, but could not. She related how she had sought the Spirit of the Hill, and what reply he had given.

"He was right!" she said faintly, for her voice was growing weaker each moment, and the shades of death were creeping across her pale face. "The Spirit was right. I am dying in your arms, Connor; and is that not finding rest?"

Sadly and sorrowfully did Connor hang over the dying girl. Pained by her sad history, wrung with despair at having been the innocent cause of her death, nought but the remembrance that he had some one to live for prevented him from terminating his existence with his own hand. But he knew that there were longing eyes and anxious hearts which awaited his return, and lie refrained. Aileen was now speechless, and the coldness of death was chilling her frame. Yet still her dying eyes sought his, and her white lips moved and told him, though he heard no sound, that her heart was uttering a fond farewell. This lasted but a few moments. When the last sunbeam had ceased to cast its golden shadow on the heavens and the ocean, her spirit fled.

1908

THE MONKS OF SAINT BRIDE

Herminie Templeton Kavanagh

The Irish author Herminie Templeton Kavanagh (1861–1933) was the creative mind behind the funny, spirited and mischievous figure of the Irish farmer Darby O'Gill, the protagonist of a series of short stories imbued with elements of lore; these modern Irish fairy tales, playfully presented as real incidents, were collected in *Darby O'Gill and the Good People* (1903) and *The Ashes of Old Wishes and Other Darby O'Gill Tales* (1926). Darby O'Gill's adventurous encounters with the fairies even led to the release of the Disney film *Darby O'Gill and the Little People* (1959). Despite living in the United States, Kavanagh carried with her a love for Irish folk tales, and her inventiveness was regularly galvanised by the shadowy kingdom of elves, fairies and banshees of her ancestral land.

"The Monks of Saint Bride" was first published in *Collier's Magazine* in 1908 and although it was included in *Darby O'Gill and the Crocks of Gold* (1926) it does not feature the titular character of Darby O'Gill. Furthermore it is overwhelmingly sombre, presenting the readers with an awful curse, forbidden love and a spooky abbey, while Kavanagh's vivid descriptions of the wild landscape render this bleakness an integral part of the tale's desolate mood. In her short preface to the collection the author implies that the preternatural stories that comprise it are a marvellous blend of fiction and folk tradition: "The garments these legends wear are my own; the stories themselves are as old, as deeply planted, and as real as the grey sentinel cliffs along the Antrim coast."

THERE was a decent bit of a man, yer honour, named Michael Bresnahan, who till a few years ago lived over in that little fisher village under the cliff, and he had a good, sensible lump of a woman for a wife, named Katie.

No one could say a word against Katie—she was thrifty, she was clean, she was hard-working—only she used to be faulting Michael, and faulting him, and faulting him. If the decent man happened home of an evening with a sign of a little drop of drink on him, one would think from the way Katie went on that it was after robbing a church he was.

Well, one day Michael said to himself that he'd bear it no longer, so he up and went to his wife's relations, especially her sisters' husbands, to ask their advice about what he should do. They pitied him indeed—sure no one could do less—but all the counsel they could scrape together to give the unfortunate man was just the kind of encouragement relations always give.

"Arrah, God help ye, me poor man, and bear it the best ye can!"

Well, there wasn't much comfort in that, so Michael put in the next day going around asking the neighbours what he'd do with Katie, and every one freely gave the advice the neighbours always give under such circumstances: "Musha, God help ye, me poor man, and ye're a fool for standing it!"

Now, taking public advice on family matters soon grows into a pleasant habit with any one, so, after Michael had exhausted the cottages on both sides of the village street, he took the road in his hands, and was making his way down to Haggarty's public-house at the cross-roads when who should he meet up with, ambling along on the grey pony, but his Reverence Father John Driscoll.

"This is me chance to get in the first word before Katie sees his Reverence," he thought.

And what does the blundering lad do but stop the priest in the middle of the road and there make his bitter complaint. That was the rock Michael split on, for the clergyman, without a word of warning, up with his whip and hit Bresnahan two rousing welts over the legs, and then when the poor man took to his heels Father Driscoll galloped after, larruping Michael down the road and calling him such heart-scalding names that the very crows wouldn't pick his bones.

That same night Michael made up his mind to do something tremendous; so bright and early the next morning the desperate man slipped from the blue teapot on the dresser the last shilling in the house, and, taking the road in his hands again, off with him to Ballinderg to get the grand advice from Sheila McGuire, the fairy doctor. And the advice that Sheila gave him would raise the hair on your head.

"Hand me the shillin'! All Souls' night'll be here soon, and whin it comes d'ye go up to the monastery of Saint Bride an' help the monks an' they'll help you."

When Michael heard that same advice the cold sweat broke out on his forehead, for no man in five hundred years had ever been bold enough to face the monks of Saint Bride.

"Where are the monks of Saint Bride?" is it yer honour? Why, God rest their souls, they're dead a thousand years! That old ruin up on the cliff is where the monastery used to be. Troth and I must tell you of the monks of Saint Bride, or you'll never be able to rightly appreciate the terrible thing that happened to Michael Bresnahan that Hallowe'en night.

Do you see that high bare cliff beyant?—Aill Ruahd they do be calling it—well, in the days when the five kings ruled over Ireland—and many a year ago that was—Black Roderick O'Carrioll with three hundred of his fighting men lived perched upon the very pinpoint of the hill. Right opposite, on that other bold headland where you see the ruins lying tumbled, dwelt the far-famed Monks of Saint Bride. And just as you see it now, between their stout old monastery and the castle of the O'Carrioll, the blue sea curved in like the half of a cartwheel.

Barring these two habitations there wasn't another strong house within forty miles; but only the cottages of the cowherds and of the swineherds and the low mud huts of the kerns.

However, it's little the O'Carrioll cared for near neighbours, and it's little he bothered the monks with his visiting, and as for the monks, it's far from being sorry the holy men were to have the O'Carrioll keeping that way to himself.

A fierce, proud man was Black Roderick, and the greatest pleasure he took in life was in leading a hundred or two of his spears over the walls of some nobleman's castle and leaving its roof glowing blood-red against the midnight sky. But though half the province of Leinster hated and feared the O'Carrioll, it wasn't that way at all with him in his own household, for, whatever was the reason, with all his stern, cold ways there was many a man-at-arms who sat at the chief's table that would willingly have laid down his life to serve Black Roderick. But if the chief himself had any great liking for his men, he wasn't the one to be making much talk about it. And indeed they used to be saying that there was only one mortal man that he showed any fondness for and that same his only brother, the yellow-haired, pleasant-faced young Turlough. And it was no wonder for him to be fond of the lad the way he was, for a brighter-minded, comelier young fellow there wasn't to be found in the seven counties. Indeed, it's more like father and son the two men were than like brother and brother. All their days they lived that way together, with their foraging and their game and their hunting and their feasting, happy and contented enough I dare say, though it's little enough attention the two paid to prayers or to fasting or to any other pious thing. Nor at Christmas, nor Easter, nor on any other holy day did either of the two go next or near the monastery chapel of Saint Bride. Now what could any one expect from the likes of that but misfortune and bad luck?

Well, the misfortune came at last, and when it did a bitter, burning misfortune it was.

One black midnight the holy monks were awakened by a great noise of confused shouting and cheering that was passing along the road in the valley below them. And what should the good men see but the flare of a hundred torches held high by O'Carrioll's men above a dim crush of hard-driven cattle.

"The O'Carrioll is home from his raiding," said Brother John. "I wonder who was the unfortunate that felt the edge of his sword."

"God help him the night whoever he was," sighed Brother Andrew. "And than isn't it the marvel that Heaven has spared the heartless spoiler so long!"

While the monks stood wondering that way what depredation Black Roderick was after doing, there suddenly fell a hard rapping upon the convent gate, and a voice strident as a trumpet startled the monastery.

"Open, open, I say! 'Tis the O'Carrioll bids ye!"

And the drawbridge was let down, indeed, and the gate was opened, as it needs must be, and then two shadowy horses crossed the wide moat and stumbled into the abbey court.

First of all came the O'Carrioll himself on the tall black horse that people used to be saying could fight as well as his master. And the figure of a woman is what Roderick carried in front of him, and she wrapped in his wide cloak; and at the black steed's haunches rode Turlough, the brother, and by the strange, wild look on his face the monks thought at first that maybe it was a bad wound that was on him and that it was for a leech the two men were coming.

"Come, Sir Abbot," cried the dark man, "out with your book and marry the both of us here, for when this lady crosses my threshold I wish her to go as my wife. That much I'll do for her father's daughter." So saying he leaped to the ground and stood beside the girl and lifted her hand in his.

And Brother Paul was telling the next day how when Black Roderick took the lady's hand young Turlough's face went deadly white and the lad's hand made a sudden reach toward the sword at his side; and sure every one saw how the colleen (it's little more than a child she was) tottered and would have fallen if the O'Carrioll himself had not held her up.

I never rightly heard the truth about the three of them, but I think that there must have been something that time between Turlough and the young colleen. Who was the lady and how came the friendship between herself and young Turlough was, we may be sure, more than a nine days' wonder at Saint Bride's.

One morning a rumour reached the monastery that the colleen was the O'Coffey's daughter, and that she had been stolen out of the West, but that couldn't be, for O'Coffey's daughter was being reared in France; and after that some pilgrims were saying that the lady was the child of O'Donavon from Munster, but if that was true half of Ireland would have been in arms against the O'Carrioll. So, one way and another, the matter was bothering the friars at their beads and distracting them at their vespers till they could get no good of their prayers, when lo and behold, one morning about three months after the wedding, an astonishing thing happened: the Lady O'Carrioll herself, and no other, came riding up to the monastery again. This time, however, she came hurrying alone up the winding path, her mist of brown hair streaming in the wind and a look of terror frozen on her white face. At the same time came galloping in furious pursuit Lord Roderick O'Carrioll.

"Open and let me in," she called to the warder. "I claim the protection of this holy place."

And the draw was let down to her when they heard that cry, but when she rode over the bridge the O'Carrioll was at her heels, and when they drew bridle in the midst of the crowd of curious friars one horse's head was beside the other horse's head.

The man's eyes gleamed on her like coals of living fire, and what he said was:

"Is it to escape you thought you would! Return to your house and to your duty, shameless woman!"

The Lady O'Carrioll didn't answer him then, but slipped quickly down from the horse, and it's on her two bended knees she went before the abbot.

The old monk looked in stern amazement from the dark, threatening brow of the angry man to the death-white cheeks of the girl at his feet.

"Stop where you are, O'Carrioll," was what he said as the chief dismounted, "and come not a foot nearer, for, though I'm a priest of God, now if you so much as lift a finger to this woman it's little help that sword you're striving to draw will be to ye then."

At that the abbot turned, and it's what he called to the warder:

"Brother John, raise the drawbridge." And while the bridge was clanking up a score of stalwart monks armed, some with staves, some with spears, and two or three with naked swords, came hurrying up and grouped themselves around their abbot.

"And now, Roderick O'Carrioll," demanded the soldierly old friar, "what means this rude pursuit?"

"By the cross it's what it means, that she is a disobedient wife," haughtily replied the O'Carrioll, "and it's more than that you shall not know!"

"It's more than that I shall know indeed," said the abbot; "for unless you swear by the cross on your sword-hilt never to harm a hair of the woman's head, it's not one foot she'll stir beyond this gate."

"Most willingly do I take that oath," spoke the O'Carrioll, "though it's not through any dread of this nest of scurrying grey mice. An O'Carrioll never did anything yet through fear; but I'll take the oath you say to ease the fears of this woman."

And straightway, holding up the gold hilt of his sword, he swore by it blunt and plain like a soldier to keep her safe from any hurt or harm or shame that might come through himself or through another.

The monks of Saint Bride never saw her again and for two months it's little they heard of her, and then a dark rumour crept over the valley. And when two cowherds stood together out on the lonely hills they whispered the rumour to each other, and when any two men were alone together in their currach on the ocean they talked of it and it's what they said:

"The O'Carrioll has reddened his hands with his wife and he has reddened his hands with his brother Turlough that she had the love for, and the both of them are lying beside each other cold and dead at the bottom of the sea."

At last one day a fisherman found a lady's blue cloak washed up between two rocks, and it was the Lady O'Carrioll's gold-embroidered cloak they were saying.

Now when the abbot of Saint Bride heard this thing and of the way the sword oath that had been put upon the O'Carrioll was broken, it's great indeed the wrath that was on the good man, for such treachery never had been heard of before in all Ireland.

The evening of the day that the word was brought to him he called all the monks together in the chapel, and there they consulted one with the other what was a just and worthy punishment to put upon the O'Carrioll. It was the turn of midnight before they decided that and went to their cells. And then on the morning of the morrow, just when the great round sun was reddening the foreheads of the hills, they all gathered again on the east turret of the monastery, and when the abbot found that they were all about him he fronted the castle of the O'Carrioll and raised his oaken cross. Then, with the cross, he cursed that house, and he cursed the chief of that house. And it wasn't the O'Carrioll alone he cursed, but he banned him and all who cleaved to him with the curse of sleepless nights, which is the most agonising of all curses, and he doomed them with the curse of friendless days, which is the most terrible of all curses, and he cursed them with the blight of a quick-coming death, which is the surest of all curses. And he put excommunication upon the lord of the castle, so that he would be banished from out the ways of living men.

And no wonder it is, at all, at all, that quick and heavy that curse fell. For from that day out, the kerns began to steal away from Black Roderick's land, the way they were afraid of the curse; and the fighting men deserted him, at first by twos and threes, and then by scores; and then the women of the house crept away in the night; so that presently he that used to be counting five hundred spears was left with but a dozen or so of the old retainers.

And that is how Black Roderick's power went from him, so that he was forced at last to pay tribute to the O'Driscolls that he might save the roof of his castle from the torches of the MacDonoughs.

And that's the way it was with him when the red plague came sweeping up from Ath Cliath, as they used to be calling the city of Dublin then, and it leaving in its track no living man, woman, or child.

One morning six men lay dead in the castle of the O'Carrioll, and within the hour the master of the house, in the way that he would be ready if his own turn came, sent a quick messenger over for one of the monks of Saint Bride to come and shrive him. But the abbot sent a stern answer back, and it's what he said:

"Let Roderick O'Carrioll come himself to this monastery, and on his bare knees make public confession of the murder of his brother, and of his wife, and full acknowledgment of his other crimes, and then let him humbly take on himself the penance I'll impose, and it's no light penance that will be either; and let him not be sending here for a priest again, for it's to the chapel he himself must come, and it's my own tongue, and no other, that shall ask the forgiveness for him, and until I do that same it's unshriven he will be, and it's neither ease for his body, nor rest for his soul, he may expect in this world, or in the next."

When the frightened messenger went back and told that, it's what the O'Carrioll answered:

"It's a hard saying that is, and the curse they put on me I send back to them, and let it be laid against their souls that as I am innocent of the crime they say, they shall pray for me until I am blessed, whether in this world or in the next!"

The words were no sooner out of his mouth than he felt the sickness of the plague on him, and he turned to the serving-men, and what said was:

"The hand of death is on me now, and after all I'd wish to die at peace with God so lay me on the litter there and carry me with what haste you can to the monastery of Saint Bride. And when they hear what I have to say, it's well I know they'll shrive me then."

And the serving-men were loath to go, for the night was on, and it was All Souls' night, and wild with the wind, and the thunder, and the rain. But for love of the old times they took the master up between them at last, and it's how they carried him out into the darkness, and down into the valley, and by every short way toward the monastery.

By the time the serving-men had reached the path on the edge of the high cliff, which was half-way between the two places, they were as frightened as four shivering hares, and they set down the litter to rest themselves. When they did that there sprang across the sky a long flame of green lightning, and when it was over a man of them said:

"We need go no further. The O'Carrioll is dead."

And they crossed themselves then, but not one of them dared say: "God have mercy on his soul," because of the curse that was on him. Then one of them said: "What shall we do with him now?"

And the waves were leaping up against the rocks, the way they were striving to drag the men down into the sea.

Then the oldest of them answered, and what he said was: "The sea is calling for him, because he cannot be buried in the consecrated ground. We shall bury him in the sea."

And they flung him far out over the cliff, and the strong waves of the green sea leaped up to meet him as he fell, and there was his grave.

At sunrise, on the morning of the morrow, the red plague stalked into the monastery of Saint Bride, and the first token of its presence was when it put its hot breath upon the old abbot himself so that he withered within the hour. And it's the dying that was burying the dead from that hour on, until the last friar of them all, with his spade in his hand, tumbled, stricken, into the half-filled grave.

Then the loneliness and bleakness of desolation settled down on miles of hills and leagues of plains.

For three times ten years the deer browsed under the castle walls, and the badgers dug their lairs in the dry convent moat; and then the O'Broders sent their herds and their cattle and their swine down into the fat grass lands which for so long had lain fallow. But for years after that no one had the courage in his four bones to take shelter in the castle, or the convent, for fear of the sickness and the misfortune that was on the two places.

But after a time there came an old swineherd of the O'Broders—Brown Shamus, he was called—and on winter nights he used to be driving his pigs into the castle yard and to be building a great blaze on the hearth of the hall, the way he would be sleeping in the warmth of it.

One night as he sat huddled before the fire with his chin on his knees there fell a hard rap on the hall door behind him. Brown Shamus never turned his head, for he'd often heard sounds like that before at night in the castle, and he had seen strange shapes, and well he knew that it's from the grave they were, and what he'd do then was to be shutting his eyes and striving not to be thinking of them.

But the rap came again, and after it a blast of cold air. By that Shamus knew the door was open. He turned around then, and what he saw was a very old man and a very old woman, and they perishing with the cold. At that Shamus began on his prayers, for he made no doubt but what it was two spirits standing forninst him.

Then the old man, seeing the fright that was on Shamus, spoke up, and it's what he said:

"Have no fear, swineherd of the brown beard, it is I, Turlough O'Carrioll; and this is the Lady O'Carrioll, my brother's wife, that has come back with me."

At that the terror was all the greater on Shamus, for he was sure the two had been dead at the bottom of the sea those forty years. But when they drew nearer to the fire, and he heard the fall of their shoes on the stones of the floor, he knew by that it was living creatures they were, for the others, that used to be coming and going there, made no sound at all.

And sure enough, Turlough O'Carrioll it was, coming back after all these years, and his brother's wife along with him. Instead of being murdered and killed, as the report was out, they had taken a currach at night, and had slipped away to foreign parts, where they lived together until the hour I'm telling you about. And the pride of Black Roderick O'Carrioll, and his bitter shame, and maybe a bit of love for the both of them as well, had kept their flight and their crime secret—even when the dark man was excommunicated, and cursed, and forsaken on account of them, he made no sign. Sure you can never tell what good or evil thing is working hidden inside the mind of a man.

How long Turlough and the Lady O'Carrioll remained living I'm not very sure. It may have been one year, or it may have been two years, but it wasn't very long. At any rate, the two of them died, and were put in the one grave, and that was the end of the world for them, and they came back no more. You may see the wide brown flag that covers them to this day.

And wouldn't it have been a good thing, too, if Roderick O'Carrioll, and the monks of Saint Bride with him, could have found untroubled graves in consecrated ground? But an unjust curse is a dreadful thing. And through five hundred years, as sure as the night of All Souls' came, the friars of the abbey, and the lord of the castle, did bitter penance for their sin.

The dead make no account of time, they say—and, indeed, why should they?—and so one generation followed another generation, and the story of the curse came down with the years and the weary penance was still unfinished.

By and by the castle of O'Carrioll melted away. One by one its great stones were rolled down the mountainside to build the fishers' village of Killgillam, which was growing up on the ribbon of sandy beach below—the same village that I was telling you about, where Michael Bresnahan lived.

But no man was hardy enough to take a single stone from the haunted abbey, for fear of the bad luck it might bring him. So it crumbled away in the sun, and in the storms, and the grey rocks that tumbled lay where they fell.

And many's the strange whisper that went around about things that were seen at night on the top of that lonely hill. And I myself knew an old man, who once lived in that village, and his name was Thomas O'Deegan, and it's what he told me:

One All Souls' night when he was out on the bay alone, fixing his nets, and the wind was sweeping down from the face of the cliff, he heard the sound of many voices chanting together, and it was the litany for the dead they were singing.

Now, it's in the prayer-book, as every one knows, that the living may pray for the dead, and the dead may pray for the living, but the sorrow of it is, that the dead may not pray for the dead. It's a queer way that is, but they do be saying that there's a stranger thing still, and I'm greatly bothered sometimes to know the reason, and it's what it is: Though the dead can not pray for the dead, if one among the living say a prayer for the departed, then the dead may join his prayer to the living prayer, and so it makes one prayer, and they'll both be heard.

And this was the penance that was put on the monks of Saint Bride:

Once a year, upon All Souls' night—the night O'Carrioll died—they were to come out of their graves, every one, and to pray for the dead man's soul, and this until the day of judgment came, with no release unless some living voice would join itself to their dead voices.

And it was a punishment put upon Black Roderick, too, for his red deeds, that his soul should attend them there and find no ease until it felt the blessing of the abbot of Saint Bride. And so the useless prayers went on through all the generations, for sure what man in all the country was brave enough to climb that lonely road at midnight on Hallowe'en?

So by this time your honour will understand the hard task that Sheila McGuire put upon Michael Bresnahan: He was to go alone, d'ye mind, at midnight of All Souls', to the ruined monastery and there to face the unhappy spirits of the monks of Saint Bride, and to join his living prayers with their own, over the body of Black Roderick.

On the way home from Ballinderg, after seeing Sheila, Michael turned over and over in his mind the advice the fairy doctor had given him, and it's what he decided at last:

"Well, after all, I think I'd better try to stand the faulting of Katie for a while longer, and if the worst comes to the worst," said the persecuted man to himself, "maybe I'll stop a trifle of the drink for peace' sake." With that he tossed the matter from his mind and did the best he could with Katie.

Be that as it may, one afternoon not long after, as the lad was on his way home from the village of Ballyslane (where he was after selling a fine cow to his uncle, Ned Corrigan, who kept the public-house by the bridge), he took for a short cut home the path along the cliff. When he reached the top of the hill there was a weariness on him from his journey and a bit of a weakness maybe, besides, so he stopped to clear his wits and to rest a while on the sunny side of the old abbey.

As Michael sat comfortably reclining with his back to the wall and he smoking his pipe, the boy could see far down below him where the little village straggled lazily along the yellow beach. About a stone's throw from the edge of the green cliff stood his own white cottage, with the grey nets drying on its roof, and he could make out, too, Katie herself moving around in the thumb-nail of a garden with one of the children clinging to her petticoat, and it's what he thought:

"Oh, wouldn't I be the foolish man to be going down there now the way I am with the sign of the drop of drink on me after the hard warning about the public-houses she was putting on me when I went away this morning! No, no, Michael, take my advice, be a wise lad, and do you go in there now to the old chapel, where no one will be seeing you, and take a matter of forty winks or so, the way you'll have a sober and a clear head going down to her while it is still in the light of the evening."

So saying, Michael rose, stepped carefully over the fallen arch stones that locked the doorway of the ruined chapel, and, after picking out a soft green mound for a pillow on the sunny side of the wall, laid himself down and fell asleep. But sure it wasn't forty winks nor forty hundred winks the poor man took. The afternoon shadowed into evening, and the evening darkened into night, and Michael says he was sleeping like one of the cold stones when, suddenly, something like the skim of a bird's wing, or the brush of a passing garment across his face, startled every vein in his body, and he was wide awake at once and sitting up.

The full moon was sailing swiftly out to sea through a bank of fleecy clouds, and it took a wondering second or two to place rightly in the lad's mind the tumbled, roofless walls and the tall, broken arches of the ruin. And it's ghostly and solemn enough the place was, too, in the moonlight, with the sighing of the wind in the yew trees, and the whispering of the restless ivy on the walls, and far away the lonesome chirping of a cricket.

As Bresnahan hesitated, round-eyed and breathless, suddenly from the gaping tower of the abbey, soft and muffled, stole the boom of a tolling bell. Its toll was like the hollow moan of the shoal bell when the fog lies heavy on the sea—it was the mere ghost of a sound.

"My grief and my wo, where am I at all, at all," he began, "and what's this awful place?" The jump of his heart up into his throat took the breath from his lips, for the truth flashed into Michael's mind that this was the ruined abbey on the cliff where he had lain down for a minute's sleep; and, O Father in Heaven! wasn't tonight All Souls' night, when the terrible monks of Saint Bride walked in their awful penance?

The tolling ceased.

"The saints preserve us, 'tis the abbey!" whispered Michael. "Maybe I'll be able to slip down the hill before they come." He was half to his feet when there broke from the court outside the chapel a low wailing cry that froze the blood in his heart. It was as if some one in deep torment were begging for a drop of pity.

"Remember not his iniquities," pleaded the terrible voice. "Nor let Thine anger encompass him."

Instantly the mournful chant of many lips, like the moan of the ocean, took up the response of the litany.

"O Lord, we beseech Thee to hear us."

Michael crouched breathless behind a broken pillar. To the day of his death the bitter beseeching of that litany rang in his ears.

"From Thy wrath and from everlasting death," wailed the first supplicant.

And then the response, growing wild and dismal as the winter wind:

"O Lord, deliver him."

"I'm lost," groaned Michael. "'Tis the monks of Saint Bride, and they're coming in." Twice he tried to look, but the courage wasn't in him, so he just huddled there cowering. At the same time the ghostly chant kept swelling nearer and nearer, and every wild prayer for the dead, with its pitiful response, went driving through the heart of poor Bresnahan.

Presently he felt that the monks were near the chapel door behind him, and, compelled by very terror, Michael glanced shrinkingly back over his shoulder.

By this time the great white moon was flinging a soft steady light over the old ruin, and clearly, through the archway of the chapel, the crouching man saw approaching a sight terrible for mortal eyes.

Marching, two by two, moved a shadowy procession of grey-robed monks, and they chanting the litany for the dead as they came. The spectres walked with arms folded, and each bowed head was hidden in its cowl. There must have been fifty of them. The fallen stones along their way were no hindrance to their feet any more than if those same stones had been moon-shadows.

A few paces in front of the procession, slow, solemn, and silent, the abbot marched alone, a tall, stately figure. Just behind him four monks carried something between them on a litter. As the abbot entered the ruined chapel, soft and low again the bell in the tower began tolling.

Michael saw that they were going to pass by within a yard of him, so he strained every nerve and sinew to move aside, but the arms and legs of the poor lad were as heavy and had as little life in them as the stones lying scattered about the ground. When the monks drew near, the night air grew cold and damp and close as an open vault.

"Out of Thy great pity pardon his infirmities," chanted the abbot.

"O Lord, we beseech Thee to hear us," answered the monks.

When they were within five feet of him, Michael could see the abbot's hands crossed humbly upon the sunken breast: and, oh, achone mavrone! they were the long, thin, fleshless hands of a skeleton.

One face in all the ghastly train was visible, and that one was the still, white face of a dead man, who was being carried past on the bier. And a dreadful thing he was to see, with his long silken tunic dripping wet with the sea-brine, and the heavy seaweed clinging to him.

"Merciful Father!" gasped Bresnahan; "isn't it Black Roderick himself that I'm looking at, an' him drowned an' dead these five hundred years?"

It's well Michael Bresnahan marked that as the monks passed him by not one of them cast a shadow on the ground. And they turned neither to the right nor to the left, nor changed their pace, nor made any kind of sign, till they reached the place where the old altar used to be standing. There they stopped, and the four set the litter on the ground.

It was the abbot himself, then, that moved solemnly to the head of the bier, and, kneeling down as though before an altar, stretched wide his arms. He was praying there, but what he said Michael couldn't hear because the chanting had begun again. But at any rate, there they were, the dead praying for the dead. Here was the chance at last for poor Bresnahan to escape. And so, with teeth chattering and knees quaking, he turned him round and began creeping over toward the black, gaping archway.

There isn't a doubt but what Michael, if he had had the strength, would have opened his lips and prayed aloud with the monks, for he remembered the legend well of how the tormented spirits needed only a living voice to join its prayer with their own, the way they would have rest in quiet graves, but the fear was heavy on the poor man, and so he couldn't do that.

But just as he reached the archway the heart-broken wail rose higher and higher and more despairing, so that he could bear the sorrow of it no longer, and, turning where he stood, he bent his knee and cried aloud with the others: "O Lord, we beseech Thee to hear us."

Those were the happy words, for as Bresnahan scrambled over the fallen stones of the threshold, and darted down the hill with all the strength of his legs, the wail of the solemn chant for the dead changed to the glorious burst of the "Te Deum Laudamus." And no wonder: the curse was broken, the punishment of the centuries was ended, for the prayer of the living had been joined to the prayer of the dead. In that way Bresnahan knew that the spirits were released from their penance. And ye may not believe it, but it's as true as the Book that from that good day to this the monks of Saint Bride walk the ruin no more.

As for Katie Bresnahan, the kind-hearted woman, when she heard of the great miracle that her husband Michael had performed that night, she quit faulting him about the little drop of liquor he used to be taking, and on account of all that had happened to him Michael grew to be a hero throughout the countryside, and was looked up to as a knowledgeable man to the day he died.

Some Rural Ghosts and Uncanny Sounds

1836

THE DROWNED FISHERMAN

Anna Maria Hall

Anna Maria Hall (1800–1881), who published as Mrs S. C. Hall, was an Irish author deeply invested in exploring and depicting the cultural peculiarities of her fellow countrymen and their ways, notably in her short story collection *Sketches of Irish Character* (1829). Although she relocated to London early in life, Hall frequently returned to Ireland, delving into the customs and manners of the west during her tours there with her husband, the writer and editor Samuel Carter Hall (1800–1889), an experience which led them to pen together such non-fiction accounts as *Ireland: Its Scenery, Character and History* (1841–43). Although there are often scraps of folklore in her writings, Hall's tales of the supernatural are not abundant; the most memorable specimen is considered to be "The Dark Lady" (1847), a spectral narrative that, curiously, takes place not in rural Ireland but in the Swiss Alps and has been anthologised more than any other of her short stories. She was a Christian feminist and philanthropist and her tales are often didactic, while at the same time she highlights female characters and even challenges the subordinate status of women.

"The Drowned Fisherman", published in 1836 in *The Amulet*, an annual publication edited by Samuel Carter Hall, is a ghostly dramatic tale that unfolds in a seaside community, a tragic story of the common people; it is about maternal intuition, youthful romance, male stubbornness and female bonding, with the pervading sense of imminent danger casting its shadow over idyllic coastal scenery.

In the immediate neighbourhood of Duncannon Fort, along that portion of the coast which contracts into the Waterford river, there are a number of scattered cottages standing either singly or in small clusters along a wild and picturesque sea-shore—more wild, perhaps, than beautiful, although the infinite number of creeks, and bays, and overhanging rocks, vary the prospect at every hundred yards; and I know nothing more delightful than to row during a long summer-evening, from the time when the sun abates his fierceness until the moon has fairly risen upon the waters, nothing more delightful than to row—now in, now out, now under the hanging rocks, now close upon the silver-sanded bays, where thousands of many-coloured shells form the most beautiful Mosaic beneath the transparent waters. So deep is the tranquillity of land and sea during these happy hours, that travellers would find it difficult to believe they were really floating beneath the shadow of the Irish coast: that the lovely village of Templemore smiling on the brink of the Waterford river, was inhabited by the "savage cut-throats," which it is the delight of a peculiar party to denominate the suffering peasantry of a land who for centuries have "laughed and laboured" upon worse food and worse treatment, than we in rich and happy England, bestow upon our dogs—oh, it makes my heart ache, and my blood boil, when I think of what I have seen, and contrast it with what I hear; when I remember that whether priest-ridden or law-ridden, the heads of either party have been fanatics or worse—but what have I to do with this? I love the green turf of my native country, I laugh at its follies, I weep over its sorrows and grieve for its crimes; ah! a woman's smiles and a woman's tears are alike useless—but what have you, gentle reader, to do with that? I have never entered upon, and do not wish to enter upon, any subject that trenches on the *political* grievances of Ireland: I can only pray—which I do with all my heart and soul!—that times may mend, and speedily. I have endeavoured to win the suffrages of my dear English friends for the virtues and domestic privations of my *humble* countrywomen; and I have endeavoured to show to Irish people how their besetting sins of carelessness and inconsiderateness might be corrected—corrected without much trouble, and with great advantage to themselves; as far as Ireland is concerned I have no ambition beyond what I have stated, and having so said, I will tell my story:—

"And what 'ud ail the boat but to do? Sure she's done, ay, and done a dale for us, this ten years; and as to the hole, Jemmy 'ill plug his hat into it, or stick in a piece of *sail-cloth*, and what 'ud ail her then, but sail, God bless her!—like a swan or a curlew, as she always does?"

"Dermot—Dermot, darling! listen to me for onc't!"

"Faith," replied Dermot to his better half, Kate Browne, while his keen blue eye twinkled with that mixture of wit and humour so truly Irish, "Faith, my dear, I'll accommodate you in any way I can, for I'll listen to you onc't for three speakings—come, out with it, and don't stand twisting your face that was onc't so purty as to win the heart and hand of the handsomest man in the parish, and that is—myself, Dermot Browne at your sarvice, Mistress Kate Browne, madam! Don't keep lengthening your face to the length of a herring-net, but out with it!—out with it!—at onc't!"

"Dermot, I've got the box of tools quite convanient; I brought it with me to the shore, and the last time I was in Waterford I bought all sortings of nails, large and small; and there's plenty of *boord* in the shed—and Dermot, mend the hole, and God bless you!—sure its the sore heart I'd have when you'd be on the wather, to think that any harm would happen you—it won't take you any thing like an hour—"

"An hour! God bless the woman, why a body would think you had never been a fisherman's wife! An hour would turn the tide—and the luck!—an hour! Why, the herrings out yonder would miss my company if I waited; and all for what? To go to the trouble of nailing a bit o' boord on a mite of a hole, when it will be just as easy to stop it with a hat!"

"But not as safe, Dermot!"

"Be asy with your safety! You're always touching on that;—ay, will it, and as safe too; havn't I done it before?—Why, turn up every one of the boats along the shore, and I'll bet you the cod I mean to catch against a branyan that there isn't as sound a boat as my own on the sands; doesn't Harrison's go without a rudder?—doesn't Micban's go without a mast—barring a gag of a gate-post that he pulled out of Lavery's field? I'm sure Michael Murphy's craft is bang full of dowshy holes like a riddle: and a good noggin he won on that, for he betted Lanty Moore that at the present time the keel of his boat had more holes in it than Lanty's English sieve which he had for winnowing corn; and sure enough he won; for the holes in the sieve were all stopped up with the dirt! Lend a hand, old girl, and help me and the boy to shove her off!" He continued appealing to his wife, "What!—you won't? Why thin, Kate agra, what ails ye?—I've been your true and faithful husband next Candlemas will be seventeen years, and you never refused me a hand's turn before!" Still Kate Browne moved not; and her husband, using, with his eldest son, considerable exertion to push off the boat, became annoyed at her obstinacy.

Kate saw, but, contrary to her usual habit, heeded it not. She stood, with folded arms and tearful eyes, surveying the proceedings, without possessing the power of putting a stop to preparations, of the termination of which she had a fearful presentiment.

"Why, thin, look at your mother, Benje!" exclaimed Browne to his son, "sure she's enough to set a man mad, and her's the help that's as good as five—she has such a knowledge of setting every thing straight. Kate," he exclaimed to his wife:—

"Let her alone, father dear," interrupted the boy, "let her alone, and don't vex her more, *don't ye see there's a tear in her eye?*"

"And how can I help that?" expostulated the father, looking kindly towards his wife at the same time; "them women are ever so hard to manage, and manage as ye will, ye can't find 'em out;—there's the sun shining above her head, the waters dancing and capering, like jewels, at her feet, the herrings crying 'Come, catch me,' and Benje, between you and I, as handsome a husband, and as fine, ay, and for the matter of that, as good a boy for a son as woman's heart could wish, and yet the tears are in her eyes, and the corners of her mouth drawn as far down as if she did nothing but sup sorrow all her life." Benjamin, the fisher's only child, made no reply; and, after a moment's pause, his father looked at him and said, "Why, boy, you look as much cast down as your mother—stay on shore, and good luck to you!"

"No, father, that I won't! I'll not put more to the throuble she's in, by letting you go by yourself; I wish from my heart the boat was mended, if it would make her easy."

"Don't bother about the boat, boy," replied Browne, "I never meddle or make with her house, or land business; hasn't she got a back-door for the cabin?—a sty for the poor pig?—a *chaney* dish for the pratees, and a white table-cloth for saints'-days and bonfire-nights?—can't she stay at home and mind them, and let me and the cobble alone?" Benjamin loved the wild and careless spirit of his father better than the prudence and forethought of his mother; yet did he not forget that the very arrangements and luxuries to which his father alluded, were solely the effects of her care and industry.

"Won't you say, God speed me, Kate?" inquired the fisherman as he pushed off his dangerous craft with a broken oar, "Won't you say, God speed me and the boy?" The woman clasped her hands suddenly and fervently together, and dropping on her knees without moving from the spot on which she had been standing, uttered a few earnest words of supplication for their safety. Benjamin sprang on the shingles, and raising his mother affectionately in his arms, whispered—

"Keep a good heart, we will back with such bouncing fish, before morning, any how; and mother, darling, if you see Statia Byrne, here is the neckerchief she promised to hem for me; tell her not to forget her promise." The kisses Mrs Browne bestowed on her son were mingled with tears. She watched the boat until it had dwindled to a small speck on the horizon. As she turned to ascend the cliff, she saw the round laughing face of Statia Byrne peer from behind a rock, and withdraw itself instantly on being perceived. She called to her; and after a little time Statia came blushing, and smiling, and lingering by the way to pluck every sprig of samphire, every root of sea-pink, that grew within her reach.

"I just came down to gather a few bits of herbs for the granny's cures, and a few shells to keep the childre asy," said Statia—pulling her sea-pinks to pieces at the same time.

"And what does the granny cure with these?" inquired Mrs Browne.

"Sorra a know I know," replied the girl, blushing still more deeply.

"Maybe," continued Mrs Browne, gravely, "maybe, Stacy honey, there's a charm in them like the yarrow you put under your pillow last Holy-eve night?"

"Ah, thin, Mistress Browne, ma'am, let me alone about the yarrow—sure it was only out of innocent mirth I did it, and no harm; and, any way, I've no belief in such things at all, at all."

"And why do you disbelieve them?" inquired the fisherman's wife. Statia made no reply. "I can tell you," she continued; "because though you neither spoke nor laughed that blessed night, my poor girl, after you placed the yarrow under your pillow—still you did *not* dream of Benje Browne. Stacy, Stacy, I mind the time myself when, if a spell worked contrary, I'd disbelieve it directly—it's only human natur, darling."

Statia Byrne flung her handful of sea-pinks upon the shingles, and passed the back of her hand across her eyes, for they were filled with tears.

"You have thrown away the granny's pinks," said Kate, pointing to the flowers that the sea-breeze was scattering far and wide.

"Ah, thin, let me alone Mistress Browne dear!" exclaimed the girl. "And good bye, for the present, ma'am; I'm sure the child 'ill be woke before this, and mother is carding wool, so she'll want me now."

"Good bye, Statia—but stop child: Benje desired me to put you in mind, that you promised to hem this neckerchief for him; and tell your mother, jewel, that if she'll let you come down to my cabin tonight, when the *grawls* are all in bed, I'll be for ever obliged to her; Browne and the boy are out to sea, and there's something over me that I don't care to be quite alone this blessed night: so come down, a lannan,—and thin you can hem the neckerchief—before morning."

"I will, I will," said the maiden, with whom smiles had already taken the place of tears, for she loved Mrs Browne's cottage almost better than her own; "I will, and I've learnt a new song; oh, I shall be so happy!" and she danced up the cliffs with all the light gaiety of fifteen!

The fisherman's wife set her house in order and then commenced mending her husband's nets. It would have been evident to any observer, that her mind was ill at ease, for instead of pursuing her occupation with her usual steadiness, she frequently suffered the hard meshes to drop from her bony fingers, and the wooden needle to lie idle on her lap. She would rise and peer from her small window, or more frequently still from the open door, into the heavens, but there was no cause for disquiet in their aspect—the moon was in her full, calm glory; and the stars, bright, glittering, and countless, waited round her throne as handmaids silently attending upon their mistress. She could see the reflection of the moon-beams on the far-away waters—but her ear, practised as it was, could hardly catch the murmur of the ocean, so profound was its repose: and yet Kate continued restless and feverish. Benjamin was her only surviving child—although five others had called her mother—and, indeed, while he was absent from her, she felt that undefined, but perfectly natural, dread which steals over a sensitive mind for the welfare of a beloved object, whenever the one is separated from the other.

It was a great relief to her spirits when she heard the light foot of Statia Byrne on her threshold, and she felt new-sprung hope within her heart when she looked into the bright eyes and observed the full smile of the joyous girl.

"They're all a-bed, and the babby went off to sleep without an *hushow!* and mother says, as you're all alone by yourself, I might stay with you all night, Mrs Browne; and so I will, if you please—and I've brought my needle, and—I'll hem the handkerchief, if you please—and then, maybe—maybe you'd shew me how you mend nets—I should so like to mend Mister Browne's herring net; he gave mother (God bless him!) as many herrings last year as lasted all Lent!—I'm sure we can never forget it to him."

"Pray for him then, Stacy—pray on your bended knees—for Dermot and Benjamin Browne this night."

"Why so I will," rejoined the girl—astonished at the woman's earnestness of manner—"but the night is fine, the sky is blue, the waters clear as chryshtal; they've been out many a night when the winds do be blowing the waves into the sky, and I've wondered to see you heart-easy about them—what, then, ails you tonight?"

"God knows!" replied Kate Browne, with a heavy sigh, "I think I'll go over my *bades* a bit; ough, Stacy darling, it's a fine thing to have the religion to turn to when the heart turns against every thing else." Kate sprinkled herself with holy water out of a small chalice, and knelt down, with a "decket" of beads in her hands, to "say her prayers;" almost unwittingly, she repeated them aloud, but they had, in a degree, lost their soothing power, and she mingled the anxieties of earth with her petitions, not to heaven but to its inhabitants; her "mingled yarn" ran thus:—

"'Holy Mary, mother of God, pray for us'—Statia, open the door, agra, and listen, myself thinks the wind's rising—'now, and in the hour'—the cat! avourneen, don't you see the cat at the herring-tub, bad luck to that cat!—'now, and in the hour of our death!'" There was a long pause, and she continued murmuring her petitions, and speaking aloud her anxieties, while Statia went on hemming the handkerchief; at last she looked up at her young companion and inquired, "Where did I leave off, my darling, was it at 'Virgin most powerful,' or at 'Queen of Confessors?'"

"I did not hear," replied the industrious maiden.

"Hear what?" exclaimed Kate Browne, starting off her knees.

"Lord defend us, you startle the very life out of me!" ejaculated the girl, devoutly crossing herself.

"But what did you hear, Stacy?"

"Nothing. I told you I did not hear where you left off."

"Ough! ay, ay!" exclaimed Mrs Browne, "God forgive me, I am a poor sinful thing; quite full of sin; I must give up the prayers for tonight, I can't steady my heart to them, good nor bad; there! finish your work, and we'll go to bed, jewel—it is, as you say, a beautiful night, thanks be to God for his mercies! and I ought to have more faith."

Long did they both remain awake during that calm moonlight: the fisherman's wife muttering prayers and fears, and raising her eyes to the little window which opened at the foot of her bed, and from which, as she lay, she could catch a view of the distant sea—at last she fell off into a deep, deep sleep. But Statia, though free from all anxiety as to the fate of the absent, could not close her eyes—poor girl! her young imagination had passed a gulf of years, and she was thinking, that perhaps she might be to the young fisher what Kate was to the old; and she thought how good he was—and how handsome; and how happy she should be to mend his nets, and watch the return of his boat from the highest cliff that "toppled o'er the deep." The grey morning was stealing on the night, yet still Kate slept—and still Statia Byrne continued with her eyes fixed on the window, creating—not castles but—nets, and boats, and cottages in the air; when, suddenly, before the window stood Benjamin Browne—she had not seen his shadow pass—she had heard no step—no voice—no sound; nor did she see a figure, but there was his face almost pressed to the glass—his long, uncurled hair hung down either cheek—and his eyes were fixed on her with a cold, unmoving, rayless gaze—she endeavoured to sit up—she felt suddenly paralysed—she could not move—she tried to speak, to call Mrs Browne who still slept heavily, heavier than before—she could make no sound—still her lover gazed—gazed on. And what occurred to her (for she afterwards declared, she never, for a moment, was deprived of consciousness) as most strange was, that though the room within was dark, and his head obscured the window, still she could see his features (to use her own expressive phrase) "Clear like wax;" while as he gazed, their beautiful form assumed the long, pale hue of death—by a sudden effort she closed her eyes, but only for a brief, brief moment. When she re-opened them, he was gone—and she only looked upon the grey mingling of sea and sky; trembling and terror-stricken she at last succeeded in awakening her companion. Mrs Browne heard her story with apparent calmness, and putting her lips close to the ear of the fainting girl, whispered—"HE IS DEAD!"

It was long, long before Statia recovered from her swoon, for when she did, the morning sun was shining on her face—and she was alone, quite alone in the fisherman's cottage; at first, she thought she had fearfully dreamed, but the realities around her recalled her to herself; she flew to the same cliff where, the evening before, unconscious of the strong affection which bound her almost childish heart to her young lover, she had watched his departure; and looking down on the beach, her painful vision was too truly realised—Dermot Browne was leading his wife from a group of persons who were bearing the corpse of the young fisherman to the shore; in the distance could be seen the keel of the doomed boat floating upwards, while crowds of sea-birds overhead screamed the youth's funeral dirge!

It might be about two months after this occurrence—which plunged the warm-hearted people of the neighbouring villages into deep sorrow—that Kate Browne visited the cottage of Statia Byrne; it was the first time the bereaved mother had entered any cottage, save her own, since "her trouble." As soon as Statia saw her, she flung herself upon her neck and sobbed as if her heart would break; the fisherman's wife held her from her, and parting her hair from off her brow, said,

"Sorrow has worked with you, and left his mark upon your face, avourneen; and though, my darlint, you did not drame of *him that's gone* last Holy-eve, you've dramed of him often since."

The poor girl wept still more bitterly.

"You must have been very dear, very dear entirely, to him," continued Kate Browne, "for his blessed spirit found it harder quitting you than his own mother, who nursed him a babby at her breast; but whisht, darlint, don't I love you better for that now? Sure every thing—let alone every one that he regarded—that his regard only rested on, is more to me than silver or goold, or the wealth of the whole world! Didn't the bright eyes of his spirit look from the heavens on you, my jewel? And what I'm come here for Mistress Byrne, ma'am, is, that as you have so many childre, (and God keep them to you!) maybe you'd spare Statia to bind *my heart from breaking*, and let her bide entirely with us—we have prosperity enough, for when the Lord takes one thing away, why he gives another—blessed be his holy name! And sure, since the boy's gone, nothing can equal Dermot's industry and carefulness, stopping every hole in every fisherman's boat—when he's ashore the hammer and nails is never out of his hand. Let her be to me as my own child, Mistress Byrne, and you'll have a consolation that will never lave you, no! not on your death-bed. Sure you'll see her every day the sun rises—let her bide with me, for I am very desolate!"

The mother, as she looked round upon seven rosy, healthy children, felt, that indeed her neighbour was desolate, and in a voice hoarse with emotion, she said,

"Statia may go, and take our blessing with her, if she likes!"

Many little voices wept aloud in that cottage, although they knew they should see their sister daily; but the maiden was firm in her resolve, and that night greeted, as a father, the father of him whom her young heart had loved with an entireness of affection which the heart can know but once.

Statia is now long past the age of girlhood, and it is pleasant to see how perfectly her simple life is an illustration of the pathetic exclamation of the Jewish damsel, "Thy people, shall be my people, and thy God, my God!" She manages admirably between her "two mothers," as she calls them, so that the one may not be jealous of the other: but though she has had many suitors for her hand, she has never forgotten—the drowned fisherman!

1894

A SCRAP OF IRISH FOLKLORE

Rosa Mulholland

Rosa Mulholland was born in Belfast in 1841. Though she wrote in a wide variety of literary genres, modern readers enjoy her work almost exclusively for her contributions to the ghost story. Initially she moved to London to study art yet by the 1860s she had built a career as a writer and became a regular contributor of uncanny tales to Charles Dickens's *All the Year Round*, sharing pages with such popular authors as Wilkie Collins and Elizabeth Gaskell. Among her stories published in *All the Year Round* was the much anthologised "Not to Be Taken at Bedtime" (1865), a harrowing witchcraft narrative reminiscent of a horror fairy tale. The ghost story aficionados and the lovers of supernatural tales must also be familiar with her spooky "The Haunted Organist of Hurly Burly" and "Ghost at the Rath" – both published in *All the Year Round* in 1866 – which have made regular appearances in anthologies of the fantastic and the Gothic throughout the years. In the 1870s Mulholland returned to Dublin and became a popular and highly accomplished novelist focusing on rural Ireland settings and characters. In the following decades she continued to write supernatural tales for London magazines but also for *The Irish Monthly*. She died in 1921 in Dublin.

The short story "A Scrap of Irish folklore", which appeared in the December 1894 issue of *The Irish Monthly*, is a chilling first person narrative possibly inspired by a folk tale, reviving the beauty and the forwardness of oral tradition. Moreover, it is a story endowed with authentic rural atmosphere and vivid descriptions that add a realist touch to its macabre qualities.

I WAS resting in the grass on a summer evening when the following little story dropped down upon me.

"Whisht, honey! Don't let the waft of such a word pass your lips to the child!"

The speaker was an old woman in a blue hooded cloak and white cap, and was sitting in a bank of foxgloves in a green dell of Wicklow. Beside her was the stick that had helped her out to enjoy the sweet after-coolness of the remnant of a day in July. Along the sky behind spread a lake of gold to which the darkening oak-trees made a serrated shore; opposite to her the summer night was creeping leisurely up the dewy shamrock pastures. A triplet of little grey cabins with their snubby chimneys emitting peat-smoke, fragrant as incense, were huddled together for a few perches away in the twilight, and out of one of them had come the neighbour whose rude words to the child on her arm had called forth the aged grandame's remonstrance.

"You mane no harm, Nora honey, no more than I did meself whin my Larry came back from the other world to check me!"

Nora sat down with a shiver on the bank, caressing her child's little sleepy head against her shoulder.

"Is it a ghost you're talkin' about, granny?"

"He died whin you were both young," continued the old woman, "and left me with three o' them, and hard-set I was to keep the life in them. Many's the time whin my body was tired and my heart sore, I did let out an impatient word at the childher. I didn't mane any harm by it. Only a bad habit I had.

"Wan night I was sayin' my prayers down on my knees at the ould broken chair, and Johnny the eldest (him that wint to say) was answerin' the prayers with me. I looked up and I seen that the door I thought I barred was open, and I said to Johnny out o' the prayers, to stand up and shut it for me. Whin I turned my head again, it was open still, and I spoke out sharp to the boy to get up off his knees and do what I had bid him to do. The child declared he had done it, and he upped and wint to do it again, but, whin I lifted my head after sayin' the Litany, my word to you but the door was as wide open still as if I had set it that way a-purpose, to give a good airin' to the place. I was tired and I was cross (God forgive me, and me at my prayers!) and I let a bit of a curse at the boy.

"'Bad luck to you, Johnny!' I said, 'have you no hands on you at all that you make three tries at a door and can't manage to shut it?'

"The child cried and crept into bed and fell asleep, and whin I had well barred the door, meself turned in after him. But before I settled rightly to my rest, I took a back-glance at the door: and there it was standin' open as wide, like as it was rale politeness to somebody that was just expected.

"I jumped out of bed in a passion, but before I reached the door there was some wan standin' in it—Larry, my husband, and he carryin' a child on each arm, the two that was buried with him in the graveyard at the Kill.

"The sweat teemed off my face, and my tongue dried up, but he looked in my eyes so kind-like that at last I gother up my courage to spake to him.

"'Larry,' I said, 'will you sit down at your own fireside, and I'll make up a fire; for you look cowld and pale,' says I, 'and so does the childher that you niver thought to see again. Give me little Mary into my arms, that I may comb her yellow hair,' says I, 'and give her a sup of milk to bring the rosy colour that she used to have, back into her cheeks. And let me wake up Dermot that I may see his blue eyes that were the light of our first wedded years, my husband,' says I. For a sort of madness had come over me at seein' them, and I seemed to think they were rale livin' again, and come back to me to stay.

"'I can't, my woman,' says Larry, says he, 'for I only came to you on a God's-errand. And I brought the childher with me for a warnin' to you. Don't let the waft of a curse iver pass your lips any more to thim you have still with you, my girl,' says he. 'Oh Molly, don't curse the childher! Look at these two on my arms,' he says. 'These little innocent childher with their love and their prayers have been my salvation. Your curse will poison their innocence,' says he, 'and you'll have to answer for it.'

"'I'll niver do it again, Larry,' says I, 'but will you put them childher into my arms for a minute, and will you give me wan kiss, as it's yourself that used to know how to do without the asking?'

"Well, he came near me and let the childher in me arms, and he leaned over and put his lips upon my own, and oh, the cowld of them!—the dead cowld of the little cratures on my breast, and the ice of himself's face agin' mine—they wint through and through me, and froze me up and killed me. And I cried out loud like a mad woman, and fell down on the flure in a hape. And whin I came to meself, there was nothin' but the stars shinin' through the open door where he had left it open for a sign. I heard a big sigh and a couple of little twitters like the young birds at the dawn, as if him and the childher had been watchin' till they seen I was better, and only passed way whin I came back to my sinces."

"Maybe you dhreamt it all," said Nora, whose sun-burnt cheeks had been growing paler as the story approached its climax.

"No," said granny, "for as if like a kind of token, my lips where he kissed them was iver and always after that the colour of blue purple, like the lips of a body that does be froze with the cold. And I have two white marks on my breast where the heads of the little dead childher lain, same as if the chill and druv the blood out o' that part o' my bosom back into my heart, druv it so hard that it never could return."

She ceased, and I, the eaves-dropper, had no mind to rise up and try to argue the old woman out of her faith. She remained sitting on the bank after Nora had gone away to put her sleeping child in its nest under the poor cabin thatch. Presently the aged seer drew forth some large rosary beads and began to pray out loud in a continuous murmur.

The greys of the landscape deepened; the green-purple of the trees sank into gulfs of black all around; a few poplars beyond the cabins stirred faintly in the sky, and the white-blossomed boughs of an alder-tree glimmered out of the deepest darkness down the vanished road, and suggested the hovering nearness, yet aloofness of a reserve of sympathetic and vigilant spirits.

1900

THE STRANGE VOICE

Dora Sigerson Shorter

Dora Sigerson Shorter was born in 1866 in Dublin and grew up in a literary family; her literary accomplishments had to do mainly with poetry, while her artistic concerns rendered her an aspirant painter. Being at the heart of the literary scene of late-Victorian Dublin, she gradually became a prominent figure of the Irish Literary Revival. Prompted by her restless spirit, she also became politically active, namely a supporter of Irish independence, while several of her poems paid a tribute to the Easter Rising of 1916. She died in London in 1919 where she lived a considerable part of her later years. Although she had integrated supernatural elements in her poems, she is not known as an author of the fantastic since her prose contributions to the genre are not profuse – though this remains to be more adequately explored.

"The Strange Voice" was included in her volume *Father Confessor: Stories of Death and Danger* which was published in 1900. It is a rural uncanny story whose unearthly qualities are primarily associated with the auditory sphere; it is also a heartbreaking tale of young love, and at the same time an eerie paranormal narrative that maintains a sense of elusiveness all the way to its ambivalent conclusion; while also conveying perfectly the rustic ambiance and the nocturnal countryside terrors of that era.

EILEEN sat very silent amongst the group that gathered around the turf fire in the low thatched cottage.

"What has come to your light heart?" one said to her. "You are that quiet, I keep forgetting Eileen Murphy is with us at all."

But the head of the old grandmother nodded slowly, and it was she who answered for Eileen.

"I'm afeard," she said, "the boy is gone. It is seven days since he walked from that door, and not a word or sight of him since. I'm afeard the boy is gone."

Eileen drew her bare feet from the fire, as though a spark had fallen upon them. She shrank further into the shadow.

"I met him that night outside your door," the neighbour said, knocking the ashes from his pipe upon the stone hearth. "He borrowed a match from me, to light his pipe. He told me he was to be married as soon as the banns were called. He seemed very light-hearted." The man glanced pitifully at the girl's figure hiding in the shadow. "I never seen or heard of him since."

"He said he had business to do when he left us, and that a lamb of his had strayed, that he must look for before morning; but it was not dark, and the lamb was there next day, but he had gone."

The girl's little sister drew her chair to the fire, looking fearfully behind her. "Maybe he walked on the sleeping grass," she whispered, thinking of the fairies, but nobody heeded her.

"Maybe he ran from the wedding," a bold young voice giggled from near the door. "Maybe he's off to Dublin, and some of the grand ladies have caught hold of him."

"Shame upon you! Kathleen O'Grady." The girl's mother spied into the darkness where her daughter sat so quiet. "Well you know he was after Eileen since they were children together."

"And he is going to give her the jackdaw you wanted, Kathleen," the girl's sister said, with childish triumph. "He said he was teaching it to speak."

"I remember them well," the old grandmother said, "the two children; and with him it was, 'Follow me, Eileen,' and she was after him wherever he went."

A faint giggle from Kathleen and a whispered "She was" drew the stern eye of the neighbour upon her face. She flushed, and said, "I mean no harm; sure the boy is all right."

"'Follow me, Eileen,'" the old woman muttered. "I seem to hear his voice; only a few weeks ago he came to the door and cried to her, then ran like a child, jumping the heather before her."

"It was his way of getting her to himself," the mother said. "God be with him, wherever he is!"

The girl threw her chest out with a long breath, but stifled the sob before it was heard.

"He was for selling every stick and beast about his place," Kathleen said in a hard voice. She once fancied that he cared for her, and the mistake still stabbed her. "Yesterday the bargain was to have come off. Did he tell ye?"

"That's true," the neighbour said, filling his pipe and crushing the tobacco in with his finger. "Mike Doherty told me he paid him good money that evening. He was going to take his bride to America, and he was right; there is more chance there for a man than here."

"It's to Dublin he's gone," Kathleen muttered, "and forgotten ye all; he was always a rag on every bush."

The girl in the shadow clenched her hands, but did not speak.

"He promised to send for me," the old grandmother muttered, "in a year; but I'll be buried by that, glory be to God!"

"I'm told America's a great place for the poor," the mother said, looking round the dim cabin it would have broken her heart to leave; "a great place entirely."

"And Eileen will be a grand lady there," the grandmother continued, breaking into a cackle of laughter. "For it's over the sea with O'Rouark she is going. 'Follow me, Eileen,' he said."

Kathleen sprang to her feet.

"My God!" she cried; "did you hear that?"

There was a sudden rustling in the cabin of startled people settling into silence, then the quiet of listening. Outside the door a voice was heard, loud and distinct,—

"Follow me, Eileen."

Then came a burst of joyous clatter in the room.

"Open the door for him!"

"He's right welcome!"

Eileen stood up in her corner, the hot blood rushing back to her heart, suffocating her.

Kathleen opened the door with a sullen face; she would not be glad to see him. She opened the door wide, and all faces were turned to the darkness outside; but no one entered.

There was a moment's silence, and then from a distance the voice again,—

"Follow me, Eileen."

Kathleen sprang towards the group at the fire, hiding her face amongst them.

"Lord have mercy upon us! It's his ghost I'm after seeing."

The little child began to scream, and the women made the sign of the cross upon themselves.

"Holy Mother, protect us!" they said; but the neighbour shook the ashes from his pipe and stood up.

"You're a fool, Kathleen O'Grady!" he said, and he went outside.

Eileen laid her hands upon her heart. "He wants me," she whispered, "but I cannot stir; I am too glad—too glad!"

The neighbour re-entered; he closed the door behind him, and, as though unintentionally, slipped the bar across it.

"There's nothing there, sure enough," he said, and pulled his chair closer to the fire.

Again came the cry, "Follow me, Eileen," and the bar fell with a clatter from the door.

The women rose with a shriek, which ended in a hysterical laugh.

"It's only Eileen," Kathleen said; "she slipped out."

"Holy Mother and the saints, preserve her!" the mother said. She put a lighted candle in the window. "She will see it when she is tired of her foolishness."

They sat down in silence and waited.

But Eileen ran out into the night, listening for the voice she loved, for in the dark she heard it again,—

"Follow me, Eileen."

"I am coming," she answered; "wait for me: I cannot see you." She ran fast along the rough mountain road, till her breath failed her.

"Oh! wait for me!" she gasped; "it is so dark."

"Follow me, Eileen." The voice was close beside her—amongst the few fir trees that clustered together beside a murmuring brook.

She sprang from the road with a laugh, and bounded amongst the deep fern and pricking gorse. The briars caught her dress and tore it, they clung about her ankles, leaving red marks of their caresses. She stretched her arms wide, to hold the beloved. "Follow me, Eileen." The voice was far away. She struggled back to the road, sobbing and crying, "Ah, you are cruel; I will follow you no more."

"Follow me, Eileen." The voice had a plaintive note now. She stretched her hands towards it, but did not answer. She crouched by the wayside, and hid her face. Surely he was playing with her, to treat her so; and yet—she raised her head to listen.

"Follow me, Eileen." The voice grew fainter, further off. She sprang to her feet and ran, afraid to lose the sound. Once again she thought she had come upon him. The voice seemed only a few feet away from her. She opened her arms with a glad cry:—

"Ah! I have found you at last."

Then a crushing blow upon the forehead knocked her to the earth. She had run against a tree in the darkness. She drew herself up beneath it and moaned. Far away she could hear the voice again, "Follow me, Eileen."

A great terror came to her; she shivered, and hid her bruised face in her hands. He was dead—oh, yes! dead; it was his ghost who was calling to her, and flying before her like a false marsh-light. She shuddered with the fear of death upon her. He was near, she felt him; in a moment he would put his cold, dead hands upon her. She shrieked, "Don't touch me!" and heard his voice far away calling to her pitifully,—

"Follow me, Eileen."

She sprang up, all her love awake for him. "Living or dead, I will follow you." She cast her fear from her.

"Where are you, Alanna?"

All around her came the singing of grasshoppers amongst the rough grass and heather. The sound seemed to her like the turning of fairy spinning wheels. She imagined the tiny figures sitting there among the ferns spinning. Whiz! whiz! whiz! What were they spinning? Over her face came spiders' webs, blown by the wind,—fine silk, floating from place to place in the breeze—lying on her nervous, bruised forehead like ropes. She brushed them aside.

"You will not bind me," she said; "spin as you may, I will follow him for ever."

She started running again; and ran gasping and stumbling after the strange voice for hours. Her dress was torn half away, her hands and feet red with her rough travelling, her brain was hot and mad with weariness and despair, her breath came in harsh sobs through the quiet of the night.

Now she would say, "I hate you; you are cruel." And again, "I love you; wait for me; I love you."

Suddenly again, close beside her, came the voice, "Follow me, Eileen."

"I follow you till death." She staggered aside off the little foot-track across the bog. In a moment she felt herself caught; something cool, and soft, and strong was dragging her down.

"Is it you, Alanna?" she gasped but got no answer, and was too tired to wonder. She was benumbed and foolish with weariness, yet surely she was in his arms.

"You are so cold," she muttered, yet thought it should be so, seeing he was dead. "I do not care if you are living or dead, now I have found you." She felt the cold chill of his soft clasp move upward, now to her waist, now to her shoulders. She struggled a moment, then was quiet—she sank lower. "I am in the bog," she shrieked. Then again, "I am so tired; kiss me, Alanna!" And for a moment the kiss was bitter on her lips, then the bog closed above her soft hair, and she slept.

But still in the little village they tell the story of Eileen and her lover, and bar the door and draw near the fire in the telling; for though one old man always believed it was the jackdaw's voice that frightened them that night, calling as its lost master had taught it, he was always a foolish old man, and he is dead now, and his story forgotten. The others, and especially the young folk, will tell you it was the ghost of Eileen's lover who called her forth, and Kathleen O'Grady saw him with her two eyes standing before the door beckoning and calling.

1903

THE WEE GRAY WOMAN

Ethna Carbery

Ethna Carbery was the pen name of Anna Johnston McManus (1866–1902) who was born in Co. Antrim in Northern Ireland. She was a poet, journalist, feminist, passionate nationalist and accomplished writer of ballads. She was also co-founder and member of The Daughters of Ireland, a nationalist women's organisation coordinated by Maud Gonne, revolutionary, artist and writer of the Celtic Twilight, also known on account of her relationship with William Butler Yeats. Carbery felt a romantic connection to old Ireland and this perfectly mirrored the cultural context of her era. Her poetry collection *The Four Winds of Eirinn* (1902) celebrates Irish Gaelic tradition with much fervour, while her collection of short fiction *In the Celtic Past* (1904) is based on famous Irish myths and legends. She died quite young, at the age of thirty-five, while being recently wed to the writer and folklorist Seumas McManus.

"The Wee Gray Woman" was included in her short story volume *The Passionate Hearts* (1903); one of Carbery's few spectral tales, this is a melancholy eerie narrative about loss, memory, remorse and loneliness, distinguished by beautiful prose and distinct poetic qualities, where imagination merges with reality in either literal or figurative hauntings.

His cabin stood by the side of a burn into which the sally-trees drooped from either side, making a thick fringe of green that met overhead and cast dappled shadows on the clear water when the sun stood high and fierce in the heavens. Little ripples broke in white bubbles around the stones that made the crossing-places, and the speckled trout darted like tiny silver spears through their haunts below the overhanging banks.

It was a tranquil, lonely spot; eerie, too, in the autumn twilight, when the slow-creeping mists rose up from the bog for miles around, and many were the tales told of an evening, by the folk living on the high land, of lights that flashed all over the bog at the very moment that Jamie Boyson set his candle in his cottage window to guide the Wee Gray Woman up the rugged loaning to her seat in the chimney corner.

Once it happened that the wild young fellows of Glenwherry came in the dead of night to play a trick on Jamie. They stole over the stepping-stones of the burn and noiselessly reached the one-paned window, half hidden by thatch, in which the light gleamed. A red turf fire blazing on the hearth lit up the interior of the old man's kitchen; it shone on the battered ancient dresser, and on the store of carefully-kept delf that had been his mother's. For Jamie had the name of being cleanly and thrifty in his ways. The hearth was carefully swept, the flat stones at front and sides whitened by a practised hand, and no ragged streaks wandered over the edges on to the clay floor beyond. A three-legged stool stood in front of the fire, placed there for the convenience of the unearthly visitant who, Jamie said, came nightly to sit and rest herself by the *greesaugh* until the black cock should crow in the rafters above the settle-bed, invariably awaking him at the same moment that the Wee Gray Woman got warning to leave. That was why he could never get a right look at her, he lamented. Sometimes he opened his eyes in time to see the flutter of her grey cloak as she passed out of his door, and once he caught a gleam of red. It was a red hood she wore, not like anything that mortal ever saw before, but just as if a big scarlet tulip had been crushed down over her head with all the leaves sticking out round her face. And his blood always curdled when she gave a cry going over the threshold, as if she was being dragged away into some dreaded torment from which she had had a respite.

"It would break the heart in yer breast to hear it, just for all the worl' like the whine of a dog when there's death aroun'," he would say.

But no one could get him to commit himself as to a theory about the comings and goings of the Wee Woman. Whether he fancied her a friendly denizen of fairyland, or a poor wandering ghost dreeing her purgatory for her own sake or the sake of some one loved and living, the inquisitive people of the bog-side could never learn, yet night after night the hearth was swept, and the stool placed that she might have her rest until dawn broke in a flame of gold and pale chilly green over the hill-tops.

So the ghostly story spread, as such stories will, through the country, finding by turns sympathiser and sceptic alike, who yearned, though fear of the supernatural kept most of them away, for a peep through Jamie's window before the black cock gave the signal. But the young fellows from Glenwherry, daring and mischievous as they were, had made up their minds to solve the mystery, and nothing daunted, holding their breath steadily, they drew close to the little window, and out of the thick blackness of the last night-hour glared into the haunted kitchen.

The firelight flickered fitfully at first, so that their eyes, half blinded with the darkness, saw nothing save shadows; then, suddenly, a gleam shot from the heart of the dying turf, and showed a vision that drove them back from the window, saddened and ashamed.

It was only the old man asleep in his settle-bed, his thin, wrinkled profile outlined like a cameo against the background of dark wood, and the patient old hands, that were so gentle and capable, folded upon his breast, as when he had lain down to sleep.

After that the Wee Gray Woman might come and go, without dread of being watched for, or disturbed, and among the Glenwherry lads Jamie found a set of stalwart partisans, whose judgment in his favour dare not be gainsaid.

He was not altogether devoid of occupation and amusement in his lonely existence. The little one-roomed cabin was tidy as a woman might have kept it. And though he harboured neither cat nor dog, during one winter at least—the severest winter known for many years in that locality—he had a pet, and the pet was a cricket. Imported from a neighbouring fireside, he had trained it with the utmost patience and skill until the diminutive dusty-looking object learned to jump out from behind the big pot in the chimney-corner at his call. The story of his having accomplished such a marvel scarcely gained credence; it was not to be compared to that of his ghostly guest; but the country children cherished it and repeated it in wide-eyed wonder, when they gathered round their elders' knees before the unwelcome bedtime; while the more superstitious asserted that it was the Wee Gray Woman come to bide with Jamie Boyson by day in another guise. It certainly looked uncanny enough, hop-hopping over the floor, chirruping in a shrill, faint treble to his deeper intonation, and, when he lifted it, creeping into the shelter of his hand, as a home bird might that has known and loved and trusted in the kind guardianship.

But once upon a time Jamie Boyson had need of neither ghost nor cricket for company. That was in the days of his early manhood, when, stalwart, supple, and strong, he led the boys of Crebilly to victory on many a hard-fought field of a Sunday, proving himself a champion to be proud of, in throwing the shoulder-stone, and wielding the *camán* against the athletic Glenwherry lads, with big Dan O'Hara at their head. Then, where was his equal to be found at dance or christening? Why, half the girls in the country were in love with him, and hopelessly, too, as they learned to admit to their own sad hearts, that fluttered so uncomfortably under the

Sunday 'kerchiefs when he passed, his black head erect, and his shoulders squared like a militia major's, without a look at one of them, up the chapel aisle to his seat next his mother in the old family pew.

The family pew held something else besides his mother; something the very sight of which was enough to bring the red blood in a rush to the roots of his curly dark hair, and make his heart almost leap out of his breast for gladness; something that was small, and fair, and blue-eyed, half-hidden behind his mother's ample form, and scarcely lifting her white lids from the beads she was passing through her fingers.

She was no stranger to him; he had many opportunities of watching her pale sweetness by his own fireside at night, without embarrassing her with that burning gaze of his under the disapproving eyes of all the congregation; but he was wont to say to himself, as a sort of justification that little Rosie at her prayers taught him more about heaven and holiness than the priest could do with all his preaching.

His brother Hugh used to joke him often and often about his fancy for the little orphan girl whom his mother had saved from the poorhouse, and Jamie's brow would glow with the angry red that warned Hugh's tongue to stop, and the laughter to die out of his merry brown face. There were only the two of them left to his mother, and one took little Rosie into his life as a sister, while to the other she, whom the country lads in general had called "a poor, pale wisp o' a thing", became his all, his world, his gateway of Paradise. How the love for her grew up in his heart was a mystery to him. Perhaps it took root when as a little child—the evening she came home to them—she laid her flaxen head on the bashful lad's broad shoulder and would not be parted from him until sleep stole on her unawares and released the tiny hands from their grasp on his strong ones. Or perhaps it came later as he learned to watch delightedly her deft, gentle household ways, and heard her crooning to herself over her flowering, in the rare leisure moments the active, bustling mother allowed.

There was an old song he was very fond of singing about "Lord Edward"—an old song she loved to listen to—and he was always sure of a grateful glance from the shy eyes, when of a winter's night he favoured the little circle around the hearth of Lisnahilt with the stanzas set to an air that was very popular in the district:—

"The day that traitors sold him an' enemies bought him,
The day that the red gold and red blood was paid;
Then the green turned pale and trembled like the dead leaves in
autumn.
An' the heart an' hope of Ireland in the cold grave was laid.

"The day I saw you first, with the sunshine fallin' round ye,
My heart fairly opened with the grandeur of the view;
For ten thousand Irish boys that day did surround ye,
An' I swore to stand by them till death, an' fight for you.

"Ye wor the bravest gentleman an' the best that ever stood,
An' yer eyelids never trembled for danger nor for dread,
An' nobleness was flowin' in each stream of your blood—
My blessin' on ye day and night, an' Glory be your bed.

"My black and bitter curse on the head an' heart an' hand
That plotted, wished, an' worked the fall of this Irish hero bold,
God's curse upon the Irishman that sould his native land,
And hell consume to dust the hand that held the traitor's gold."

Sometimes tired with the day's hard work, she would rest her head against the wall with a low sigh of weariness. She must often be tired, he thought; those little feet had run about so nimbly since early morning, and the little red hands had washed and baked, without a moment's pause; but, please God, that would be all ended soon, when his wife should reign over a home of her own, and he had taken her into the shelter of his strong arms for evermore.

Yet no word of this crossed his lips, though the desire that filled his heart beat like a strong ceaseless wave within his breast, giving him an almost unbearable pain, and he never dreamt but that she knew. In the very effort to control himself, his voice was, curiously, harsh when he spoke to her; and while the poor child trembled at the rude accents, her faltering reply aroused in the big, tender-hearted fellow a wild feeling that was half exquisite pity, and half hate. Ah! if he had only spoken then, the grim tragedy of his life might have been spared him.

One bleak night in autumn a sound outside drew him to the door, and opening it, he stood listening.

"John Conan's calves are in the clover-field," he said; "go and put them out."

Rose lifted her timid blue eyes to him questioningly.

"Do you hear me?" he asked.

"But I'm afraid," she murmured; "it's so dark, an'—"

He pointed his finger to the open door and the black stormy night outside.

"Go," he repeated fiercely, turning to his chair, and lifting his pipe off the shelf, and the girl passed into the darkness without another word.

What madness was on him that he had spoken to the little girl, and sent her on such an errand? he asked himself when she had gone. He had been conscious of a strange, sore sensation all day, since at Crebilly Fair, that forenoon, Tom M'Mullan had proposed a match between her and his son Jack, one of the wildest young scamps in the whole countryside, and the unreasoning jealousy grew and grew until he had wreaked his pain in vengeance on his poor Rosie's unoffending head.

"Oh! amn't I the queer, ungrateful fool," he muttered, "to trate the wee lass this way."

An hour passed, he waiting every moment to hear her footfall on the threshold, and his mother speculating comfortably that she had gone in for a gossip to John Conan's. At last he could bear his regret and the suspense no longer, and went out to seek her.

It was only a step or two to the clover-field, and reaching the low stone wall he called to her eagerly in the darkness. The startled calves, still enjoying their forbidden banquet, lowed back in answer.

He vaulted the gate, every step of the way familiar to him by night as by noon, and called anxiously and long. Then he remembered his mother's surmise, and turned across the field to Conan's.

There was no little Rosie sitting with the laughing girls grouped together in the corner, over a quilting frame, and in response to his husky demand a couple of Conan's young sons volunteered to accompany him on his search—Hugh, his brother, being away for the night in a market town many miles off.

He walked on, quickly, in the direction of the bog, guided only by his intimate knowledge of the treacherous path that wound like a serpent across the marshy windswept surface. He heard the small waves beat against each other with a faint sad sound, while overhead not one solitary star glimmered, to light his heart with hopefulness. Through the terrible night, and into the dawn, his frantic search continued, calling her name in a hoarse agony that wrung the souls of those who heard him.

"Rosie, Rosie, my little girl, it's Jamie's callin'. Ah! come, can't ye, an' don't be hidin' there. Don't ye hear me darlin', it's Jamie, an' the supper's waitin' on us. Let Conan's calves go—they're always a trouble to somebody, but *you* come home. Here, take my han'"—stretching out his arms into the empty shadows—"take it, love, an' don't be afeard, nothin' can touch ye, pulse o' my heart, when I'm beside ye, Rosie! Rosie!"

And so on through the dreary hours, over the wild bogland, his voice rang in pitiful entreaty, until jagged streaks of golden red flamed like trailing banners in the East, and the birds, wide-awake, took up in a chorus, clear-tongued and grateful, the morning song; but alas! for him, whose song-bird had flown afar, and for whom the dawn henceforth should hold no radiance, nor the rose-flushed mellow evening any passion.

Yet his frantic cry broke in upon the happy choir, and the blackbird and thrush, from hedge and beechentree, watched him staggering home in the sunshine, murmuring through lips that scarcely knew the words they uttered—"Rosie, Rosie, girl dear, come home."

Some hours later a turf-cutter, crossing the burn to his work, caught a gleam of something bright under the cold running water. It was little Rosie's fair head lying against the stones in the shade of the drooping sally-trees, whither through the darkness, blinded by her sorrow, she had wandered to her death.

Jamie Boyson aged suddenly after that. When the friends of his boyhood had grown into sturdy, middle-aged men, strong and hearty, he was already old, with a gloom upon him that no smile was ever known to lighten. In time, when his mother died, and Hugh had married, he grew unable to bear the sound of children's chatter through the rooms where he had once hoped to see his own little ones at play, and came to live his life alone in the cabin by the burnside, from whence he could watch the very spot where poor Rosie's gentle head had lain under the clear cold ripples.

So the country folk, noting his absent dim blue eyes, and wandering talk about the Wee Gray Woman, grew to believe that it was little Rosie's ghost come to bear him company until the call should sound for him, and his broken and desolate heart should find peace.

That was many, many years ago; and, perhaps, they have met long since in heaven, where Jamie Boyson, young, and straight, and strong again, with all the bitterness gone from his heart, has taken little Rosie in his arms and told her the truth at last.

1928

TALE OF THE PIPER

Donn Byrne

Donn Byrne became chiefly known for his romance and adventure novels and not due to his forays into the supernatural. He was born in New York in 1889 to Irish emigrants but from his school years onwards he grew up in Ireland. Back in his parental homeland at the turn of the century the idea of Irish identity was immensely stressed through the preservation of native language and culture in the context of the Celtic Revival. In this respect, as a young boy Byrne was fascinated by Irish Gaelic and delved with enthusiasm in ancient Irish lore; he even managed to become bilingual by coming into contact with native speakers of Irish. Notwithstanding his involvement in all things Irish, in 1911 he left for New York where he gradually became a successful writer of short stories and novels. He died in Cork in 1928 in a car accident shortly after his relocation to Ireland. He never became actively involved in political matters, and his contemporaries described him as a very imaginative man unable to cope with modern reality.

The "Tale of the Piper" was included in Byrne's short story collection *Destiny Bay* which was published in 1928. It is a rather short yet powerful narrative of the strange and the uncanny open to different interpretations.

I FIRST saw him as I rode from the Irish village into the gates of Destiny—a burly man with a moustache, a cheap suit of Glasgow reach-me-downs, a cap with a twisted brim, and the most evilly insolent eyes I have ever seen in a human face. At the sight of him Pelican, that wisest and steadiest of horses, reared; and I felt a savage gust of hatred rise in me.

"Now, who are you?" I asked; "and what are you doing here?"

"The same question from me to you." And his eyes were studiedly insulting.

An unaccountable rage made me tremble. I shook out the thong of the hunting-crop, and edged Pelican towards him.

"I am the Younger of Destiny," I informed him; "and when I pass, all folk in Destiny do me the honour of uncovering."

He fumbled with his cap and took it off. His hair was shaggy and matted, like a wild man's.

"I am a piper your uncle, Sir Valentine Macfarlane, sent from the High Country of Scotland home here to await his coming."

I said no more and rode in. My Aunt Jenepher told me of my Uncle Valentine's letter which Morag, her Islay maid, had read to her. My Uncle Valentine had met the man in an inn in Argyllshire, where he was stalking deer. "None knows anything about him, and he is most reticent about himself; but I am persuaded he is the best piper in the world. Also, he may help revive the lost art of piping in Ireland."

"Now, if he had only sent me a pair of Ayrshire ploughmen," I grumbled.

At dinner that night the man threw his reeds over his shoulder and played outside the dining-room window. He broke into the rollicking country air of the "Palatine's Daughter." I don't know what he did to it with the knowledge of his art, but out of that tune of frolicsome rural love-making he produced an atmosphere which made me uncomfortable, as though some cad were telling foul stories. He swung from that into "Thorroo a Warralla," the "Funeral of the Barrel,"—a noted drinking song of how a barrel of porter went dry after a day's flax-pulling. But the picture evoked was not that of country men drinking healthily at a cross-roads, but of a thieves' kitchen, where dreadful blowsy women, as of Hogarth, lay drunk with their rat-faced cut-purses…

"Stop that man, James Carabine," said my Aunt Jenepher.

He played no more under our window, but in the Irish village the next day he piped "The Desperate Battle," that music that only a great piper can touch, and that night the only faction fight we had had in Destiny for forty years broke out and raged until the police from the neighbouring villages were rushed in. He played "The Belles of Perth" to the men from the fields, and for days afterwards I saw maidservants and young girls in the farmhouses around with red eyelids. And a young under-gardener flung down his spade and said out of nothing, to nobody: "I'm sick of the women in this untoward place." And one morning I heard him play, "Iss fada may an a walla shuh"—"I'm a long time in this one town"—and my own feet took an itch for the road.

I said to my Aunt Jenepher at luncheon, "I was thinking now, with the winter coming, I'll give up hunting for this one season, and go and see Egypt maybe, or go as far as India. A young man ought to see the world a bit."

"Shall we talk about it tonight, Kerry?" said my Aunt Jenepher.

She asked me to go with her into the garden after luncheon, and sent Carabine for the piper. He arrived with his instrument under his arm.

"You have never played for me yet, piper."

"Your ladyship has never asked me." There was a solid dignity about him.

"I suppose you have many tunes," said my Aunt Jenepher.

"What I say now would be immodest in another man but true in me: no piper has more tunes. I have the lost tunes of McCrimmon. I have tunes that were lost before McCrimmon's day—old, dark tunes. Also tunes of my own making."

"Will you play me the tune of the fishermen, piper, as they raise the brown sails: 'Christ, Who walked on the sea, guard us poor fisher folk'!"

"I am sorry, my lady, but I have not that tune."

"Please play me Bruce's Hymn: 'God of Battles'!"

"That also, my lady, is a tune I have not."

"Then a merry song, piper, which you must know: 'The Marriage Feast which took place in Cana'!"

He was stolid as a rock. "I am afraid I have not that either."

"One of your favourite tunes is: 'I'm a long while in this one town'?"

He bowed with a nobleman's courtesy.

"It is a choice tune," he said slowly, "a darling tune."

"Then play it, piper, then play it," said my Aunt Jenepher. "And as you are playing it"—she rose up suddenly from the seat and looked at him with her blind eyes—"in God's name, go!"

"I was to wait," said the piper, "until Sir Valentine returned."

Both Carabine and I made a step towards him. My Aunt Jenepher must have felt us. "Please, Kerry! Please, James Carabine!"

"Piper, my brother Valentine will not wish you to stay here an instant longer than I would have you stay, and I would not have you stay at all."

"Then I had better go," the piper said. And he swung his reeds to his shoulder; struck the piper's swagger.

"Do you need money for the road?" my Aunt Jenepher asked.

"I need nothing."

"But you do, piper," said my Aunt Jenepher softly. "I shall pray for you tonight."

He dropped the pipes from his shoulder and turned around. "I thank your ladyship," he said simply; "but I fear it is late for that."

"Nevertheless, I shall," said my Aunt Jenepher.

He turned and went away from us down the garden path, and what became of him is not known. He did not play his pipes as he went, but held them crumpled under his arm, and his walk was more like the rapid amble of an animal than the step of a man. I was convinced that were I to look in the gravel I should find not a footprint of a man, but the slot of an animal. But I did not look. I was afraid.

Gothic Chills

1888

THE LAST OF SQUIRE ENNISMORE

Charlotte Riddell

Charlotte Riddell (1832–1906), also known as Mrs J. H. Riddell, was a very popular and prolific Irish writer of the Victorian period who lived most of her life in London. Her numerous romantic and realist novels have been neglected and are rarely reprinted nowadays; however, she is considered to be a prominent author of the Victorian ghost story and has been steadily included in horror anthologies throughout the decades. The settings of her uncanny narratives are rarely Irish with a few exceptions such as the much anthologised "Hertford O'Donnell's Warning" (1867) sometimes called "The Banshee's Warning". Her supernatural tales are distinguished by more or less common motifs and tropes of traditional ghost stories and gothic fiction: haunted houses and vengeful apparitions, murder, premonitions, ghastly women, uncanny warnings, curses, evil spirits, and tragic turns of fate, through which she managed to evoke authentic feelings of uneasiness and terror in Victorian readers and even in today's audience. Her collection *Weird Stories,* which was published in 1882, is regarded as an excellent sample of the Victorian ghost story genre. Her other supernatural and gothic works include the novellas *The Uninhabited House* (1875) and *The Haunted River* (1877), as well as the novel *The Nun's Curse* (1888).

"The Last of Squire Ennismore" was included in the collection *Idle Tales* published in 1888; it is a fascinating gothic narrative of unrivalled craft, a mysterious Faustian tale and a genuinely frightening account enveloped with the aura of a riddle, which renders it engaging all the way to its harrowing end.

"DID I see it myself? No, sir; I did not see it; and my father before me did not see it; or his father before him, and he was Phil Regan, just the same as myself. But it is true, for all that; just as true as that you are looking at the very place where the whole thing happened. My great-grandfather (and he did not die till he was ninety-eight) used to tell, many and many's the time, how he met the stranger, night after night, walking lonesome-like about the sands where most of the wreckage came ashore."

"And the old house, then, stood behind that belt of Scotch firs?"

"Yes; a fine house it was, too. Hearing so much talk about it when a boy, my father said, made him often feel as if he knew every room in the building, though it had all fallen to ruin before he was born. None of the family ever lived in it after the Squire went away. Nobody else could be got to stop in the place. There used to be awful noises, as if something was being pitched from the top of the great staircase down into the hall; and then there would be a sound as if a hundred people were clinking glasses and talking all together at once. And then it seemed as if barrels were rolling in the cellars; and there would be screeches, and howls, and laughing, fit to make your blood run cold. They say there is gold hid away in those cellars; but not one has ever ventured to find it. The very children won't come here to play; and when the men are ploughing the field behind, nothing will make them stay in it, once the day begins to change. When the night is coming on, and the tide creeps in on the sand, more than one thinks he has seen mighty queer things on the shore there."

"But what is it really they think they see? When I asked my landlord to tell me the story from beginning to end, he said he could not remember it; and, at any rate, the whole rigmarole was nonsense, put together to please strangers."

"And what is he but a stranger himself? And how should he know about the doings of real quality like the Ennismores? For they were gentry, every one of them—good old stock; and as for wickedness, you might have searched Ireland through and not found their match. It is a sure thing, though, that if Riley can't tell you the story, I can; for, as I said, my own people were in it, of a manner of speaking. So, if your honour will rest yourself off your feet, on that bit of a bank, I'll set down my creel and give you the whole pedigree of how Squire Ennismore went away from Ardwinsagh."

It was a lovely day, in the early part of June; and, as the Englishman cast himself on a low ridge of sand, he looked over Ardwinsagh Bay with a feeling of ineffable content. To his left lay the Purple Headland; to his right, a long range of breakers, that went straight out into the Atlantic till they were lost from sight; in front lay the Bay of Ardwinsagh, with its bluish-green water sparkling in the summer sunlight, and here and there breaking over some sunken rock, against which the waves spent themselves in foam.

"You see how the currents set, sir? That is what makes it dangerous, for them as doesn't know the coast, to bathe here at any time, or walk when the tide is flowing. Look how the sea is creeping in now, like a race-horse at the finish. It leaves that tongue of sand bare to the last, and then, before you could look round, it has you up to the middle. That is why I made bold to speak to you; for it is not alone on the account of Squire Ennismore the bay has a bad name. But it is about him and the old house you want to hear. The last mortal being that tried to live in it, my great-grandfather said, was a creature, by name Molly Leary; and she had neither kith nor kin, and begged for her bite and sup, sheltering herself at night in a turf cabin she had built at the back of a ditch. You may be sure she thought herself a made woman when the agent said, 'Yes: she might try if she could stop in the house; there was peat and bog-wood,' he told her, 'and half-a-crown a week for the winter, and a golden guinea once Easter came,' when the house was to be put in order for the family; and his wife gave Molly some warm clothes and a blanket or two; and she was well set up.

"You may be sure she didn't choose the worst room to sleep in; and for a while all went quiet, till one night she was wakened by feeling the bedstead lifted by the four corners, and shaken like a carpet. It was a heavy four-post bedstead, with a solid top: and her life seemed to go out of her with the fear. If it had been a ship in a storm off the Headland, it couldn't have pitched worse; and then, all of a sudden, it was dropped with such a bang as nearly drove the heart into her mouth.

"But that, she said, was nothing to the screaming and laughing, and hustling and rushing that filled the house. If a hundred people had been running hard along the passages and tumbling downstairs, they could not have made a greater noise.

"Molly never was able to tell how she got clear of the place; but a man coming late home from Ballycloyne Fair found the creature crouched under the old thorn there, with very little on her—saving your honour's presence. She had a bad fever, and talked about strange things, and never was the same woman after."

"But what was the beginning of all this? When did the house first get the name of being haunted?"

"After the old Squire went away: that was what I purposed telling you. He did not come here to live regularly till he had got well on in years. He was near seventy at the time I am talking about; but he held himself as upright as ever, and rode as hard as the youngest; and could have drunk a whole roomful under the table, and walked up to bed as unconcerned as you please at the end of the night.

"He was a terrible man. You couldn't lay your tongue to a wickedness he had not been in the fore-front of—drinking, duelling, gambling—all manner of sins had been meat and drink to him since he was a boy almost. But at last he did something in London so bad, so beyond the beyonds, that he thought he had best come home and live among people who did not know so much about his goings on as the English. It was said he wanted to try and stay in this world for ever; and that he had got some secret drops that kept him well and hearty. There was something wonderful queer about him, anyhow.

"He could hold foot with the youngest; and he was strong, and had a fine fresh colour in his face; and his eyes were like a hawk's; and there was not a break in his voice—and him near upon threescore and ten!

"At long and at last it came to be the March before he was seventy—the worst March ever known in all these parts—such blowing, sleeting, snowing, had not been experienced in the memory of man; when one blusterous night some foreign vessel went to bits on the Purple Headland. They say it was an awful sound to hear the death-cry that went up high above the noise of the wind; and it was as bad a sight to see the shore there strewed with corpses of all sorts and sizes, from the little cabin-boy to the grizzled seaman.

"They never knew who they were or where they came from, but some of the men had crosses, and beads, and such like, so the priest said they belonged to him, and they were all buried decently in the chapel graveyard.

"There was not much wreckage of value drifted on shore. Most of what is lost about the Head stays there; but one thing did come into the bay—a queer thing—a puncheon of brandy.

"The Squire claimed it; it was his right to have all that came on his land, and he owned this sea-shore from the Head to the breakers—every foot—so, in course, he had the brandy; and there was sore ill-will because he gave his men nothing—not even a glass of whiskey.

"Well, to make a long story short, that was the most wonderful liquor anybody ever tasted. The gentry came from far and near to take share, and it was cards and dice, and drinking and storytelling night after night—week in, week out. Even on Sundays, God forgive them! the officers would drive over from Ballycloyne, and sit emptying tumbler after tumbler till Monday morning came, for it made beautiful punch.

"But all at once people quit coming—a word went round that the liquor was not all it ought to be. Nobody could say what ailed it, but it got about that in some way men found it did not suit them.

"For one thing, they were losing money very fast.

"They could not make head against the Squire's luck, and a hint was dropped the puncheon ought to have been towed out to sea, and sunk in fifty fathoms of water.

"It was getting to the end of April, and fine, warm weather for the time of year, when first one, and then another, and then another still, began to take notice of a stranger who walked the shore alone at night. He was a dark man, the same colour as the drowned crew lying in the chapel graveyard, and had rings in his ears, and wore a strange kind of hat, and cut wonderful antics as he walked, and had an ambling sort of gait, curious to look at. Many tried to talk to him, but he only shook his head; so, as nobody could make out where he came from or what he wanted, they made sure he was the spirit of some poor wretch who was tossing about the Head, longing for a snug corner in holy ground.

"The priest went and tried to get some sense out of him.

"'Is it Christian burial you're wanting?' asked his reverence; but the creature only shook his head.

"'Is it word sent to the wives and daughters you've left orphans and widows, you'd like?' but no; it wasn't that.

"'Is it for sin committed you're doomed to walk this way? Would masses comfort ye? There's a heathen,' said his reverence; 'did you ever hear tell of a Christian that shook his head when masses were mentioned?'

"'Perhaps he doesn't understand English, Father,' says one of the officers who was there; 'try him with Latin.'

"No sooner said than done. The priest started off with such a string of aves and paters that the stranger fairly took to his heels and ran.

"'He is an evil spirit,' explained the priest, when he had stopped, tired out, 'and I have exorcised him.'

"But next night my gentleman was back again, as unconcerned as ever.

"'And he'll just have to stay,' said his reverence, 'for I've got lumbago in the small of my back, and pains in all my joints—never to speak of a hoarseness with standing there shouting; and I don't believe he understood a sentence I said.'

"Well, this went on for awhile, and people got that frightened of the man, or appearance of a man, they would not go near the sands; till in the end Squire Ennismore, who had always scoffed at the talk, took it into his head he would go down one night, and see into the rights of the matter himself. He, maybe, was feeling lonesome, because, as I told your honour before, people had left off coming to the house, and there was nobody for him to drink with.

"Out he goes, then, as bold as brass; and there were a few followed him. The man came forward at sight of the Squire and took off his hat with a foreign flourish. Not to be behind in civility, the Squire lifted his.

"'I have come, sir,' he said, speaking very loud, to try to make him understand, 'to know if you are looking for anything, and whether I can assist you to find it.'

"The man looked at the Squire as if he had taken the greatest liking to him, and took off his hat again.

"'Is it the vessel that was wrecked you are distressed about?'

"There came no answer, only a forbye mournful shake of the head.

"'Well, *I* haven't your ship, you know; it went all to bits months ago; and as for the sailors, they are snug and sound enough in consecrated ground.'

"The man stood and looked at the Squire with a queer sort of smile on his face.

"'What *do* you want?' asked Mr Ennismore, in a bit of a passion. 'If anything belonging to you went down with the vessel it's about the Head you ought to be looking for it, not here—unless, indeed, it's after the brandy you're fretting.'

"Now, the Squire had tried him in English and French, and was now speaking a language you'd have thought nobody could understand; but, faith, it seemed natural as kissing to the stranger.

"'Oh! that's where you are from, is it?' said the Squire. 'Why couldn't you have told me so at once? I can't give you the brandy, because it's mostly drunk; but come along, and you shall have as stiff a glass of punch as ever crossed your lips.' And without more to-do off they went, as sociable as you please, jabbering together in some outlandish tongue that made moderate folks' jaws ache to hear.

"That was the first night they conversed together, but it wasn't the last. The stranger must have been the height of good company, for the Squire never tired of him. Every evening, regularly, he came up to the house, always dressed the same, always smiling and polite, and then the Squire called for brandy and hot water, and they drank and played cards till cock-crow, talking and laughing into the small hours.

"This went on for weeks and weeks, nobody knowing where the man came from, or where he went; only two things the old housekeeper did know—that the puncheon was nearly empty, and that the Squire's flesh was wasting off him; and she felt so uneasy she went to the priest, but he could give her no manner of comfort.

"She got so concerned at last that she felt bound to listen at the dining-room door; but they always talked in that foreign gibberish, and whether it was blessing or cursing they were at she couldn't tell.

"Well, the upshot of it came one night in July—on the eve of the Squire's birthday—there wasn't a drop of spirit left in the puncheon—no, not as much as would drown a fly. They had drunk the whole lot clean up—and the old woman stood trembling, expecting every minute to hear the bell ring for more brandy, for where was she to get more if they wanted any?

"All at once the Squire and the stranger came out into the hall. It was a full moon, and light as day.

"'I'll go home with you tonight by way of a change,' says the Squire.

"'Will you so?' asked the other.

"'That I will,' answered the Squire.

"'It is your own choice, you know.'

"'Yes; it is my own choice: let us go.'

"So they went. And the housekeeper ran up to the window on the great staircase and watched the way they took. Her niece lived there as housemaid, and she came and watched too; and, after a while, the butler as well. They all turned their faces this way, and looked after their master walking beside the strange man along these very sands. Well, they saw them walk out and out to the very ebb-line—but they didn't stop there—they went on, and on, and on, and on, till the water took them to their knees, and then to their waists, and then to their arm-pits, and then to their heads; but long before that the women and the butler were running out on the shore as fast as they could, shouting for help."

"Well?" said the Englishman.

"Living or dead, Squire Ennismore never came back again. Next morning, when the tide ebbed again, one walking over the sand saw the print of a cloven foot—that he tracked to the water's edge. Then everybody knew where the Squire had gone, and with whom."

"And no more search was made?"

"Where would have been the use searching?"

"Not much, I suppose. It's a strange story, anyhow."

"But true, your honour—every word of it."

"Oh! I have no doubt of that," was the satisfactory reply.

1838

THE FORTUNES OF SIR ROBERT ARDAGH

Joseph Sheridan Le Fanu

Although Joseph Sheridan Le Fanu has been generally acknowledged as an influential and pioneering master of the Victorian ghost story, the broader audience of gothic and horror fiction remains unacquainted with many aspects of his intriguing literary work. Mostly known for his emblematic vampire novella "Carmilla" included in his seminal collection *In a Glass Darkly* (1872), and Victorian gothic novels such as *Uncle Silas* (1864) and *The Wyvern Mystery* (1869), Le Fanu had also penned a wonderful plethora of shorter tales of the otherworldly and the macabre distinguished by his remarkably suggestive style and singular treatment of his themes.

Joseph Sheridan Le Fanu, who was descended from a Huguenot family, was born in Dublin in 1814 and studied law at Trinity College but never practised; instead, he became a journalist and in 1838 started contributing his writings to *Dublin University Magazine*—for which he became proprietor and editor in 1861—whereas in later years he published tales in Charles Dickens's periodical *All the Year Round*. Furthermore, he had come "under the spell" of the mystical writings of eighteenth-century theologian and philosopher Emmanuel Swedenborg, who had a significant impact on his later works; he also got the nickname "The Invisible Prince" due to his reclusiveness in the years following his wife's death and until his own demise in 1873.

"The Fortunes of Sir Robert Ardagh" is one of his earliest tales, subtle and evasive, yet spine-chilling as most of his writings. It was first published in *Dublin University Magazine* in 1838 and became part of the posthumous collection *The Purcell Papers* (1880). Employing gothic tropes in his own idiosyncratic manner, Le Fanu delivers a masterfully sinister and almost cryptic tale about an inexplicable attachment, with hints of lurking insanity and a tormented double self.

BEING A SECOND EXTRACT FROM THE PAPERS OF THE LATE FATHER PURCELL

"The earth hath bubbles as the water hath—
And these are of them."

In the south of Ireland, and on the borders of the county of Limerick, there lies a district of two or three miles in length, which is rendered interesting by the fact that it is one of the very few spots throughout this country, in which some vestiges of aboriginal forest still remain. It has little or none of the lordly character of the American forest, for the axe has felled its oldest and its grandest trees; but in the close wood which survives, live all the wild and pleasing peculiarities of nature: its complete irregularity, its vistas, in whose perspective the quiet cattle are peacefully browsing; its refreshing glades, where the grey rocks arise from amid the nodding fern; the silvery shafts of the old birch trees; the knotted trunks of the hoary oak, the grotesque but graceful branches which never shed their honours under the tyrant pruning-hook; the soft green sward; the chequered light and shade; the wild luxuriant weeds; the lichen and the moss—all, all are beautiful alike in the green freshness of spring, or in the sadness and sere of autumn. Their beauty is of that kind which makes the heart full with joy—appealing to the affections with a power which belongs to nature only. This wood runs up, from below the base, to the ridge of a long line of irregular hills, having perhaps, in primitive times, formed but the skirting of some mighty forest which occupied the level below.

But now, alas! whither have we drifted? whither has the tide of civilisation borne us? It has passed over a land unprepared for it—it has left nakedness behind it; we have lost our forests, but our marauders remain; we have destroyed all that is picturesque, while we have retained everything that is revolting in barbarism. Through the midst of this woodland there runs a deep gully or glen, where the stillness of the scene is broken in upon by the brawling of a mountain-stream, which, however, in the winter season, swells into a rapid and formidable torrent.

There is one point at which the glen becomes extremely deep and narrow; the sides descend to the depth of some hundred feet, and are so steep as to be nearly perpendicular. The wild trees which have taken root in the crannies and chasms of the rock have so intersected and entangled, that one can with difficulty catch a glimpse of the stream, which wheels, flashes, and foams below, as if exulting in the surrounding silence and solitude.

This spot was not unwisely chosen, as a point of no ordinary strength, for the erection of a massive square tower or keep, one side of which rises as if in continuation of the precipitous cliff on which it is based. Originally, the only mode of ingress was by a narrow portal in the very wall which overtopped the precipice, opening upon a ledge of rock which afforded a precarious pathway, cautiously intersected, however, by a deep trench cut with great labour in the living rock; so that, in its original state, and before the introduction of artillery into the art of war, this tower might have been pronounced, and that not presumptuously, almost impregnable.

The progress of improvement and the increasing security of the times had, however, tempted its successive proprietors, if not to adorn, at least to enlarge their premises, and at about the middle of the last century, when the castle was last inhabited, the original square tower formed but a small part of the edifice.

The castle, and a wide tract of the surrounding country, had from time immemorial belonged to a family which, for distinctness, we shall call by the name of Ardagh; and owing to the associations which, in Ireland, almost always attach to scenes which have long witnessed alike the exercise of stern feudal authority, and of that savage hospitality which distinguished the good old times, this building has become the subject and the scene of many wild and extraordinary traditions. One of them I have been enabled, by a personal acquaintance with an eye-witness of the events, to trace to its origin; and yet it is hard to say whether the events which I am about to record appear more strange or improbable as seen through the distorting medium of tradition, or in the appalling dimness of uncertainty which surrounds the reality.

Tradition says that, sometime in the last century, Sir Robert Ardagh, a young man, and the last heir of that family, went abroad and served in foreign armies; and that, having acquired considerable honour and emolument, he settled at Castle Ardagh, the building we have just now attempted to describe. He was what the country people call a *dark* man; that is, he was considered morose, reserved, and ill-tempered; and, as it was supposed from the utter solitude of his life, was upon no terms of cordiality with the other members of his family.

The only occasion upon which he broke through the solitary monotony of his life was during the continuance of the racing season, and immediately subsequent to it; at which time he was to be seen among the busiest upon the course, betting deeply and unhesitatingly, and invariably with success. Sir Robert was, however, too well known as a man of honour, and of too high a family, to be suspected of any unfair dealing. He was, moreover, a soldier, and a man of an intrepid as well as of a haughty character; and no one cared to hazard a surmise, the consequences of which would be felt most probably by its originator only.

Gossip, however, was not silent; it was remarked that Sir Robert never appeared at the race-ground, which was the only place of public resort which he frequented, except in company with a certain strange-looking person, who was never seen elsewhere, or under other circumstances. It was remarked, too, that this man, whose relation to Sir Robert was never distinctly ascertained, was the only person to whom he seemed to speak unnecessarily; it was observed that while with the country gentry he exchanged no further communication than what was unavoidable in arranging his sporting transactions, with this person he would converse earnestly and frequently. Tradition asserts that, to enhance the curiosity which this unaccountable and exclusive preference excited, the stranger possessed some striking and unpleasant peculiarities of person and of garb—she does not say, however, what these were—but they, in conjunction with Sir Robert's secluded habits and extraordinary run of luck—a success which was supposed to result from the suggestions and immediate advice of the unknown—were sufficient to warrant report in pronouncing that there was something *queer* in the wind, and in surmising that Sir Robert was playing a fearful and a hazardous game, and that, in short, his strange companion was little better than the devil himself.

Years, however, rolled quietly away, and nothing novel occurred in the arrangements of Castle Ardagh, excepting that Sir Robert parted with his odd companion, but as nobody could tell whence he came, so nobody could say whither he had gone. Sir Robert's habits, however, underwent no consequent change; he continued regularly to frequent the race meetings, without mixing at all in the convivialities of the gentry, and immediately afterwards to relapse into the secluded monotony of his ordinary life.

It was said that he had accumulated vast sums of money—and, as his bets were always successful, and always large, such must have been the case. He did not suffer the acquisition of wealth, however, to influence his hospitality or his housekeeping—he neither purchased land, nor extended his establishment; and his mode of enjoying his money must have been altogether that of the miser—consisting merely in the pleasure of touching and telling his gold, and in the consciousness of wealth.

Sir Robert's temper, so far from improving, became more than ever gloomy and morose. He sometimes carried the indulgence of his evil dispositions to such a height that it bordered upon insanity. During these paroxysms he would neither eat, drink, nor sleep. On such occasions he insisted on perfect privacy, even from the intrusion of his most trusted servants; his voice was frequently heard, sometimes in earnest supplication, sometime as if in loud and angry altercation with some unknown visitant; sometimes he would, for hours together, walk to and fro throughout the long oak wainscoted apartment, which he generally occupied, with wild gesticulations and agitated pace, in the manner of one who has been roused to a state of unnatural excitement by some sudden and appalling intimation.

These paroxysms of apparent lunacy were so frightful, that during their continuance even his oldest and most faithful domestics dared not approach him; consequently, his hours of agony were never intruded upon, and the mysterious causes of his sufferings appeared likely to remain hidden for ever.

On one occasion a fit of this kind continued for an unusual time, the ordinary term of their duration—about two days—had been long past, and the old servant who generally waited upon Sir Robert after these visitations, having in vain listened for the well-known tinkle of his master's hand-bell, began to feel extremely anxious; he feared that his master might have died from sheer exhaustion, or perhaps put an end to his own existence during his miserable depression. These fears at length became so strong, that having in vain urged some of his brother servants to accompany him, he determined to go up alone, and himself see whether any accident had befallen Sir Robert.

He traversed the several passages which conducted from the new to the more ancient parts of the mansion, and having arrived in the old hall of the castle, the utter silence of the hour, for it was very late in the night, the idea of the nature of the enterprise in which he was engaging himself, a sensation of remoteness from anything like human companionship, but, more than all, the vivid but undefined anticipation of something horrible, came upon him with such oppressive weight that he hesitated as to whether he should proceed. Real uneasiness, however, respecting the fate of his master, for whom he felt that kind of attachment which the force of habitual intercourse not unfrequently engenders respecting objects not in themselves amiable, and also a latent unwillingness to expose his weakness to the ridicule of his fellow-servants, combined to overcome his reluctance; and he had just placed his foot upon the first step of the staircase which conducted to his master's chamber, when his attention was arrested by a low but distinct knocking at the hall-door. Not, perhaps, very sorry at finding thus an excuse even for deferring his intended expedition, he placed the candle upon a stone block which lay in the hall, and approached the door, uncertain whether his ears had not deceived him. This doubt was justified by the circumstance that the hall entrance had been for nearly fifty years disused as a mode of ingress to the castle. The situation of this gate also, which we have endeavoured to describe, opening upon a narrow ledge of rock which overhangs a perilous cliff, rendered it at all times, but particularly at night, a dangerous entrance. This shelving platform of rock, which formed the only avenue to the door, was divided, as I have already stated, by a broad chasm, the planks across which had long disappeared by decay or otherwise, so that it seemed at least highly improbable that any man could have found his way across the passage in safety to the door, more particularly on a night like that, of singular darkness. The old man, therefore, listened attentively, to ascertain whether the first application should be followed by another. He had not long to wait; the same low but singularly distinct knocking was repeated; so low that it seemed as if the applicant had employed no harder or heavier instrument than his hand, and yet, despite the immense thickness of the door, with such strength that the sound was distinctly audible.

The knock was repeated a third time, without any increase of loudness; and the old man, obeying an impulse for which to his dying hour he could never account, proceeded to remove, one by one, the three great oaken bars which secured the door. Time and damp had effectually corroded the iron chambers of the lock, so that it afforded little resistance. With some effort, as he believed, assisted from without, the old servant succeeded in opening the door; and a low, square-built figure, apparently that of a man wrapped in a large black cloak, entered the hall. The servant could not see much of this visitant with any distinctness; his dress appeared foreign, the skirt of his ample cloak was thrown over one shoulder; he wore a large felt hat, with a very heavy leaf, from under which escaped what appeared to be a mass of long sooty-black hair; his feet were cased in heavy riding-boots. Such were the few particulars which the servant had time and light to observe. The stranger desired him to let his master know instantly that a friend had come, by appointment, to settle some business with him. The servant hesitated, but a slight motion on the part of his visitor, as if to possess himself of the candle, determined him; so, taking it in his hand, he ascended the castle stairs, leaving his guest in the hall.

On reaching the apartment which opened upon the oak-chamber he was surprised to observe the door of that room partly open, and the room itself lit up. He paused, but there was no sound; he looked in, and saw Sir Robert, his head and the upper part of his body reclining on a table, upon which burned a lamp; his arms were stretched forward on either side, and perfectly motionless; it appeared that, having been sitting at the table, he had thus sunk forward, either dead or in a swoon. There was no sound of breathing; all was silent, except the sharp ticking of a watch, which lay beside the lamp. The servant coughed twice or thrice, but with no effect; his fears now almost amounted to certainty, and he was approaching the table on which his master partly lay, to satisfy himself of his death, when Sir Robert slowly raised his head, and throwing himself back in his chair, fixed his eyes in a ghastly and uncertain gaze upon his attendant. At length he said, slowly and painfully, as if he dreaded the answer:

"In God's name, what are you?"

"Sir," said the servant, "a strange gentleman wants to see you below."

At this intimation Sir Robert, starting on his feet and tossing his arms wildly upwards, uttered a shriek of such appalling and despairing terror that it was almost too fearful for human endurance; and long after the sound had ceased it seemed to the terrified imagination of the old servant to roll through the deserted passages in bursts of unnatural laughter. After a few moments Sir Robert said:

"Can't you send him away? Why does he come so soon? O God! O God! let him leave me for an hour; a little time. I can't see him now; try to get him away. You see I can't go down now; I have not strength. O God! o God! let him come back in an hour; it is not long to wait. He cannot lose anything by it; nothing, nothing, nothing. Tell him that; say anything to him."

The servant went down. In his own words, he did not feel the stairs under him till he got to the hall. The figure stood exactly as he had left it. He delivered his master's message as coherently as he could. The stranger replied in a careless tone:

"If Sir Robert will not come down to me, I must go up to him."

The man returned, and to his surprise he found his master much more composed in manner. He listened to the message, and though the cold perspiration rose in drops upon his forehead faster than he could wipe it away, his manner had lost the dreadful agitation which had marked it before. He rose feebly, and casting a last look of agony behind him, passed from the room to the lobby, where he signed to his attendant not to follow him. The man moved as far as the head of the staircase, from whence he had a tolerably distinct view of the hall, which was imperfectly lighted by the candle he had left there.

He saw his master reel, rather than walk down the stairs, clinging all the way to the banisters. He walked on, as if about to sink every moment from weakness. The figure advanced as if to meet him, and in passing struck down the light. The servant could see no more; but there was a sound of struggling, renewed at intervals with silent but fearful energy. It was evident, however, that the parties were approaching the door, for he heard the solid oak sound twice or thrice, as the feet of the combatants, in shuffling hither and thither over the floor, struck upon it. After a slight pause he heard the door thrown open with such violence that the leaf seemed to strike the side-wall of the hall, for it was so dark without that this could only be surmised by the sound. The struggle was renewed with an agony and intenseness of energy that betrayed itself in deep-drawn gasps. One desperate effort, which terminated in the breaking of some part of the door, producing a sound as if the door-post was wrenched from its position, was followed by another wrestle, evidently upon the narrow ledge which ran outside the door, overtopping the precipice. This proved to be the final struggle, for it was followed by a crashing sound as if some heavy body had fallen over, and was rushing down the precipice, through the light boughs that crossed near the top. All then became still as the grave, except when the moan of the night wind sighed up the wooded glen.

The old servant had not nerve to return through the hall, and to him the darkness seemed all but endless; but morning at length came, and with it the disclosure of the events of the night. Near the door, upon the ground, lay Sir Robert's sword-belt, which had given way in the scuffle. A huge splinter from the massive door-post had been wrenched off by an almost superhuman effort—one which nothing but the gripe of a despairing man could have severed—and on the rock outside were left the marks of the slipping and sliding of feet.

At the foot of the precipice, not immediately under the castle, but dragged some way up the glen, were found the remains of Sir Robert, with hardly a vestige of a limb or feature left distinguishable. The right hand, however, was uninjured, and in its fingers were clutched, with the fixedness of death, a long lock of coarse sooty hair—the only direct circumstantial evidence of the presence of a second person. So says tradition.

This story, as I have mentioned, was current among the dealers in such lore; but the original facts are so dissimilar in all but the name of the principal person mentioned and his mode of life, and the fact that his death was accompanied with circumstances of extraordinary mystery, that the two narratives are totally irreconcilable (even allowing the utmost for the exaggerating influence of tradition), except by supposing report to have combined and blended together the fabulous histories of several distinct bearers of the family name. However this may be, I shall lay before the reader a distinct recital of the events from which the foregoing tradition arose. With respect to these there can be no mistake; they are authenticated as fully as anything can be by human testimony; and I state them principally upon the evidence of a lady who herself bore a prominent part in the strange events which she related, and which I now record as being among the few well-attested tales of the marvellous which it has been my fate to hear. I shall, as far as I am able, arrange in one combined narrative the evidence of several distinct persons who were eye-witnesses of what they related, and with the truth of whose testimony I am solemnly and deeply impressed.

Sir Robert Ardagh, as we choose to call him, was the heir and representative of the family whose name he bore; but owing to the prodigality of his father, the estates descended to him in a very impaired condition. Urged by the restless spirit of youth, or more probably by a feeling of pride which could not submit to witness, in the paternal mansion, what he considered a humiliating alteration in the style and hospitality which up to that time had distinguished his family, Sir Robert left Ireland and went abroad. How he occupied himself, or what countries he visited during his absence, was never known, nor did he afterwards make any allusion or encourage any inquiries touching his foreign sojourn. He left Ireland in the year 1742, being then just of age, and was not heard of until the year 1760—about eighteen years afterwards—at which time he returned. His personal appearance was, as might have been expected, very greatly altered, more altered, indeed, than the time of his absence might have warranted one in supposing likely. But to counterbalance the unfavourable change which time had wrought in his form and features, he had acquired all the advantages of polish of manner and refinement of taste which foreign travel is supposed to bestow. But what was truly surprising was that it soon became evident that Sir Robert was very wealthy—wealthy to an extraordinary and unaccountable degree; and this fact was made manifest, not only by his expensive style of living, but by his proceeding to disembarrass his property, and to purchase extensive estates in addition. Moreover, there could be nothing deceptive in these appearances, for he paid ready money for everything, from the most important purchase to the most trifling.

Sir Robert was a remarkably agreeable man, and possessing the combined advantages of birth and property, he was, as a matter of course, gladly received into the highest society which the metropolis then commanded. It was thus that he became acquainted with the two beautiful Miss F——ds, then among the brightest ornaments of the highest circle of Dublin fashion. Their family was in more than one direction allied to nobility; and Lady D——, their elder sister by many years, and sometime married to a once well-known nobleman, was now their protectress. These considerations, beside the fact that the young ladies were what is usually termed heiresses, though not to a very great amount, secured to them a high position in the best society which Ireland then produced. The two young ladies differed strongly, alike in appearance and in character. The elder of the two, Emily, was generally considered the handsomer—for her beauty was of that impressive kind which never failed to strike even at the first glance, possessing as it did all the advantages of a fine person and a commanding carriage. The beauty of her features strikingly assorted in character with that of her figure and deportment. Her hair was raven-black and richly luxuriant, beautifully contrasting with the perfect whiteness of her forehead—her finely pencilled brows were black as the ringlets that clustered near them—and her blue eyes, full, lustrous, and animated, possessed all the power and brilliancy of brown ones, with more than their softness and variety of expression. She was not, however, merely the tragedy queen. When she smiled, and that was not seldom, the dimpling of cheek and chin, the laughing display of the small and beautiful teeth—but, more than all, the roguish archness of her deep, bright eye, showed that nature had not neglected in her the lighter and the softer characteristics of woman.

Her younger sister Mary was, as I believe not unfrequently occurs in the case of sisters, quite in the opposite style of beauty. She was light-haired, had more colour, had nearly equal grace, with much more liveliness of manner. Her eyes were of that dark grey which poets so much admire—full of expression and vivacity. She was altogether a very beautiful and animated girl—though as unlike her sister as the presence of those two qualities would permit her to be. Their dissimilarity did not stop here—it was deeper than mere appearance—the character of their minds differed almost as strikingly as did their complexion. The fair-haired beauty had a large proportion of that softness and pliability of temper which physiognomists assign as the characteristics of such complexions. She was much more the creature of impulse than of feeling, and consequently more the victim of extrinsic circumstances than was her sister. Emily, on the contrary, possessed considerable firmness and decision. She was less excitable, but when excited her feelings were more intense and enduring. She wanted much of the gaiety, but with it the volatility of her younger sister. Her opinions were adopted, and her friendships formed more reflectively, and her affections seemed to move, as it were, more slowly, but more determinedly. This firmness of character did not amount to anything masculine, and did not at all impair the feminine grace of her manners.

Sir Robert Ardagh was for a long time apparently equally attentive to the two sisters, and many were the conjectures and the surmises as to which would be the lady of his choice. At length, however, these doubts were determined; he proposed for and was accepted by the dark beauty, Emily F——d.

The bridals were celebrated in a manner becoming the wealth and connections of the parties; and Sir Robert and Lady Ardagh left Dublin to pass the honeymoon at the family mansion, Castle Ardagh, which had lately been fitted up in a style bordering upon magnificent. Whether in compliance with the wishes of his lady, or owing to some whim of his own, his habits were henceforward strikingly altered; and from having moved among the gayest if not the most profligate of the votaries of fashion, he suddenly settled down into a quiet, domestic, country gentleman, and seldom, if ever, visited the capital, and then his sojourns were as brief as the nature of his business would permit.

Lady Ardagh, however, did not suffer from this change further than in being secluded from general society; for Sir Robert's wealth, and the hospitality which he had established in the family mansion, commanded that of such of his lady's friends and relatives as had leisure or inclination to visit the castle; and as their style of living was very handsome, and its internal resources of amusement considerable, few invitations from Sir Robert or his lady were neglected.

Many years passed quietly away, during which Sir Robert's and Lady Ardagh's hopes of issue were several times disappointed. In the lapse of all this time there occurred but one event worth recording. Sir Robert had brought with him from abroad a valet, who sometimes professed himself to be French, at others Italian, and at others again German. He spoke all these languages with equal fluency, and seemed to take a kind of pleasure in puzzling the sagacity and balking the curiosity of such of the visitors at the castle as at any time happened to enter into conversation with him, or who, struck by his singularities, became inquisitive respecting his country and origin. Sir Robert called him by the French name, JACQUE, and among the lower orders he was familiarly known by the title of "Jack, the devil," an appellation which originated in a supposed malignity of disposition and a real reluctance to mix in the society of those who were believed to be his equals. This morose reserve, coupled with the mystery which enveloped all about him, rendered him an object of suspicion and inquiry to his fellow-servants, amongst whom it was whispered that this man in secret governed the actions of Sir Robert with a despotic dictation, and that, as if to indemnify himself for his public and apparent servitude and self-denial, he in private exacted a degree of respectful homage from his so-called master, totally inconsistent with the relation generally supposed to exist between them.

This man's personal appearance was, to say the least of it, extremely odd; he was low in stature; and this defect was enhanced by a distortion of the spine, so considerable as almost to amount to a hunch; his features, too, had all that sharpness and sickliness of hue which generally accompany deformity; he wore his hair, which was black as soot, in heavy neglected ringlets about his shoulders, and always without powder—a peculiarity in those days. There was something unpleasant, too, in the circumstance that he never raised his eyes to meet those of another; this fact was often cited as a proof of his being something not quite right, and said to result not from the timidity which is supposed in most cases to induce this habit, but from a consciousness that his eye possessed a power which, if exhibited, would betray a supernatural origin. Once, and once only, had he violated this sinister observance: it was on the occasion of Sir Robert's hopes having been most bitterly disappointed; his lady, after a severe and dangerous confinement, gave birth to a dead child. Immediately after the intelligence had been made known, a servant, having upon some business passed outside the gate of the castle-yard, was met by Jacque, who, contrary to his wont, accosted him, observing, "So, after all the pother, the son and heir is still-born." This remark was accompanied by a chuckling laugh, the only approach to merriment which he was ever known to exhibit. The servant, who was really disappointed, having hoped for holiday times, feasting and debauchery with impunity during the rejoicings which would have accompanied a christening, turned tartly upon the little valet, telling him that he should let Sir Robert know how he had received the tidings which should have filled any faithful servant with sorrow; and having once broken the ice, he was proceeding with increasing fluency, when his harangue was cut short and his temerity punished, by the little man raising his head and treating him to a scowl so fearful, half-demoniac, half-insane, that it haunted his imagination in nightmares and nervous tremors for months after.

To this man Lady Ardagh had, at first sight, conceived an antipathy amounting to horror, a mixture of loathing and dread so very powerful that she had made it a particular and urgent request to Sir Robert, that he would dismiss him, offering herself, from that property which Sir Robert had by the marriage settlements left at her own disposal, to provide handsomely for him, provided only she might be relieved from the continual anxiety and discomfort which the fear of encountering him induced.

Sir Robert, however, would not hear of it; the request seemed at first to agitate and distress him; but when still urged in defiance of his peremptory refusal, he burst into a violent fit of fury; he spoke darkly of great sacrifices which he had made, and threatened that if the request were at any time renewed he would leave both her and the country for ever. This was, however, a solitary instance of violence; his general conduct towards Lady Ardagh, though at no time uxorious, was certainly kind and respectful, and he was more than repaid in the fervent attachment which she bore him in return.

Some short time after this strange interview between Sir Robert and Lady Ardagh; one night after the family had retired to bed, and when everything had been quiet for some time, the bell of Sir Robert's dressing-room rang suddenly and violently; the ringing was repeated again and again at still shorter intervals, and with increasing violence, as if the person who pulled the bell was agitated by the presence of some terrifying and imminent danger. A servant named Donovan was the first to answer it; he threw on his clothes, and hurried to the room.

Sir Robert had selected for his private room an apartment remote from the bed-chambers of the castle, most of which lay in the more modern parts of the mansion, and secured at its entrance by a double door. As the servant opened the first of these, Sir Robert's bell again sounded with a longer and louder peal; the inner door resisted his efforts to open it; but after a few violent struggles, not having been perfectly secured, or owing to the inadequacy of the bolt itself, it gave way, and the servant rushed into the apartment, advancing several paces before he could recover himself. As he entered, he heard Sir Robert's voice exclaiming loudly—"Wait without, do not come in yet;" but the prohibition came too late. Near a low truckle-bed, upon which Sir Robert sometimes slept, for he was a whimsical man, in a large armchair, sat, or rather lounged, the form of the valet Jacque, his arms folded, and his heels stretched forward on the floor, so as fully to exhibit his misshapen legs, his head thrown back, and his eyes fixed upon his master with a look of indescribable defiance and derision, while, as if to add to the strange insolence of his attitude and expression, he had placed upon his head the black cloth cap which it was his habit to wear.

Sir Robert was standing before him, at the distance of several yards, in a posture expressive of despair, terror, and what might be called an agony of humility. He waved his hand twice or thrice, as if to dismiss the servant, who, however, remained fixed on the spot where he had first stood; and then, as if forgetting everything but the agony within him, he pressed his clenched hands on his cold damp brow, and dashed away the heavy drops that gathered chill and thickly there.

Jacque broke the silence.

"Donovan," said he, "shake up that drone and drunkard, Carlton; tell him that his master directs that the travelling carriage shall be at the door within half-an-hour."

The servant paused, as if in doubt as to what he should do; but his scruples were resolved by Sir Robert's saying hurriedly, "Go—go, do whatever he directs; his commands are mine; tell Carlton the same."

The servant hurried to obey, and in about half-an-hour the carriage was at the door, and Jacque, having directed the coachman to drive to B——n, a small town at about the distance of twelve miles—the nearest point, however, at which post-horses could be obtained—stepped into the vehicle, which accordingly quitted the castle immediately.

Although it was a fine moonlight night, the carriage made its way but very slowly, and after the lapse of two hours the travellers had arrived at a point about eight miles from the castle, at which the road strikes through a desolate and heathy flat, sloping up distantly at either side into bleak undulatory hills, in whose monotonous sweep the imagination beholds the heaving of some dark sluggish sea, arrested in its first commotion by some preternatural power. It is a gloomy and divested spot; there is neither tree nor habitation near it; its monotony is unbroken, except by here and there the grey front of a rock peering above the heath, and the effect is rendered yet more dreary and spectral by the exaggerated and misty shadows which the moon casts along the sloping sides of the hills.

When they had gained about the centre of this tract, Carlton, the coachman, was surprised to see a figure standing at some distance in advance, immediately beside the road, and still more so when, on coming up, he observed that it was no other than Jacque whom he believed to be at that moment quietly seated in the carriage; the coachman drew up, and nodding to him, the little valet exclaimed:

"Carlton, I have got the start of you; the roads are heavy, so I shall even take care of myself the rest of the way. Do you make your way back as best you can, and I shall follow my own nose."

So saying, he chucked a purse into the lap of the coachman, and turning off at a right angle with the road, he began to move rapidly away in the direction of the dark ridge that lowered in the distance.

The servant watched him until he was lost in the shadowy haze of night; and neither he nor any of the inmates of the castle saw Jacque again. His disappearance, as might have been expected, did not cause any regret among the servants and dependants at the castle; and Lady Ardagh did not attempt to conceal her delight; but with Sir Robert matters were different, for two or three days subsequent to this event he confined himself to his room, and when he did return to his ordinary occupations, it was with a gloomy indifference, which showed that he did so more from habit than from any interest he felt in them. He appeared from that moment unaccountably and strikingly changed, and thenceforward walked through life as a thing from which he could derive neither profit nor pleasure. His temper, however, so far from growing wayward or morose, became, though gloomy, very—almost unnaturally—placid and cold; but his spirits totally failed, and he grew silent and abstracted.

These sombre habits of mind, as might have been anticipated, very materially affected the gay housekeeping of the castle; and the dark and melancholy spirit of its master seemed to have communicated itself to the very domestics, almost to the very walls of the mansion.

Several years rolled on in this way, and the sounds of mirth and wassail had long been strangers to the castle, when Sir Robert requested his lady, to her great astonishment, to invite some twenty or thirty of their friends to spend the Christmas, which was fast approaching, at the castle. Lady Ardagh gladly complied, and her sister Mary, who still continued unmarried, and Lady D—— were of course included in the invitations. Lady Ardagh had requested her sisters to set forward as early as possible, in order that she might enjoy a little of their society before the arrival of the other guests; and in compliance with this request they left Dublin almost immediately upon receiving the invitation, a little more than a week before the arrival of the festival which was to be the period at which the whole party were to muster.

For expedition's sake it was arranged that they should post, while Lady D——'s groom was to follow with her horses, she taking with herself her own maid and one male servant. They left the city when the day was considerably spent, and consequently made but three stages in the first day; upon the second, at about eight in the evening, they had reached the town of K——k, distant about fifteen miles from Castle Ardagh. Here, owing to Miss F——d's great fatigue, she having been for a considerable time in a very delicate state of health, it was determined to put up for the night. They, accordingly, took possession of the best sitting-room which the inn commanded, and Lady D—— remained in it to direct and urge the preparations for some refreshment, which the fatigues of the day had rendered necessary, while her younger sister retired to her bed-chamber to rest there for a little time, as the parlour commanded no such luxury as a sofa.

Miss F——d was, as I have already stated, at this time in very delicate health; and upon this occasion the exhaustion of fatigue, and the dreary badness of the weather, combined to depress her spirits. Lady D——had not been left long to herself, when the door communicating with the passage was abruptly opened, and her sister Mary entered in a state of great agitation; she sat down pale and trembling upon one of the chairs, and it was not until a copious flood of tears had relieved her, that she became sufficiently calm to relate the cause of her excitement and distress. It was simply this. Almost immediately upon lying down upon the bed she sank into a feverish and unrefreshing slumber; images of all grotesque shapes and startling colours flitted before her sleeping fancy with all the rapidity and variety of the changes in a kaleidoscope. At length, as she described it, a mist seemed to interpose itself between her sight and the ever-shifting scenery which sported before her imagination, and out of this cloudy shadow gradually emerged a figure whose back seemed turned towards the sleeper; it was that of a lady, who, in perfect silence, was expressing as far as pantomimic gesture could, by wringing her hands, and throwing her head from side to side, in the manner of one who is exhausted by the over indulgence, by the very sickness and impatience of grief, the extremity of misery. For a long time she sought in vain to catch a glimpse of the face of the apparition, who thus seemed to stir and live before her. But at length the figure seemed to move with an air of authority, as if about to give directions to some inferior, and in doing so, it turned its head so as to display, with a ghastly distinctness, the features of Lady Ardagh, pale as death, with her dark hair all dishevelled, and her eyes dim and sunken with weeping. The revulsion of feeling which Miss F——d experienced at this disclosure—for up to that point she had contemplated the appearance rather with a sense of curiosity and of interest, than of anything deeper—was so horrible, that the shock awoke her perfectly. She sat up in the bed, and looked fearfully around the room, which was imperfectly lighted by a single candle burning dimly, as if she almost expected to see the reality of her dreadful vision lurking in some corner of the chamber. Her fears were, however, verified, though not in the way she expected; yet in a manner sufficiently horrible—for she had hardly time to breathe and to collect her thoughts, when she heard, or thought she heard, the voice of her sister, Lady Ardagh, sometimes sobbing violently, and sometimes almost shrieking as if in terror, and calling upon her and Lady D——, with the most imploring earnestness of despair, for God's sake to lose no time in coming to her. All this was so horribly distinct, that it seemed as if the mourner was standing within a few yards of the spot where Miss F——d lay. She sprang from the bed, and leaving the candle in the room behind her, she made her way in the dark through the passage, the voice still following her, until as she arrived at the door of the sitting-room it seemed to die away in low sobbing.

As soon as Miss F——d was tolerably recovered, she declared her determination to proceed directly, and without further loss of time, to Castle Ardagh. It was not without much difficulty that Lady D—— at length prevailed upon her to consent to remain where they then were, until morning should arrive, when it was to be expected that the young lady would be much refreshed by at least remaining quiet for the night, even though sleep were out of the question. Lady D—— was convinced, from the nervous and feverish symptoms which her sister exhibited, that she had already done too much, and was more than ever satisfied of the necessity of prosecuting the journey no further upon that day. After some time she persuaded her sister to return to her room, where she remained with her until she had gone to bed, and appeared comparatively composed. Lady D—— then returned to the parlour, and not finding herself sleepy, she remained sitting by the fire. Her solitude was a second time broken in upon, by the entrance of her sister, who now appeared, if possible, more agitated than before. She said that Lady D—— had not long left the room, when she was roused by a repetition of the same wailing and lamentations, accompanied by the wildest and most agonised supplications that no time should be lost in coming to Castle Ardagh, and all in her sister's voice, and uttered at the same proximity as before. This time the voice had followed her to the very door of the sitting-room, and until she closed it, seemed to pour forth its cries and sobs at the very threshold.

Miss F——d now most positively declared that nothing should prevent her proceeding instantly to the castle, adding that if Lady D—— would not accompany her, she would go on by herself. Superstitious feelings are at all times more or less contagious, and the last century afforded a soil much more congenial to their growth than the present. Lady D—— was so far affected by her sister's terrors, that she became, at least, uneasy; and seeing that her sister was immovably determined upon setting forward immediately, she consented to accompany her forthwith. After a slight delay, fresh horses were procured, and the two ladies and their attendants renewed their journey, with strong injunctions to the driver to quicken their rate of travelling as much as possible, and promises of reward in case of his doing so.

Roads were then in much worse condition throughout the south, even than they now are; and the fifteen miles which modern posting would have passed in little more than an hour and a half, were not completed even with every possible exertion in twice the time. Miss F——d had been nervously restless during the journey. Her head had been constantly out of the carriage window; and as they approached the entrance to the castle demesne, which lay about a mile from the building, her anxiety began to communicate itself to her sister. The postillion had just dismounted, and was endeavouring to open the gate—at that time a necessary trouble; for in the middle of the last century porter's lodges were not common in the south of Ireland, and locks and keys almost unknown. He had just succeeded in rolling back the heavy oaken gate so as to admit the vehicle, when a mounted servant rode rapidly down the avenue, and drawing up at the carriage, asked of the postillion who the party were; and on hearing, he rode round to the carriage window and handed in a note, which Lady D—— received. By the assistance of one of the coach-lamps they succeeded in deciphering it. It was scrawled in great agitation, and ran thus:

"My Dear Sister—My Dear Sisters both,—In God's name lose no time, I am frightened and miserable; I cannot explain all till

> you come. I am too much terrified to write coherently; but understand me—hasten—do not waste a minute. I am afraid you will come too late.
>
> "E. A."

The servant could tell nothing more than that the castle was in great confusion, and that Lady Ardagh had been crying bitterly all the night. Sir Robert was perfectly well. Altogether at a loss as to the cause of Lady Ardagh's great distress, they urged their way up the steep and broken avenue which wound through the crowding trees, whose wild and grotesque branches, now left stripped and naked by the blasts of winter, stretched drearily across the road. As the carriage drew up in the area before the door, the anxiety of the ladies almost amounted to agony; and scarcely waiting for the assistance of their attendant, they sprang to the ground, and in an instant stood at the castle door. From within were distinctly audible the sounds of lamentation and weeping, and the suppressed hum of voices as if of those endeavouring to soothe the mourner. The door was speedily opened, and when the ladies entered, the first object which met their view was their sister, Lady Ardagh, sitting on a form in the hall, weeping and wringing her hands in deep agony. Beside her stood two old, withered crones, who were each endeavouring in their own way to administer consolation, without even knowing or caring what the subject of her grief might be.

Immediately on Lady Ardagh's seeing her sisters, she started up, fell on their necks, and kissed them again and again without speaking, and then taking them each by a hand, still weeping bitterly, she led them into a small room adjoining the hall, in which burned a light, and, having closed the door, she sat down between them. After thanking them for the haste they had made, she proceeded to tell them, in words incoherent from agitation, that Sir Robert had in private, and in the most solemn manner, told her that he should die upon that night, and that he had occupied himself during the evening in giving minute directions respecting the arrangements of his funeral. Lady D—— here suggested the possibility of his labouring under the hallucinations of a fever; but to this Lady Ardagh quickly replied:

"Oh! no, no! Would to God I could think it. Oh! no, no! Wait till you have seen him. There is a frightful calmness about all he says and does; and his directions are all so clear, and his mind so perfectly collected, it is impossible, quite impossible." And she wept yet more bitterly.

At that moment Sir Robert's voice was heard in issuing some directions, as he came downstairs; and Lady Ardagh exclaimed, hurriedly:

"Go now and see him yourself. He is in the hall."

Lady D—— accordingly went out into the hall, where Sir Robert met her; and, saluting her with kind politeness, he said, after a pause:

"You are come upon a melancholy mission—the house is in great confusion, and some of its inmates in considerable grief." He took her hand, and looking fixedly in her face, continued: "I shall not live to see tomorrow's sun shine."

"You are ill, sir, I have no doubt," replied she; "but I am very certain we shall see you much better tomorrow, and still better the day following."

"I am *not* ill, sister," replied he. "Feel my temples, they are cool; lay your finger to my pulse, its throb is slow and temperate. I never was more perfectly in health, and yet do I know that ere three hours be past, I shall be no more."

"Sir, sir," said she, a good deal startled, but wishing to conceal the impression which the calm solemnity of his manner had, in her own despite, made upon her, "Sir, you should not jest; you should not even speak lightly upon such subjects. You trifle with what is sacred—you are sporting with the best affections of your wife—"

"Stay, my good lady," said he; "if when this clock shall strike the hour of three, I shall be anything but a helpless clod, then upbraid me. Pray return now to your sister. Lady Ardagh is, indeed, much to be pitied; but what is past cannot now be helped. I have now a few papers to arrange, and some to destroy. I shall see you and Lady Ardagh before my death;

try to compose her—her sufferings distress me much; but what is past cannot now be mended."

Thus saying, he went upstairs, and Lady D—— returned to the room where her sisters were sitting.

"Well," exclaimed Lady Ardagh, as she re-entered, "is it not so?—do you still doubt?—do you think there is any hope?"

Lady D—— was silent.

"Oh! none, none, none," continued she; "I see, I see you are convinced." And she wrung her hands in bitter agony.

"My dear sister," said Lady D——, "there is, no doubt, something strange in all that has appeared in this matter; but still I cannot but hope that there may be something deceptive in all the apparent calmness of Sir Robert. I still must believe that some latent fever has affected his mind, or that, owing to the state of nervous depression into which he has been sinking, some trivial occurrence has been converted, in his disordered imagination, into an augury foreboding his immediate dissolution."

In such suggestions, unsatisfactory even to those who originated them, and doubly so to her whom they were intended to comfort, more than two hours passed; and Lady D—— was beginning to hope that the fated term might elapse without the occurrence of any tragical event, when Sir Robert entered the room. On coming in, he placed his finger with a warning gesture upon his lips, as if to enjoin silence; and then having successively pressed the hands of his two sisters-in-law, he stooped sadly over the fainting form of his lady, and twice pressed her cold, pale forehead, with his lips, and then passed silently out of the room.

Lady D——, starting up, followed to the door, and saw him take a candle in the hall, and walk deliberately up the stairs. Stimulated by a feeling of horrible curiosity, she continued to follow him at a distance. She saw him enter his own private room, and heard him close and lock the door after him. Continuing to follow him as far as she could, she placed herself at the door of the chamber, as noiselessly as possible, where after a little time she was joined by her two sisters, Lady Ardagh and Miss

F——d. In breathless silence they listened to what should pass within. They distinctly heard Sir Robert pacing up and down the room for some time; and then, after a pause, a sound as if some one had thrown himself heavily upon the bed. At this moment Lady D——, forgetting that the door had been secured within, turned the handle for the purpose of entering; when some one from the inside, close to the door, said, "Hush! hush!" The same lady, now much alarmed, knocked violently at the door; there was no answer. She knocked again more violently, with no further success. Lady Ardagh, now, uttering a piercing shriek, sank in a swoon upon the floor. Three or four servants, alarmed by the noise, now hurried upstairs, and Lady Ardagh was carried apparently lifeless to her own chamber. They then, after having knocked long and loudly in vain, applied themselves to forcing an entrance into Sir Robert's room. After resisting some violent efforts, the door at length gave way, and all entered the room nearly together. There was a single candle burning upon a table at the far end of the apartment; and stretched upon the bed lay Sir Robert Ardagh. He was a corpse—the eyes were open—no convulsion had passed over the features, or distorted the limbs—it seemed as if the soul had sped from the body without a struggle to remain there. On touching the body it was found to be cold as clay—all lingering of the vital heat had left it. They closed the ghastly eyes of the corpse, and leaving it to the care of those who seem to consider it a privilege of their age and sex to gloat over the revolting spectacle of death in all its stages, they returned to Lady Ardagh, now a widow. The party assembled at the castle, but the atmosphere was tainted with death. Grief there was not much, but awe and panic were expressed in every face. The guests talked in whispers, and the servants walked on tiptoe, as if afraid of the very noise of their own footsteps.

The funeral was conducted almost with splendour. The body, having been conveyed, in compliance with Sir Robert's last directions, to Dublin, was there laid within the ancient walls of St. Audoen's Church—where I have read the epitaph, telling the age and titles of the departed dust. Neither painted escutcheon, nor marble slab, have served to rescue from oblivion the story of the dead, whose very name will ere long moulder from their tracery—

"Et sunt sua fata sepulchris."*

The events which I have recorded are not imaginary. They are FACTS; and there lives one whose authority none would venture to question, who could vindicate the accuracy of every statement which I have set down, and that, too, with all the circumstantiality of an eye-witness.†

* This prophecy has since been realised; for the aisle in which Sir Robert's remains were laid has been suffered to fall completely to decay; and the tomb which marked his grave, and other monuments more curious, form now one indistinguishable mass of rubbish.

† This paper, from a memorandum, I find to have been written in 1803. The lady to whom allusion is made, I believe to be Miss Mary F——d. She never married, and survived both her sisters, living to a very advanced age.

1929

THE WATCHER O' THE DEAD

John Guinan

John Guinan (1874–1945) was an Irish playwright and writer of short stories; there is not much information available regarding his life and work. Some of his plays written for the Abbey Theatre in Dublin were *The Cuckoo's Nest* (1913), *Black Oliver* (1927) and *The Rune of Healing* (1931).

Guinan's "The Watcher o' the Dead" was first published in *Cornhill Magazine* in 1929; it was also part of the seminal anthology *Supernatural Omnibus* (1931) compiled by Montague Summers. A variation of the bizarre custom it refers to has appeared in William Le Fanu's *Seventy Years of Irish Life, Anecdotes and Reminiscences* (1893), where the author describes an old Irish superstition, according to which the last person buried in a cemetery is compelled to fetch water to everybody previously interred there, until a new "resident" replaces that unfortunate soul. Guinan's take on this odd and morbid bit of Irish tradition is a haunting macabre narrative distinguished by a sense of doom and despair.

IT is now the fall of the night. The last of the neighbours are hitting the road for home. The time they went out through that door together, for the sake of the company on the way, as they said, did they give e'er a thought at all to myself, left alone here in this desolate house? To be sure, they asked me more than once why I refuse to leave the place, and the day is in it, by the same token. But I have no call to answer them, though what I am about to set down here in black and white will settle the question, at least for myself.

A few hours ago, and the corpse of Tim McGowan was taken from under this roof and buried deep in the clay. They laid the spade and the shovel like a rude cross on the fresh sod of his grave, and they went down on their knees and said a few hasty prayers for the good of his soul. One or two, and their faces hidden in their hats, took good care not to rise from the wet ground till they got sight of others already on their two feet. Letting on that their thoughts were on higher things, they kept in mind the old belief that the first one to leave the churchyard warm in life would not be the last to come back cold in death.

The little groups moving out began to talk of the man who was gone. Their talk ran in whispers, for fear they might trouble his long sleep. They all knew, though none had the rights of it, that he was after earning his rest dearly. An old man, whose face was hard, even for his years, took a white clay pipe from the pocket of his body coat.

"God rest your soul, Tim McGowan," he cried. It was the custom to pray for the dead before taking a "draw" from a wake pipe. "God rest you in the grave," he added, "for it's little peace or ease you had and you in the world that we know!"

The bulk of those who heard his words caught, a little gladly, a mocking undertone which stole through the kindly feeling that had at first shaken his voice. A young man, with eager eyes and a desire to know and talk of things that should be left hidden, took courage and spoke out bluntly:

"For him to be haunting the graveyard like a ghost, and he a living man! That was a strange vagary, for sure."

"It was the death of the good woman a year ago," the old man went on, speaking more openly, in his turn. "It was her loss turned his poor head."

"There's no denying there was a queer strain in him already," the young man said to that. "Sure they say all of that family were a bit touched!"

They did not scruple to speak like this before myself, and I of the one blood with the man who was dead, if any of them could know or suspect that. They were after doing their duty towards his mortal remains: if there was a kink in his nature or a mystery about his life why, they might fairly ask, should it not fill the gossip of an idle hour? But it was myself only, the stranger amongst them, who knew the true reason of Tim McGowan's nightly vigils in Gort na Marbh, why he, a living man, as was said, chose to become the Watcher o' the Dead in the lonesome graveyard. It was ere yesterday morning he told me his secret. Tim was lying there in the settle-bed from which his stark body was carried feet foremost this day. I was trying to get ready a little food by the fire on the hearth, for Tim had not been able to rise, let alone to do a hand's turn for himself. Our wants were simple, and it was not for the first time that I had turned my poor endeavours to homely use.

"There are times," I made bold to remark, "there are times I feel this house to be haunted;" for every night during the short spell since I came to see my kinsman, I was sure I heard the fall of footsteps on the floor after the pair of us had gone to our beds. The rattling of the door, if it was not a troubled dream, had also startled me in my sleep. I had begun to ask myself was it one of these houses where the door must be left on the latch and the hearth swept clean for Those who come back. Always at a certain hour Tim was in a hurry to rake the fire and get shut of me out of the kitchen. A pang now shot through my breast. With the poor man hardly able to raise hand or foot, it was not kind to draw down such a thing. But he looked glad that I had given him the chance to speak out.

"As you make mention of it," he said eagerly, "I want to let you know the house is haunted, surely! But it is not by any spirit of good or evil from beyond the grave. That is a strange thing, you will be saying."

"It is a strange thing," I agreed. I had no doubt what he was going to disclose. He had already given me the story of a house built, and not without warning, on a "fairy pass", through which the Sluagh Sidhe in their hosting and revels swept gaily every night. This was the house for sure: The Gentle Folk had never passed the gates of death and know nothing of the grave.

"But," he went on, "there is one other thing as strange again. It is that same you will now be hearing, if you pay heed to me."

"You mean that this is the house"—I began, intending to say that it was the house of the story, but I checked myself—"that it is a case of a fallen angel, hanging between heaven and hell, who never had to pay the penalty of death?"

"If you let me," he made answer, "I will tell you the truth. The place is haunted by a mortal man!"

"One still in the world, one who goes about in his clothes, one to be seen by daylight?" I asked, without drawing breath.

"In troth," he declared, "it is haunted by the man who tells it, and no other, if I am still in the flesh itself!"

I lifted him slightly in the bed, not knowing what to say or think. Was this his way of speaking about some common habit, or was his reason leaving him?

"Whisper!" he said, and his face was flushed. "You came here to gather old stories out of the past, over and above seeing your last living relative in the world, leaving out Michael, my son, who should be here by this. I might do worse than give you the true version of my own trouble."

This made a double reason why I should hear him out. There is no man but carries in his breast the makings of a story, which, though never told, comes more home to him, than any the mind of another man can find and fashion in words.

"What harm if my story should turn out a poor thing in the telling?" he sighed. "It will ease my mind, if it does only that. And who knows: but we will talk of that when the times comes."

He turned aside from the food I was coaxing him to take, and started:

"It is now a year since herself was laid to rest. Laid to rest!" He laughed, a little bitterly. "That is what they call it. A week after that again, call it what you like, the graveyard was closed by orders. There are people still to the fore who have their rights under the law; but it is hardly likely that many, if any of them, will try to make good their claim to be buried in Gort na Marbh."

Gurthnamorrav, the Field of the Dead, that is what those around and about call the lonely patch to this day. Though this generation of them are "dull of" the ancient tongue, such names, of native savour, help to keep them one in soul with the proud children of Banbha who are in eternity. Vivid imagery, symbols drawn, in a manner of speaking, from the brown earth, words of strength and beauty that stud like gems of light and grace the common speech hold not merely an abiding charm in themselves. Such heritages of the mind of the Gael evoke through active fancy the fuller life of the race of kings no less surely than those relics of skill and handicraft found by chance in tilth or red bog, the shrine of bell or battle book, the bronze spear head, the torque of gold.

"But, surely," I objected, "those who are able would like to have their bones laid beside their own when their day of nature is past! Surely they would choose such a ground as the place of their resurrection, as the holy men of old used to say!"

"Time and time again," he made answer, "people have left it to their deaths not to be buried in Gort na Marbh. Man and wife have been parted, mother and child. What call have I to tell you the reason? You know it rightly. You know it is the lot of the last body brought to its long home to be from that time forth the Watcher o' the Dead?"

"I have heard tell of that queer—of that belief," I replied. "That the poor soul cannot go to its rest, if it took years itself, till another comes to fill its place; that it must wander about in the dead of the night amongst the graves where the mortal body is crumbling to dust; and, as one might say in a plain way, keep an eye over the place!"

"And who would care to be buried in ground that was shut up for ever?" he asked. "Even at the best of times people try their best endeavours to be the first through the gate with the corpse of their own friend and when two funerals happen to fall on the one day."

And then he went on to tell me, and his voice failing at that, of all he was after going through thinking of his woman, his share of the world, making the weary, dreary, rounds of the graveyard during the best part of the changing year. And, bitter agony! he felt that she could not share in the Communion of Saints, that all his good works for her sake would not hasten her release. But the thing that made it the hardest for him to bear was this: It was through his veneration for the old customs, through his great respect even for the dead, that this awful tribulation had come to the pair of them.

"Let you not be laughing at what I'm going to tell you now," he warned me: "for I won't deny there have been times when I made merry over the like myself. It was a seldom thing two funerals to be on the one day; nor would it have come to happen at the time it did if the other people had the proper spirit, like myself, or the right regard for the things good Christians hold highly. Listen! They knew the order to close the graveyard, the other people knew it was on the road, for the man who was dead and going to be buried on the same day as herself was himself on the Board of Guardians. That was why they waked him for one night only, and they people of means, and rushed with him in unseemly haste to Gort na Marbh. But we got wind of it, and would have been the first, for all that, only we followed the old road, the long road, and in a decent and becoming way walked in through the open gate while they took a short cut and got in over the stile. We did more than that, and so did they. While the savages, for they were little else, while they were trampling above the relics of the dead, we went round about the ground in the track of the sun till we came in the proper course to the side of the open grave."

This set me thinking of the ancient ritual by which the corpse is brought round to pay its respects, as a body might say, to those who have gone before. I began to ask myself was it a fragment of Druid worship that had come down even to our own day. But this is what I said to my kinsman:

"You did what was right, and no one would be better pleased than the woman who was gone!"

"That is the way I felt myself at the first going off," he agreed: "but soon I began to question myself: When I did the right thing, that the neighbours gave me full credit for, was I thinking more of what was expected from the living or what was due to the dead? Was I thinking of myself, and the great name I'd be getting from the self-same neighbours, or of the woman going into the clay, who only wanted their prayers? Many's the long night this thought kept me on the rack till I was nigh gone astray in the head. In my mind I saw her, and her brown habit down to her feet, and she looking to me for help, and it my sin of human respect, as I felt, that kept her so long from walking on the sunny hills of Glory! Funeral after funeral went the way, for people have to die; but not a one passed the rusty gate of Gort na Marbh as a poor woman of the roads might give the go-by to a stricken house.

"At length and at last, I could stand it no longer, and one night I got up from my bed and made my way to the graveyard. 'Twas in the dark hour before the crowing of the cocks, when wandering spirits are warned home to their house of clay."

"And did you half expect to see the Watcher o' the Dead?" I asked.

"Did I? And why not?" he asked in turn, by way of reply.

"With your mind disturbed that way," I went on, "the wonder is you didn't see her, if only in fancy."

I meant to be kind. He faced me testily.

"I did see her, as sure as I'm a living man!" he declared.

I had not the heart to urge my view that it was only a brain-born figure.

"I no sooner crossed the stile," he said softly, "than I got clear sight of herself. She was moving through the graves she guarded, and a kindly look in her two eyes. The dead image I thought her of the Nuns you see in the sick ward of the poorhouse in Ballybrosna, and she taking a look at the beds in their little rows, and fearing to waken the tired sleepers in her charge. There she was, in truth, as I had seen her a thousand times in my own mind."

"In your own mind!" I said after him. "It was on your eyes, so to speak, and you merely saw what was in your mind already. Was it not more natural to see the figment that never left your sight than not to see it at all?"

It was all very clear to me, and I felt this was sound talk; and isn't it a caution the way the rage of battle will rise in a body and set the tongue loose! But Tim's reply put a stop to any dispute or war of words.

"It was in my mind, for sure," he said. "But tell me, you who have the book learning, why was it in my mind? When a man's brain begins to work, what gives it the start, or sets it going—or does it start to go of itself?"

I had to give in that I always left such vexed questions to wiser heads, adding, whimsically enough as it seems to me now, that I was not such a great fool as to attempt an answer where they failed. In a way I was put out by the reflection that this old man, who "didn't know his letters", was making a mockery of me on the head of my few books and my small store of book learning.

"There is nothing hard about the case I am after putting before you," he said. "It was on my mind because the thing was taking place in Gort na

Marbh night after night, was taking place in the Field of the Dead, though there was no living eye to see it!"

I had no reply to that, whether it was a head-made ghost or not. Where was the use of starting to argue that nothing really takes place if not within the knowledge of man? I told myself weakly that such visions were due to the queer strain in the old man the neighbours spoke about this day. It might be that, in his present state, all this had only come into his head as the two of us talked together. It did not occur to me then, and I have too much respect for the dead to credit it now, that he was "taking a rise" out of me, as the plain saying is.

Tim became a little rambling in his speech and asked me to let him lie flat in the bed. I gathered from the words he mumbled and jumbled that he made a promise to the departed spirit to take her place till his own time came in real earnest: that he had bid her go to her rest, in the Name of God, much, I could not help but think, as one might banish an evil spirit to the "red sea" to make ropes of the sand; that he had kept his word, which brought great peace to his breast: and that he never set eyes on her again from that hour, there or there else.

I had no doubt he had but laid the ghost of his own troubled thoughts. It is not every poor mortal can do that same, even by dint of hard sacrifice. Tim was growing worse. I tried hard to cheer him. It was all to no use. I talked of his son, Michael, who was far away on the fishing grounds. We had already sent word for him to come home, and he might be here any stroke, if it was a long ways off, itself.

"Michael will never be here in time!" the father groaned. "That is my great trouble. I never could ask another to do it. It would be again' reason."

"There is nothing you could name I would not gladly do!" I declared; and, in all fair speaking, I meant it.

"There are things no man should ask of his friend," he said to that, with a slight shake of the head.

"And who else should he ask but his friend?" I laughed, trying to rouse him. "But, first, I'll send for the Doctor—"

"The Doctor, how are ye!" he broke in on me. "That is not what I want. What can the like of himself do for a body who has seen the Watcher o' the Dead?"

"What harm if you did itself?" I asked. "The sign of a long life it is, as likely as not. It would be another story, entirely, one's 'fetch' to be seen in the late hours of the day. An early death that would signify."

"The man," he made answer, "the man who lays eyes on the Watcher o' the Dead, late or early, if the like could come to pass at all before dark, that man will soon be only a shadow himself. I am saying, he will soon be among the silent company. The time I took the woman's place, the woman who held my heart for years, I knew rightly, it would not be for long. It is for that reason and no other I am after telling you my secret sorrow. I will never be able to put out this night, if I live through this night of the nights, or any night for the future; and if it was a thing I failed her, sure herself would be disturbed in her rest."

I took a grip of his hand and looked down steadily into his eyes.

"Put your trust in me!" I said. "I'll take your place till such time as you are laid in the clay!"

Who is it, though he might throw doubt on the very stars above his head, would not try to humour an old man or a little child?

"God sent you for a friend," he said, "praised be His holy Name! For all I know, I may not want you to do so much: I may want you to do a little more, but in another way. I want you to take my place till Michael comes, and not an hour more; I want you, as well as that, to tell him all I have told you and to give him my dying wish, if it is a thing he does not come before I go for ever. Whisper! You'll tell Michael, in case I'm too far through myself, that I am dying happy knowing he will not refuse a last favour to the father who reared him. It is this: That he will become the Watcher o' the Dead, though a living man, like myself, and let me, after so much fret and torment, go straight to herself, to his mother, in Heaven. Tell him I know he will do this, for the rest of his mortal days, if it comes to that. Tell him I know that, after that again, if he gets no release he will have his bones laid in Gort na Marbh and wait his own turn. I have done my share of watching, God knows!"

Some kind neighbours gathered during the course of the day, and the priest of the parish was sent for. Father Malachy was a man of the world, without being worldly. It is not for the knowing, and never will be in this world, whether Tim told him about the Watcher o' the Dead. As a man, his reverence knew all the customs and beliefs of the people, for he was one of them himself. Deep in his nature a body might expect to find a kindly toleration for the harmless "superstitions", as some would call them, lingering from the pagan days of Firbolg or Tuatha de Danaan. As a priest, he had, no doubt, full knowledge of the rites of the Church for dealing with "appearances" from the other world, which shows it to be no harm to give heed to such things.

Tim kept quiet till the night wore on. Then he got restless and began to mutter to himself. The use of his speech was well-nigh gone. I caught such words as "Gort na Marbh", and "Herself", and "the Watcher o' the Dead". His grip was tight on my fist when I said in his ear that I would not fail him, dead or alive, till Michael came. The kind neighbours did not let on to hear the pair of us, and I left him in their charge while I set out for the strange duty I had taken on myself so lightly, taken on, indeed, with a certain zest, in the vague hope of enlarging my experience. It was clear from Tim's behaviour that the hour of the night had come when he felt the "call" to the graveyard, and still there was no sign of Michael. The moon was in the sky. The night was cold. There was no stir. The place held no terrors for me. I set little store by Tim's story, except as a "study" in delusion. The old man was much in my thoughts, for he was passing rapidly away. I saw him in my mind, as he used to say, and he walking here and there through the graves that now held nothing but cold clay, passing by fallen stones, broken and moss-grown. I tried hard to banish such airy pictures, for I did not want to begin seeing sights.

What was that story Tim told me a few days ago as we stood before a headstone in Gort na Marbh? It was a true tale of revenge, revenge both on the living and the dead, and it was a poor sort of revenge at that. Before long I would be seeing again the spot where the dead man he spoke about was laid in the clay. His relations, in blood and law, hoped to benefit largely by his death. But he left all to his son. The boy was an only child whose mother died the hour he came into the world. He came home, a likely youth, to be at the father's funeral. For the first time in his young life he saw the place that was now to be his own. It was natural for him to ask why the usual black plumes did not wave above the hearse instead of white. The errors of the past, if any, should have been covered by charity. Feuds are forgiven, if not forgotten, in the hour of death. It is what they told him, with wild malice, that black plumes were only for people who were lawfully joined in wedlock.

Here I found the elements of tragedy, but the story only helped to keep the figure of Tim before me. I was stepping over the stile and thinking of the nights he spent walking about in the dreary waste, for, after so much neglect, that is what it had by now sunk to. I felt the nettles rank and dank as I set foot on the ground; and then—it was not wild phantasy!—I got sight of Tim moving in the moonlight among the shadows of the headstones and the trees.

"In the Name of God!" I cried, profanely, I am half afraid, "leave the place at once, and let me keep my promise in peace."

I was furious with the neighbours for letting him rise and he in a fever. But were they to be blamed? I crossed hastily and found myself alone! This gave me a start, and I began to wonder whether in that strange ground—for, surely, the place was not "right"!—I, in my turn, saw what was on my eyes only! Had Tim been there in the flesh or was it that I, in my turn, had laid but the ghost of a deranged imagination? Could it be that the queer strain of the family, if there is such a thing, runs in my own blood? Or does a sane man put such a question to himself? Without waiting for the crowing of the cocks, I made haste back to the house. My heart was beating loudly.

"We were going to call after you," the neighbours said to me. "Hardly was your back turned when the end came!"

Tim was stretched there in his long sleep, his features set free by the kindly touch of death!

Last night at the same hour we dug his grave. I was heartened by the presence of the neighbours and lingered over the work till the dawn broke, walking about from time to time, "by way of no harm", trying to keep my promise to the dead man. More than once the shadows, moving with the shifting lanthorn, took a start out of me. There were a few of the neighbours would not put out with us. One was a strong young man who was so free of the tongue this day.

"Why do you want to choose such an unreasonable hour?" they grumbled. "It is not lucky to turn up the sod in the dead of the night."

"As likely as not," I heard another make answer, "he was waiting to see would Michael come on the long car."

I did not put him right. If we were waiting for Michael only the work could have been left over till morning. It is the long wait we would have, for the same Michael, God rest the poor boy! God rest him! I say, for before Tim was taken out this day word came that the hardy young fisherman had been lost a week ago in the depths of the salt water. The hungry, angry sea did not give up its dead. And now his death comes home to me! Michael's bones will never be laid in Gort na Marbh. Michael will never, never, either in life or death, become the Watcher o' the Dead! And I have pledged my word to the man who is gone, the father, to take his place till such time as Michael should come home! That will be never, never!

What way can I break my word to the dead, whether I credit his story or doubt it? It was part of his own belief, part of himself. What odds does it make even if he was out of his mind, or if I am a madman myself? A promise, a promise to one passed away, is sacred.

Where is the good of talking of common sense? Half the world is stupid with common sense, if there is any such quality. But I see a dismal prospect before me, till the end of my days, as likely as not, let alone, for all I know, till the Day of Judgement itself! Already I feel there is a stir in my blood, the time has come for me to get up and make my lonely vigil:

for I have been putting this down in black and white for many hours. It is a true word for Tim; every man has his own story, his own agony. But I set out to tell of his troubles, which, for sure, are at an end, and not of my own, which, for all a body can see, are only in their birth throes.

Strange and Dangerous Women

1895

THE SEA'S DEAD

Katharine Tynan

Katharine Tynan (1859–1931) was a prolific and diverse Irish writer but she is mainly remembered today as a gifted poet of the Irish Literary Renaissance. Growing as an author in the fascinating late nineteenth century Dublin and its outskirts, she had many significant friends and acquaintances among the eminent members of the Irish Literary Revival such as Lady Gregory, William Butler Yeats and the mystical poet George W. Russell; she considered the latter two as major influences on her literary craft. Feeling spellbound by family ghost storytelling during her childhood and being endowed with a particular penchant for the uncanny, she became a voracious reader of gothic novels and ghost stories that inspired her to pen her own literary glimpses of the otherworldly and the fantastic. Today she is mostly regarded as a worthy but long forgotten writer, and her supernatural and horror tales have only been recently rediscovered and republished by small independent presses.

"The Sea's Dead" was included in her short story collection *An Isle in the Water*, which was published in 1895, with the title referring to the remote islands at the west of Ireland where old superstitions associated with the sea and its strange residents naturally thrived. This is the sad story of an uncommon young woman of undefined origin, who is both a wonder and an outcast in the small community in which she lives. Tynan's rich literary descriptions bring forth a highly poetic narrative evocative of enchanting fables of unearthly beauty, associating the mythical element with the unknown depths of the ocean.

In Achill it was dreary wet weather—one of innumerable wet summers that blight the potatoes and blacken the hay and mildew the few oats and rot the poor cabin roofs. The air smoked all day with rain mixed with the fine salt spray from the ocean. Out of doors everything shivered and was disconsolate. Only the bog prospered, basking its length in water, and mirroring Croghan and Slievemore with the smoky clouds incessantly wreathing about their foreheads, or drifting like ragged wisps of muslin down their sides to the clustering cabins more desolate than a deserted nest. Inland from the sheer ocean cliffs the place seemed all bog; the little bits of earth the people had reclaimed were washed back into the bog, the grey bents and rimy grasses that alone flourished drank their fill of the water, and were glad. There was a grief and trouble on all the Island. Scarce a cabin in the queer straggling villages but had desolation sitting by its hearth. It was only a few weeks ago that the hooker had capsized crossing to Westport, and the famine that is always stalking ghost-like in Achill was forgotten in the contemplation of new graves. The Island was full of widows and orphans and bereaved old people; there was scarce a window sill in Achill by which the banshee had not cried.

Where all were in trouble there were few to go about with comfort. Moya Lavelle shut herself up in the cabin her husband Patrick had built, and dreed her weird alone. Of all the boys who had gone down with the hooker none was finer than Patrick Lavelle. He was brown and handsome, broad-shouldered and clever, and he had the good-humoured smile and the kindly word where the people are normally taciturn and unsmiling. The Island girls were disappointed when Patrick brought a wife from the mainland, and Moya never tried to make friends with them. She was something of a mystery to the Achill people, this small moony creature, with her silver fair hair, and strange light eyes, the colour of spilt milk. She was as small as a child, but had the gravity of a woman. She loved the sea with a love unusual in Achill, where the sea is to many a ravening monster that has exacted in return for its hauls of fish the life of husband and son. Patrick Lavelle had built for her a snug cabin in a sheltered ravine. A little beach ran down in front of it where he could haul up his boat. The cabin was built strongly, as it had need to be, for often of a winter night the waves tore against its little windows. Moya loved the fury of the elements, and when the winter storms drove the Atlantic up the ravine with a loud bellowing, she stirred in sleep on her husband's shoulder, and smiled as they say children smile in sleep when an angel leans over them.

Higher still, on a spur of rock, Patrick Lavelle had laid the clay for his potatoes. He had carried it on his shoulders, every clod, and Moya had gathered the seaweed to fertilise it. She had her small garden there, too, of sea-pinks and the like, which rather encouraged the Islanders in their opinion of her strangeness. In Achill the struggle for life is too keen to admit of any love for mere beauty.

However, Patrick Lavelle was quite satisfied with his little wife. When he came home from the fishing he found his cabin more comfortable than is often the case in Achill. They had no child, but Moya never seemed to miss a child's head at her breast. During the hours of his absence at the fishing she seemed to find the sea sufficient company. She was always roaming along the cliffs, gazing down as with a fearful fascination along the black sides to where the waves churned hundreds of feet below. For company she had only the seagulls and the bald eagle that screamed far over her head; but she was quite happy as she roamed hither and thither, gathering the coloured seaweeds out of the clefts of the rocks, and crooning an old song softly to herself, as a child might do.

But that was all over and gone, and Moya was a widow. She had nothing warm and human at all, now that brave protecting tenderness was gone from her. No one came to the little cabin in the ravine where

Moya sat and moaned, and stretched her arms all day for the dear brown head she had last seen stained with the salt water and matted with the seaweeds. At night she went out, and wandered moon-struck by the black cliffs, and cried out for Patrick, while the shrilling gusts of wind blew her pale hair about her, and scourged her fevered face with the sea salt and the sharp hail.

One night a great wave broke over Achill. None had seen it coming, with great crawling leaps like a serpent, but at dead of night it leaped the land, and hissed on the cottage hearths and weltered grey about the mud floors. The next day broke on ruin in Achill. The bits of fields were washed away, the little mountain sheep were drowned, the cabins were flung in ruined heaps; but the day was fair and sunny, as if the elements were tired of the havoc they had wrought and were minded to be in a good humour. There was not a boat on the Island but had been battered and torn by the rocks. People had to take their heads out of their hands, and stand up from their brooding, or this wanton mischief would cost them their dear lives, for the poor resources of the Island had given out, and the Islanders were in grips with starvation.

No one thought of Moya Lavelle in her lonely cabin in the ravine. None knew of the feverish vigils in those wild nights. But a day or two later the sea washed her on a stretch of beach to the very doors of a few straggling cabins dotted here and there beyond the irregular village. She had been carried out to sea that night, but the sea, though it had snatched her to itself, had not battered and bruised her. She lay there, indeed, like that blessed Restituta, whom, for her faith, the tyrant sent bound on a rotting hulk, with the outward tide from Carthage, to die on the untracked ocean. She lay like a child smiling in dreams, all her long silver hair about her, and her wide eyes gazing with no such horror, as of one who meets a violent death. Those who found her so wept to behold her.

They carried her to her cottage in the ravine, and waked her. Even in Achill they omit no funeral ceremony. They dressed her in white and put a cross in her hand, and about her face on the pillow they set the sea-pinks from her little garden, and some of the coloured seaweeds she had loved to gather. They lit candles at her head and feet, and the women watched with her all day, and at night the men came in, and they talked and told stories, subdued stories and ghostly, of the banshee and the death-watch, and wraiths of them gone that rise from the sea to warn fishermen of approaching death. Gaiety there was none: the Islanders had no heart for gaiety: but the pipes and tobacco were there, and the plate of snuff, and the jar of poteen to lift up the heavy hearts. And Moya lay like an image wrought of silver, her lids kept down by coins over her blue eyes.

She had lain so two nights, nights of starlit calm. On the fourth day they were to bury her beside Patrick Lavelle in his narrow house, and the little bridal cabin would be abandoned, and presently would rot to ruins. The third night had come, overcast with heavy clouds. The group gathered in the death chamber was more silent than before. Some had sat up the two nights, and were now dazed with sleep. By the wall the old women nodded over their beads, and a group of men talked quietly at the bed-head where Moya lay illumined by the splendour of the four candles all shining on her white garments.

Suddenly in the quietness there came a roar of wind. It did not come freshening from afar off, but seemed to waken suddenly in the ravine and cry about the house. The folk sprang to their feet startled, and the eyes of many turned towards the little dark window, expecting to see wild eyes and a pale face set in black hair gazing in. Some who were nearest saw in the half-light for it was whitening towards day a wall of grey water travelling up the ravine. Before they could cry a warning it had encompassed the house, had driven door and window before it, and the living and the dead were in the sea.

The wave retreated harmlessly, and in a few minutes the frightened folk were on their feet amid the wreck of stools and tables floating. The wave that had beaten them to earth had extinguished the lights. When they stumbled to their feet and got the water out of their eyes the dim dawn was in the room. They were too scared for a few minutes to think of the dead. When they recovered and turned towards the bed there was a simultaneous loud cry. Moya Lavelle was gone. The wave had carried her away, and never more was there tale or tidings of her body.

Achill people said she belonged to the sea, and the sea had claimed her. They remembered Patrick Lavelle's silence as to where he had found her. They remembered a thousand unearthly ways in her; and which of them had ever seen her pray? They pray well in Achill, having a sure hold on that heavenly country which is to atone for the cruelty and sorrow of this. In process of time they will come to think of her as a mermaid, poor little Moya. She had loved her husband at least with a warm human love. But his open grave was filled after they had given up hoping that the sea would again give her up, and the place by Patrick Lavelle's side remains for ever empty.

1903

JULIA CAHILL'S CURSE

George Moore

George Moore (1852–1933) was an Irish author not particularly associated with the fantastic and the supernatural – today he is considered as part of Irish literary modernism. He lived many years in Paris in order to study art, although he later devoted himself to writing. While living and publishing in late-Victorian London, his novels caused a stir there due to their exploration of taboo subjects such as extramarital sex and lesbianism. When he returned to Dublin he became involved with the Celtic Revival movement and even co-wrote with William Butler Yeats a play inspired my Irish myths. Moreover, some of his works were admired by James Joyce who may have been influenced by Moore's highly stylistic writing. He spent his last days in London where he died in 1933.

"Julia Cahill's Curse" was included in his short story collection *The Untilled Field* (1903) and it takes place during the late nineteenth century waves of Irish emigration to the United States due to poverty and unemployment in rural areas. The supernatural element in this atypical uncanny tale is not very palpable, while the author seems to use it as a means to reflect on the fatal results of religious bigotry, prejudice, and social expulsion. Nevertheless, as the plot unfolds, the reader experiences a pervading sense of menace and uncertainty that reaches a climax, while the hidden power of the story lies in the portrayal of fear, conformity and misogyny nurtured by religion.

In '95 I was agent of the Irish Industrial Society, and I spent three days with Father O'Hara making arrangements for the establishment of looms, for the weaving of homespuns and for acquiring plots of ground whereon to build schools where the village girls could practise lace-making.

The priest was one of the chief supporters of our movement. He was a wise and tactful man, who succeeded not only in living on terms of friendship with one of the worst landlords in Ireland, but in obtaining many concessions from him. When he came to live in Culloch the landlord had said to him that what he would like to do would be to run the ploughshare through the town, and to turn "Culloch" into Bullock. But before many years had passed Father O'Hara had persuaded this man to use his influence to get a sufficient capital to start a bacon factory. And the town of Culloch possessed no other advantages except an energetic and foreseeing parish priest. It was not a railway terminus, nor was it a seaport.

But, perhaps because of his many admirable qualities, Father O'Hara is not the subject of this story. We find stories in the lives of the weak and the foolish, and the improvident, and his name occurs here because he is typical of not a few priests I have met in Ireland.

I left him early one Sunday morning, and he saying that twenty odd miles lay before me, and my first stopping place would be Ballygliesane. I could hear Mass there at Father Madden's chapel, and after Mass I could call upon him, and that when I had explained the objects of our Society I could drive to Rathowen, where there was a great gathering of the clergy. All the priests within ten miles round would be there for the consecration of the new church.

On an outside car one divides one's time in moralising on the state of the country or in chatting with the driver, and as the driver seemed somewhat taciturn I examined the fields as we passed them. They were scanty fields, drifting from thin grass into bog, and from bog into thin grass again, and in the distance there was a rim of melancholy mountains, and the peasants I saw along the road seemed a counterpart of the landscape. "The land has made them," I said, "according to its own image and likeness," and I tried to find words to define the yearning that I read in their eyes as we drove past. But I could find no words that satisfied me.

"Only music can express their yearning, and they have written it themselves in their folk tunes."

My driver's eyes were the eyes that one meets everywhere in Ireland, pale, wandering eyes that the land seems to create, and I wondered if his character corresponded to his eyes; and with a view to finding if it did I asked him some questions about Father Madden. He seemed unwilling to talk, but I soon began to see that his silence was the result of shyness rather than dislike of conversation. He was a gentle, shy lad, and I told him that Father O'Hara had said I would see the loneliest parish in Ireland.

"It's true for him," he answered, and again there was silence. At the end of a mile I asked him if the land in Father Madden's parish was poor, and he said no, it was the best land in the country, and then I was certain that there was some mystery attached to Father Madden.

"The road over there is the mearing."

And soon after passing this road I noticed that although the land was certainly better than the land about Culloch, there seemed to be very few people on it; and what was more significant than the untilled fields were the ruins, for they were not the cold ruins of twenty, or thirty, or forty years ago when the people were evicted and their tillage turned into pasture, but the ruins of cabins that had been lately abandoned. Some of the roof trees were still unbroken, and I said that the inhabitants must have left voluntarily.

"Sure they did. Arn't we all going to America."

"Then it was not the landlord?"

"Ah, it's the landlord who'd have them back if he could."

"And the priest? How does he get his dues?"

"Those on the other side are always sending their money to their friends and they pay the priest. Sure why should we be staying? Isn't the most of us over there already. It's more like going home than leaving home."

I told him we hoped to establish new looms in the country, and that Father O'Hara had promised to help us.

"Father O'Hara is a great man," he said.

"Well, don't you think that with the revival of industries the people might be induced to stay at home?"

"Sorra stay," said he.

I could see that he was not so convinced about the depopulation of Father O'Hara's parish as he was about Father Madden's, and I tried to induce him to speak his mind.

"Well, your honour, there's many that think there's a curse on the parish."

"A curse! And who put the curse on the parish?"

"Isn't that the bell ringing for Mass, your honour?"

And listening I could head a doleful pealing in the grey sky.

"Does Father Madden know of this curse?"

"Indeed he does; none better."

"And does he believe in it?"

"There's many who will tell you that he has been saying Masses for the last ten years, that the curse may be taken off the parish."

We could now hear the bell tolling quite distinctly, and the driver pointed with his whip, and I could see the cross above the fir-trees.

"And there," he said, "is Bridget Coyne," and I saw a blind woman being led along the road. At the moment I supposed he had pointed the woman out because she was blind, though this did not seem a sufficient reason for the note of wonder in his voice; but we were within a few yards of the chapel and there was no time to ask him who Bridget Coyne was. I had to speak to him about finding stabling for the horse. That, he said, was not necessary, he would let the horse graze in the chapel-yard while he himself knelt by the door, so that he could hear Mass and keep an eye on his horse. "I shall want you half an hour after Mass is over." Half an hour, I thought, would suffice to explain the general scope of our movement to Father Madden. I had found that the best way was to explain to each priest in turn the general scope of the movement, and then to pay a second visit a few weeks later. The priest would have considered the ideas that I had put into his head, he would have had time to assimilate them in the interval, and I could generally tell in the second visit if I should find in him a friend, an enemy, or an indifferent.

There was something extraordinary in the appearance of Father Madden's church, a few peasants crouched here and there, and among them I saw the blind woman that the driver had pointed out on the road. She did not move during Mass; she knelt or crouched with her shawl drawn over her head, and it was not until the acolyte rang the communion bell that she dared to lift herself up. That day she was the only communicant, and the acolyte did not turn the altar cloth over the rails, he gave her a little bit of the cloth to hold, and, holding it firmly in her fingers, she lifted up her blind face, and when the priest placed the Host on her tongue she sank back overcome.

"This blind woman," I said to myself, "will be the priest's last parishioner," and I saw the priest saying Mass in a waste church for the blind woman, everyone else dead or gone.

All her days I said are spent by the cabin fire hearing of people going to America, her relations, her brothers and sisters had gone, and every seventh day she is led to hear Mass, to receive the Host, and to sink back. Today and tomorrow and the next day will be spent brooding over her happiness, and in the middle of the week she will begin to look forward to the seventh day.

The blind woman seemed strangely symbolical and the parish, the priest too. A short, thick-set man, with a large bald head and a fringe of reddish hair; his hands were fat and short, the nails were bitten, the nose was fleshy and the eyes were small, and when he turned towards the people and said "Pax Vobiscum" there was a note of command in his voice. The religion he preached was one of fear. His sermon was filled with flames and gridirons, and ovens and devils with pitchforks, and his parishioners groaned and shook their heads and beat their breasts.

I did not like Father Madden or his sermon. I remembered that there were few young people left in his parish, and it seemed waste of time to appeal to him for help in establishing industries; but it was my business to seek the co-operation of every priest, and I could not permit myself such a licence as the passing over of any priest. What reason could I give? that I did not like his sermon or his bald head? And after Mass I went round to see him in the sacristy.

The sacristy was a narrow passage, and there were two acolytes in it, and the priest was taking off his vestments, and people were knocking constantly at the door, and the priest had to tell the acolyte what answer to give. I had only proposed to myself to sketch the objects of our organisation in a general outline to the priest, but it was impossible even to do this, so numerous were the interruptions. When I came to unfold our system of payments, the priest said:—

"It is impossible for me to listen to you here. You had better come round with me to my house."

The invitation was not quite in accordance with the idea I had formed of the man, and while walking across the fields he asked me if I would have a cup of tea with him, and we spoke of the new church at Rathowen. It seemed legitimate to deplore the building of new churches, and I mentioned that while the churches were increasing the people were decreasing, and I ventured to regret that only two ideas seemed to obtain in Ireland, the idea of the religious vocation and the idea of emigration.

"I see," said Father Madden, "you are imbued with all the new ideas."

"But," I said, "you don't wish the country to disappear."

"I do not wish it to disappear," he said, "but if it intends to disappear we can do nothing to prevent it from disappearing. Everyone is opposed to emigration now, but I remember when everyone was advocating it. Teach them English and emigrate them was the cure. Now," he said, "you wish them to learn Irish and to stay at home. And you are quite certain that this time you have found out the true way. I live very quiet down here, but I hear all the new doctrines. Besides teaching Paddy Durkin to feed his pig, I hear you are going to revive the Gothic. Music and literature are to follow, and among these resurrections there is a good deal of talk about pagan Ireland."

We entered a comfortable, well-furnished cottage, with a good carpet on the floor, and the walls lined with books, and on either side of the fireplace there were easy chairs, and I thought of the people "on the other side."

He took a pot of tea from the hob, and said:—

"Now let me pour you out a cup of tea, and you shall tell me about the looms."

"But," I said, "Father Madden, you don't believe much in the future of Ireland, you don't take very kindly to new ideas."

"New ideas! Every ten years there is a new set. If I had said teach them Irish ten years ago I should have been called a fool, and now if I say teach them English and let them go to America I am called a reactionist. You have come from Father O'Hara;" I could see from the way he said the name that the priests were not friends; "and he has told you a great many of my people have gone to America. And perhaps you heard him say that they have not gone to America for the sake of better wages but because my rule is too severe, because I put down cross-road dances. Father O'Hara and I think differently, and I have no doubt he thinks he is quite right."

While we breakfasted Father Madden said some severe things about Father O'Hara, about the church he had built, and the debt that was still upon it. I suppose my face told Father Madden of the interest I took in his opinions, for during breakfast he continued to speak his mind very frankly on all the subjects I wished to hear him speak on, and when breakfast was over I offered him a cigar and proposed that we should go for a walk on his lawn.

"Yes," he said, "there are people who think I am a reactionist because I put down the ball-alley."

"The ball-alley!"

"There used to be a ball-alley by the church, but the boys wouldn't stop playing ball during Mass, so I put it down. But you will excuse me a moment." The priest darted off, and I saw him climb down the wall into the road; he ran a little way along the road calling at the top of his voice, and when I got to the wall I saw him coming back. "Let me help you," I said. I pulled him up and we continued our walk; and as soon as he had recovered his breath he told me that he had caught sight of a boy and girl loitering.

"And I hunted them home."

I asked him why, knowing well the reason, and he said:—

"Young people should not loiter along the roads. I don't want bastards in my parish."

It seemed to me that perhaps bastards were better than no children at all, even from a religious point of view—one can't have religion without life, and bastards may be saints.

"In every country," I said, "boys and girls walk together, and the only idealism that comes into the lives of peasants is between the ages of eighteen and twenty, when young people meet in the lanes and linger by the stiles. Afterwards hard work in the fields kills aspiration."

"The idealism of the Irish people does not go into sex, it goes into religion."

"But religion does not help to continue the race, and we're anxious to preserve the race, otherwise there will be no religion, or a different religion in Ireland."

"That is not certain."

Later on I asked him if the people still believed in fairies. He said that traces of such beliefs survived among the mountain folk.

"There is a great deal of Paganism in the language they wish to revive, though it may be as free from Protestantism as Father O'Hara says it is."

For some reason or other I could see that folklore was distasteful to him, and he mentioned causally that he had put a stop to the telling of fairy-tales round the fire in the evening, and the conversation came to a pause.

"Now I won't detain you much longer, Father Madden. My horse and car are waiting for me. You will think over the establishment of looms. You don't want the country to disappear."

"No, I don't! And though I do not think the establishment of workrooms an unmixed blessing I will help you. You must not believe all Father O'Hara says."

The horse began to trot, and I to think. He had said that the idealism of the Irish peasant goes into other things than sex.

"If this be true, the peasant is doomed," I said to myself, and I remembered that Father Madden would not admit that religion is dependent on life, and I pondered. In this country religion is hunting life to the death. In other countries religion has managed to come to terms with Life. In the South men and women indulge their flesh and turn the key on religious inquiry; in the North men and women find sufficient interest in the interpretation of the Bible and the founding of new religious sects. One can have faith or morals, both together seem impossible. Remembering how the priest had chased the lovers, I turned to the driver and asked if there was no courting in the country.

"There used to be courting," he said, "but now it is not the custom of the country any longer."

"How do you make up your marriages?"

"The marriages are made by the parents, and I've often seen it that the young couple did not see each other until the evening before the wedding—sometimes not until the very morning of the wedding. Many a marriage I've seen broken off for a half a sovereign—well," he said, "if not for half a sovereign, for a sovereign. One party will give forty-nine pounds and the other party wants fifty, and they haggle over that pound, and then the boy's father will say, 'Well, if you won't give the pound you can keep the girl.'"

"But do none of you ever want to walk out with a young girl?" I said.

"We're like other people, sir. We would like it well enough, but it isn't the custom of the country, and if we did it we would be talked about."

I began to like my young carman, and his answer to my question pleased me as much as any answer he had yet given me, and I told him that Father Madden objected to the looms because they entailed meetings, etc., and if he were not present the boys would talk on subjects they should not talk about.

"Now, do you think it is right for a priest to prevent men from meeting to discuss their business?" I said, turning to the driver, determined to force him into an expression of opinion.

"It isn't because he thinks the men would talk about things they should not talk about that he is against an organisation. Didn't he tell your honour that things would have to take their course. That is why he will do nothing, because he knows well enough that everyone in the parish will have to leave it, that every house will have to fall. Only the chapel will remain standing, and the day will come when Father Tom will say Mass to the blind woman and to no one else. Did you see the blind woman today at Mass, sir, in the right-hand corner, with the shawl over her head?"

"Yes," I said, "I saw her. If any one is a saint, that woman seems to be one."

"Yes, sir, she is a very pious woman, and her piety is so well known that she is the only one who dared to brave Father Madden; she was the only one who dared to take Julia Cahill to live with her. It was Julia who put the curse on the parish."

"A curse! But you are joking."

"No, your honour, there was no joke in it. I was only telling you what must come. She put her curse on the village twenty years ago, and every year a roof has fallen in and a family has gone away."

"And you believe that all this happens on account of Julia's curse?"

"To be sure I do," he said. He flicked his horse pensively with the whip, and my disbelief seemed to disincline him for further conversation.

"But," I said, "who is Julia Cahill, and how did she get the power to lay a curse upon the village? Was she a young woman or an old one?"

"A young one, sir."

"How did she get the power?"

"Didn't she go every night into the mountains? She was seen one night over yonder, and the mountains are ten miles off, and whom would she have gone to see except the fairies? And who could have given her the power to curse the village?"

"But who saw her in the mountains? She would never walk so far in one evening."

"A shepherd saw her, sir."

"But he may have been mistaken."

"He saw her speaking to some one, and nobody for the last two years that she was in this village dared to speak to her but the fairies and the old woman you saw at Mass today, sir."

"Now, tell me about Julia Cahill; what did she do?"

"It is said, sir, she was the finest girl in these parts. I was only a gossoon at the time, about eight or nine, but I remember that she was tall, sir, nearly as tall as you are, and she was as straight as one of those poplar-trees," he said, pointing to three trees that stood against the sky. "She walked with a little swing in her walk, so that all the boys, I have heard, who were grown up used to look after her, and she had fine black eyes, sir, and she was nearly always laughing. This was the time when Father Madden came to the parish. There was courting in it then, and every young man and every young woman made their own marriages, and their marriages were made at the cross-road dancing, and in the summer evenings under the hedges. There was no dancer like Julia; they used to gather about to see her dance, and whoever walked with her under the hedges in the summer, could never think about another woman. The village was fairly mad about her, many a fight there was over her, so I suppose the priest was right. He had to get rid of her; but I think he might not have been so hard upon her as he was. It is said that he went down to her house one evening; Julia's people were well-to-do people; they kept a shop; you might have seen it as we came along the road, just outside of the village it is. And when he came in there was one of the richest farmers in the country who was trying to get Julia for his wife. Instead of going to Julia, he had gone to the father. There are two counters in the shop, and Julia was at the other, and she had made many a good pound for her parents in that shop; and he said to the father: 'Now, what fortune are you going to give with Julia?' And the father said there was many a man who would take her without any, and Julia was listening quietly all the while at the opposite counter. The man who had come to marry her did not know what a spirited girl she was, and he went on till he got the father to say that he would give £70, and, thinking he had got him so far, he said, 'Julia will never cross my doorway unless you give her £80.' Julia said never a word, she just sat there listening, and it was then that the priest came in. He listened for awhile, and then he went over to Julia and said, 'Are you not proud to hear that you will have such a fine fortune?' And he said, 'I shall be glad to see you married. I would marry you for nothing, for I cannot have any more of your goings-on in my parish. You're the beginning of the dancing and courting here; the ball-alley, too—I am going to put all that down.' Julia did not answer a single word to him, and he went over to them that were disputing about the £80, and he said, 'Now, why not make it £75,' and the father agreed to that, since the priest said it, and the three men thought the marriage was settled. And Father Tom thought that he would get not less than £10 for the marrying of her. They did not even think to ask her, and little did they think what she was going to say, and what she said was that she would not marry any one until it pleased herself, and that she would pick a man out of this parish or out of the next that pleased her. Her husband should marry her, and not so many pounds to be paid when they signed the book or when the first baby was born. This is how marriages are settled now. Well, sir, the priest went wild when he heard Julia speak like this; he had only just come to the parish, and did not know how self-minded Julia was. Her father did, though, and he said nothing; he let Julia and the priest fight it out, and he said to the man who had come to marry her, 'My good man, you can go your way; you will never get her, I can tell that.' And the priest was heard saying, 'Do you think I am going to let you go on turning the head of every boy in the parish? Do you think I am going to see fighting and quarrelling for you? Do you think I am going to see you first with one boy and then with the other? Do you think I am going to hear stories like I heard last week about poor Peter Carey, who they say, has gone out of his mind on account of your treatment? No,' he said, 'I will have no more of you; I will have you out of my parish, or I will have you married.' Julia tossed her head, and her father got frightened. He promised the priest that she should walk no more with the young men in the evenings, for he thought he could keep her at home; but he might just as well have promised the priest to tie up the winds. Julia was out the same evening with a young man, and the priest saw her; and next evening she was out with another, and the priest saw her; and not a bit minded was she at the end of the month to marry any of them. It is said that he went down to speak to her a second time, and again a third time; it is said that she laughed at him. After that there was nothing for him to do but to speak against her from the altar. The old people say there were some terrible things in the sermon. I have heard it said that the priest called her the evil spirit that sets men mad. I don't suppose Father Madden intended to say so much, but once he is started the words come pouring out. The people did not understand half of what he said, but they were very much frightened, and I think more frightened at what they did not understand than at what they did. Soon after that the neighbours began to be afraid to go to buy anything in Cahill's shop; even the boys who were most mad after Julia were afraid to speak to her, and her own father put her out. No one in the parish would speak to her; they were all afraid of Father Madden. If it had not been for the blind woman you saw in the chapel today, sir, she would have had to go to the poor-house. The blind woman has a little cabin at the edge of the bog, and there Julia lived. She remained for nearly two years, and had hardly any clothes on her back, but she was beautiful for all that, and the boys, as they came back, sir, from the market used to look towards the little cabin in the hopes of catching sight of her. They only looked when they thought they were not watched, for the priest still spoke against her. He tried to turn the blind woman against Julia, but he could not do that; the blind woman kept her until money came from America. Some say that she went to America; some say that she joined the fairies. But one morning she surely left the parish. One morning Pat Quinn heard somebody knocking at his window, somebody asking if he would lend his cart to take somebody to the railway station. It was five o'clock in the morning, and Pat was a heavy sleeper, and he would not get up, and it is said that she walked barefooted all the way to the station, and that is a good ten miles."

"But you said something about a curse."

"Yes, sir, a man who was taking some sheep to the fair saw her: there was a fair that day. He saw her standing at the top of the road. The sun was just above the hill, and looking back she cursed the village, raising both hands, sir, up to the sun, and since that curse was spoken, every year a roof has fallen in."

There was no doubt that the boy believed what he had told me; I could see that he liked to believe the story, that it was natural and sympathetic to him to believe in it; and for the moment I, too, believed in a dancing girl becoming the evil spirit of a village that would not accept her delight.

"He has sent away Life," I said to myself, "and now they are following Life. It is Life they are seeking."

"It is said, your honour, that she's been seen in America, and I am going there this autumn. You may be sure I will keep a look out for her."

"But all this is twenty years ago. You will not know her. A woman changes a good deal in twenty years."

"There will be no change in her, your honour. She has been with the fairies. But, sir, we shall be just in time to see the clergy come out of the cathedral after the consecration," he said, and he pointed to the town.

It stood in the middle of a flat country, and as we approached it the great wall of the cathedral rose above dirty and broken cottages, and great masses of masonry extended from the cathedral into the town; and these were the nunnery, its schools and laundry; altogether they seemed like one great cloud.

When, I said, will a ray from the antique sun break forth and light up this country again?

1924

THE RETURN OF NIAV

Dorothy Macardle

Dorothy Macardle, born in the coastal Co. Louth in eastern Ireland in 1889, was a journalist, historian and writer; as an author of the supernatural she is mainly remembered for her supernatural mystery novel *The Uninvited* in 1942, (first published as *Uneasy Freehold* in 1941), which was adapted for the big screen in 1944. From a young age, Macardle had started publishing articles and poems. After the events of the Easter Rising in 1916, she became politically radical and actively supported the national movement for independence. During the Irish Civil War she was captured and imprisoned by the National Army and in the time of her internment she managed to write a number of supernatural stories that were later included in her debut collection *Earth-Bound: Nine Stories of Ireland* (1924). The tales of *Earth-Bound*, narrated by a group of Irish revolutionaries exiled in the United States, reflected the author's concerns, anxieties and trauma from her experiences connected to the Irish cause, while the otherworldly element served her as a means to make a covert political commentary. In her later years and until her death in 1958 she continued to write and publish both fiction and non-fiction works, such as the historic political treatise *The Irish Republic* (1937) and the novels *The Unforeseen* (1946) and *Dark Enchantment* (1953).

"The Return of Niav", included in *Earth-Bound*, is an almost lyrical horror story, a disquieting tale indebted to fairy lore and the myth of Oisín, abounding with poetic imagery and dreamlike descriptions; moreover, it is a refined exploration of aspects of motherhood, queer sexuality, the dangers of seduction and complex relationships between women.

(For I.S.)

AN air from Errigal seemed to come to America with Maeve; that beauty of hers that subdued the heart like dé Danaan magic had changed with the sorrowful years; like sunrise once, she had a more troubled, patient, tender loveliness now. "Like to the mournful moon," Úna said.

The evenings she spent with us were wonderful, all the world's wars forgotten in the talk we had always loved—talk of the enchanted waters and hills of Ireland, of ruins and symbols and rituals and of the music that would come out of Ireland when we were free.

"Do you know that my Neoineen is making the strangest, most marvellous music already?" she said. "Her masters in Leipzig hardly know what to make of her; she is as creative, they told me, at seventeen as any composer in his prime, and makes deliriously beautiful tunes. But she won't study; while she should have been learning the history of music she was composing a symphony, I'm afraid!"

"What is her symphony?" Úna asked, and Maeve replied:

"The Children of Lir."

She looked at us then, her eyes shining, and spoke in a voice hushed with joy. "It is the sweetest, unearthliest music I have ever heard. The cold—the mortal cold of the waters! The wild lonely sorrow of the swans—the yearning for human things—the dreadful enchanted striving through water and air—nothing could describe it but music—no music but hers! She will be giving the music of Ireland to the world."

Maeve stopped, shy of so praising her own child, but I could believe it all. I had a memory of Neoineen when she was four years old and the loveliest thing, except her mother, that I had ever seen—a wind-sprite of a child with a floss of silvery-gold hair raying out like Lugh's halo round her head, and a little pointed face and dark hazel eyes. Her soul and body were all music; day-long she would be dancing to the sun or the wind or the moon, or making strange little rhymes. Maeve was making a little pagan of her, filling her imagination with the wonder-tales of Ireland, inventing druid rituals, making magical songs. I remembered an old priest warning Maeve solemnly that she was exposing her child to influences more dangerous than she knew and how Maeve, who always had an artist's recklessness, only laughed—"All beautiful things are good."

"Do you remember," I asked her, "how anxious you used to make poor Father Cahill? He thought Neoineen would lose her soul!"

I spoke laughingly, but Maeve's face, remembering, grew grave. "You don't know," she said, "how nearly he was right."

She looked at our incredulous faces and smiled, "You don't believe it? I will tell you then—I will tell you, though I was dreadfully to blame, because it is all over long ago. I think that was how her music came."

We drew close, intent, waiting, and dreamily she began to tell.

"It never could have happened but for the solitude of our home: I was so eager to welcome a companion for Neoineen. I built my house there for the glorious freedom of the place—a place unchanged, you would think, since the days of Fionn. Our home is on the very brow of the mountain where it breaks in a cliff over the loch—the water at our feet, the hawks and the clouds and the mountain peaks overhead, and steep, wooded ravines and torrents below. There we lived, just our two selves and my old Maura, as happy as human people could ever be. We had no neighbours at all except half-a-dozen families who lived fighting the mountain for a livelihood on their tiny farms. A little scamp called Seumas belonging to one of them was Neoineen's only playmate. I liked him to come because he talked such delicious Irish—I did not want her to hear English at all—but she preferred playing with me or alone.

"It was unthinkable, always, to leave Neoineen to the companionship of a nurse, impossible to find a satisfying playmate for such a child.

"That summer—the thing happened when she was five—we had the most radiant June I have ever known, full of wild scents of heather and bog, and we spent golden days. I was painting trees at the edge of the Druid's Wood—a steep, narrow glen—and Neoineen used to wander away by herself on marvellous adventures.

"We were in the Fionn cycle then! She was Osgar, I think, and I was Oisín; I was expected to make a new song every day!

"St John's Eve came, one of our Festivals; a morning of jewel colours in earth and sky. We had planned to stay out till moonrise and light our magical fire in the ravine and we had made a song with a sweet, bewitching little tune to it, to lure the fairies to our fire. While I settled to my painting Neoineen wandered away to gather wood of nine different kinds and to choose a place for the fire. She was a long time away, but she came to my whistle at last, wearing a foxglove helmet on every finger, and with her arms full of wet flowers—meadowsweet and the yellow irises that grow in pools.

"'How did you pull those, Osgar?' I asked, and she answered:

"'Niav brought them from Tír-na-n-Óg. I found Niav in the wood; she sang a most wondrous song.'

"I was accustomed to Neoineen's 'wondrous' adventures and only thought, while she told me her tale, eating her lunch under a tree, that it was the prettiest she had invented yet. She was impatient to be away, and jumped up very soon. 'Farewell, Fionn!' she called to me, kissing her hand as she ran away into the wood, and, guessing that our roles had changed, I answered, 'Farewell, Oisín!'

"You know what the silence of noon can be, the spellbound silence of a June day; it seems to well up, like clear water, from earth to heaven and hold one entranced under a still pool—it is in those silences great music is born.

"It was such a magical silence that was pierced then, suddenly, by the most rapturous music I had ever heard, wild singing, joyous and daring as a bird's. As I listened; scarcely breathing, fantastic images thronged my mind; I thought some wild swan must be singing his death-song, having strayed out of Tír-na-n-Óg. I thought it was faery music out of the mountain—I thought of Étaín and of Niav...

"The singer was coming towards me through the wood; Neoineen was holding her by the hand; I could see her between the trees. Her beauty was like the beauty of her song—daring and exquisite and free. A little high head she had with a glory of red-gold hair about it; a green, ragged gown was on her and her delicate white feet and arms were bare; she came towards me like some young, triumphant queen, leading her lover by the hand; she looked at me with soft eyes like a fawn's and smiled.

"'Come with us to Tír-na-n-Óg,' Neoineen said, and took my hand and led me down the steep, dark paths into the wood. 'This is Niav,' she said, speaking Irish, of course, and the girl looked at me joyously and said. '*Cuirim fad beannacht na gréine thú!*'—'I give you the blessing of the sun!' Her Irish was as musical as her song, soft and vigorous and rich.

"She led us down to a deep hollow in the wood, honey-fragrant, alight with the smouldering purple of foxglove, loud with the babble of a little waterfall where the brook tumbled into a pool. There, on a great flat stone, they had prepared the druid fire.

"The foxgloves were Oisín's warriors, it seemed; he went from one to another, praising them for marvellous deeds, bidding Niav lean down and kiss the best; I heard her add her praise to Oisín's with such queenly grace, speak so gravely of their perils and wounds that I became almost rapt in their illusion, too. When it was over she came and sat in a patch of pure sunlight, singing dreamy and mystical songs—songs such as I had never heard before, though I knew Irish music well—more entrancing than any I had heard.

"I spoke to her once, 'You have Irish only?' I said, and 'Irish only,' she replied.

"Tired of singing, she ran to Neoineen and they chased one another like sungleams among the trees. Neoineen like a little mad sprite of laughter, growing wilder and wilder, till she tumbled, poor baby, into the pool. Niav gave a strange, terrified cry, but Neoineen scrambled out, laughing, and shook herself like a dog. I hurried her home, leaving Niav among the trees.

"It had been an enchanted day, but it ended sadly. Neoineen had set her heart on the druid fire—she was a fire-worshipper always; but the evening was chilly and she seemed fevered with excitement and I dared not, after that wetting, let her stay out after dark. She tried all ways to persuade me, but at last, to Fionn's sorrow, Oisín cried. I remember the play I made to comfort her, with the song we had made to sing in the druid wood. She was a faery child and I was a lonely woman with no little girl and when I sang our luring little song she would creep out of faeryland, steal to me and leap into my arms at last. Again and again we played it until, drowsy and serene again, she let me sing her to sleep.

"I hardly know how to tell you how the rest of that summer passed; it is like a half-forgotten dream. Only I know that for me no less than for Neoineen there was a childish eagerness in living, a joyous wonder, from day to day—as though we lived to music. 'Niav'—we knew no other name for her, played with Neoineen and sang for me, sat in the sunlight or crouched over my fire, telling long tales, as though they were dear memories, of the old glories of the Gael. It was all what my heart's desire for Neoineen would have chosen. I listened and watched their play and painted and forgot there were sorrows in the world.

"Then, in September, quite suddenly, my dear old godmother died. She brought us up, you know—me and Hugo Blake; he was left desolate by her death. He wrote and implored me to go to him; he had always regarded me as his elder sister and he had no one else in the world. I had to go; and I had to leave Neoineen.

"I know you will think I was to blame; I know it myself now. I could have taken her, of course; but Hugo was in one of his dark, gloomy moods, and his Tower seemed no place for a child, and she was so happy, playing with Niav.

"Niav's own folk, she had told us, lived 'over the hill'. Quite poor, I imagined them, since she wore thin, ragged clothes always and could not read or write; but the gentlest, in the West, are the very poor, and Niav was as gentle as a queen. I left Neoineen to her and Maura, and went to Hugo for two months.

"He was ill and despairing. It was one of those black periods when he could not paint; there were times, you know, when we feared for his mind. November was over before I came home.

"It was a troubled letter from Maura that brought me then.

"'The darling is as good as gold,' she wrote, 'but she's not taking her food and she's too thin. She does be falling asleep in the middle of her play.'

"To my disappointment she was asleep when I came home, lying on a nest of cushions by the fire, Niav on guard. Niav rose and kissed me softly. At the very sight of her shining, serene loveliness, the old gladness flowed back, and when my Neoineen awoke and hugged me and caressed me, crooning little lyrics of her love, earth was my heaven again.

"But she was not well, my little one. I accused myself for staying so long away. Loving and contented as ever, she seemed, but she had not grown a hair's breadth and had lost weight and had become fastidious about food. Niav lived on with us; I could not do without her; no one else could make Neoineen eat at all. She never tired of the child; they would play together just as vividly, run just as lightly over the frosty ground as in those golden summer days; but after their play Neoineen would steal in to me tired—even, I sometimes fancied, a little nervous, and cuddle into my arms and fall asleep. She slept at night too deeply; nothing would wake her; her breathing was too light.

"My old friend, Dr Moore, came for a day or two, but he could not give me much help. The child's imagination seemed over-excited, he said, he found nothing else wrong.

"It was then that I began to wonder about Niav, to watch her closely and love her not quite so well—she seemed to me to have changed. She who had been so tender would not comprehend that Neoineen was ill, would not listen to my fears.

"I began to be afraid of their play, though it had grown so dreamy and quiet you would have thought it could not hurt Neoineen. One day I came upon them suddenly in the shrubbery, Neoineen lying on a bed of fallen leaves. Her eyes were shut, her arms lay limp, her face was quite colourless. I was frightened; I could not wake her or make her stir. Niav laughed at me, a little scornfully I thought. 'She is only playing! Come back, Asthore!' At that soft whisper in Niav's sweetest tones, Neoineen awoke and clung to me and cried. I looked at Niav then for the first time, coldly, and said, 'Do not play at death with her again!' She did not answer save with a smiling look, but to my imagination there was a mocking challenge in her eyes.

"My own imagination was growing morbid—tainted with jealousy perhaps—that is what I thought then. It was foolish; my Neoineen loved me; she loved no one so well as me; yet if Niav left her, I believed, so entwined was she with her life, the child would die. Then again I thought myself half-crazy in that belief, so unreasoning, so fantastical it seemed. And as the dread took hold of me, haunted me more and more terribly—the dread that I was doomed to lose Neoineen, it was my own feverish imagination that I accused. 'The more need for her,' I would say to myself then, 'to have a clear-spirited, joyous being like Niav to share her play.' So, in a nightmare duel between warning instinct and incredulous will, I wore the winter and spring away.

"Of all festivals of the year, except Saint John's Eve, we loved Beltaine best. It was then, on the last day of April, that the crisis came.

"All the Beltaine mysteries—the fire-building and songs and rituals, Neoineen had decided, were to be a surprise for me. She and Niav would prepare them alone. So all that day they were away together in the Druid Wood. They were away so long that I went out at dusk to look for them, calling 'Neoineen, Neoineen!'

"Do you remember April evenings in that glen? The sky translucent like a green faery sea, the mountain like a rock of amethyst, cut into hollow and ridge, shadow and gleam—and that evening there was a ghost of new moon. Green the woods were, too, just sprinkled with budding leaves, seeming to hold the dying light in a magical net; the long weeds and brambles were cold with dew and a silvery mist was winding among the trees. There was something tremulous, eager, pent, in the listening air.

"I stole down, calling softly, into the deep glen, till I heard the gurgle of water among the stones and came out where the little torrent breaks into a fall—where we made our Saint John's fire on the Druid stone.

"There on the flat stone lay Neoineen, in her thin white smock, quite still. Kneeling upright beside her, her hands clasped, swaying and singing softly, was Niav; my heart stood still.

"For a moment such terror was on me that I could only stand motionless, watching, while Niav laid her kiss on the child's mouth. Then I rushed down, screaming, and seized Neoineen and cried out I know not what fierce things to the girl, telling her to go back to where she came from, that never, never, should she touch or see my darling again. Niav stood up then and lifted her head and laughed—a low sweet laughter—and turned and ran and vanished into the dark.

"For dreadful hours Maura and I worked, wrapping her in hot blankets, chafing her numbed body and stiffened limbs, forcing warm milk between her clenched teeth, before the rigor passed. Her little face was terrible; I could scarcely look at it; blue and shrunken it was, like an old woman's—like a cunning old woman, dead.

"When we had won our battle with death—when her breathing was tranquil at last, and her blood flowing, and her body warm and relaxed in natural sleep, I stole into bed and held her fast in my arms. Life is wonderful when you have looked at death.

"It was late in the morning when I opened the curtains; sunlight flowed over her as she lay, and gleamed on her shining hair. As I stood, looking down at her, crying with love and joy, she opened her eyes and looked right into mine. I had been through terror, but that moment was the most horrible I have known. What looked at me out of those hazel eyes was mockery—it was mockery—triumphant—and hate.

"I turned away to the window, gasping, pressing my forehead to the cool pane, praying that I might not be mad—I tried to force myself to call her and dress her and brush her hair, chatting merrily as every day; but I could not. I knelt and held her by the shoulders at last and looked into her face and said sharply, 'Neoineen, tell me what is wrong!' She smiled. 'Nothing, Mameen,' she said softly, 'nothing, little Queen-Mother, nothing at all!' It was her lovingest name for me; it froze me to hear it spoken in that bitter-sweet tone. I tried to startle her—to shake the strange mood away; I said suddenly, 'Do you know Niav is gone?'

"'Niav has gone away,' she answered lightly.

"'We don't want Niav any more.' And she fixed me with those cold, hard eyes till my heart shrank.

"Little Seumas was calling from the garden, wild with eagerness over the May-day games. But there was no festival of Beltaine; she laughed and called and chased him up and down hill, hid and sprang out at him from trees and boulders, hooting like an owl, crying out like a curlew until he was bewildered and tired. She caught him then and laughed, but he turned and stared at her and pulled himself free and stole away home, afraid. I told her she had been rough and unkind, and she cried.

"I blamed myself bitterly then. I should have been thankful I said; it was just that her long illness had suddenly gone. Day by day now she grew healthier, browner; she ate, greedily even—was never tired—never for one moment fretted for Niav, never even mentioned her name. I walked and played, explored and gardened, sang and danced with her as of old; she went with me everywhere, responsive, caressing as ever before—yet—yet—Oh, how can I tell you the truth of those hideous days? I did not believe in her, did not want her, did not love her. I was consumed and tortured with craving for my own little lovely girl.

"I dare say I am not remembering it all quite as it was. I am sure, whatever other thing had happened, my own mind was unbalanced, my imagination distorted from the strain.

"Maura told me that I should bring Niav back. 'What she done,' Maura said, 'no other can undo,' and I used to walk wildly about the mountain seeking and enquiring for any sign, but the cottage folk knew nothing of her at all. One old woman drew from me the whole dreadful story; she sat in her corner distressfully shaking her head. 'You were mad foolish, mad foolish,' she said, 'you to lead her by the hand into your home.'

"'What can I do?' I sobbed, 'what can I do to get my baby again?'

"'I heard of them going,' she answered mournfully, 'but I never heard of one coming back.'

"I began, after crazy weeks of vain searching, to despair and try to comfort myself in childish ways, talking to Neoineen when I was quite alone, pretending that I held her in my arms. And I used to dream about her all night long—cruel, maddening dreams. I would hear her crying out to me, see her, reaching piteous arms to me from the dark, and always when I clasped her she turned to air.

"A kind of mania seized me to be going to the places where we had been together, repeating the things we had done; and the child followed me everywhere—the child that I hated—hated, now.

"I gathered wood of nine kinds on Saint John's Eve and set a fire in the glade on the druid's stone.

"Memory was vivid as an illusion—I thought there was music in the air. It was a day as golden as a year ago it had been, the air sweet with honeysuckle and with the songs of the water and the birds; there were foxgloves burning in the shadows, meadowsweet and irises in the pools. All the afternoon I was pulling weeds and flowers, strewing them around the druid stone, and sobbing, sobbing aloud. The child followed me, staring, scared and subdued; I tried to send her away, but she would not go. At moonrise I lit the fire and cried out the wild little invocation that Neoineen and I had made—gave way to all the crazy anguish within me—chanted it loud enough for the hills to hear. I was the forlorn mother in our story, playing alone, alone.

"The little brown girl sat crouching under a stone, whimpering with fear and cold. I cared nothing for her. I wanted my own baby, the child of my body and soul, wanted her more than the dying could long for life or the living for death, wanted her with an anguish that is not known.

"I flung my arms out in the darkness, walking nine times, sun-wise around the fire, singing, singing that luring, magical song; piercing sweet was the wild tune we had made!

"In the dark ravine the sparks leaped redly, terrifying the crouching child. As I passed her she sprang up shrieking and stamped her feet, but I sang on and flung ashes over her out of the fire. With a weird scream she fled from me into the darkness and I ended my ninth circling of the stone.

"When I stood still at last all was silent, and, suddenly frightened, I ran down to the stream. She was lying under the water with shut eyes.

"I lifted her; she was limp, white, unconscious. I carried her to the fire, stripped and warmed her, held her in the glow, wrapped her in my shawl, then carried her home, hugged to my heart, calling her every name she had ever heard—my star-flower, my daisy-bud, vein of my heart. Just as I crossed the threshold she opened her eyes, wide and loving and clear, but they filled with tears and she clung to me crying: 'Mameen, Mameen! Oh, hold me, little Queen-Mother! Don't let me go any more.' Then she fell asleep in my arms—my baby girl.

"No memory remains of it at all; it is gone like a dream."

KILMAINHAM.

Modern Horrors

1926

THE BACK DRAWING-ROOM

Elizabeth Bowen

Elizabeth Bowen (1899–1973) was a highly-acclaimed Anglo-Irish modernist author who was born in Dublin and died in Kent. Her life was divided between England and Ireland, with frequent travels and relocations. Her novels such as *Last September* (1929), *The House in Paris* (1935), *The Death of the Heart* (1938) and *The Heat of the Day* (1948) are highly regarded by literary critics as sophisticated literary works of profound psychological acumen. Whereas she had incorporated gothic elements in her novels, she believed that the short story was the most effective form in order to provoke a genuine sense of terror, while at the same time with her literary craft she wished to evoke "ghosts" of war, history, and gender oppression. In her non-realist tales the uncanny often invades the prosaic daily lives of the characters as being projection of haunting memories, fears and traumas, in an exploration of collective and individual feelings of repression; her most anthologised stories in this vein are "The Demon Lover" (1945), "The Happy Autumn Fields" (1945) and "Hand in Glove" (1952).

"The Back Drawing-Room", first published in Bowen's short story collection *Ann Lee's* (1926), reflects the author's own precarious sense of identity due to her Anglo-Irish descent. The tale starts off as a typical ghost story echoing Victorian Christmas discussions of the English aristocracy about seances and the world of spirits. As the plot develops an unusual guest relates the strange events he experienced in the Irish countryside some time ago rendering the Irish landscape an otherworldly presence itself, a strange unknown land with a troubled past of conflict and turmoil; a place that the English find both fascinating and uncanny.

Mrs Henneker having taken her place among them, inevitably they had begun to discuss the larger abstractions. They did not even hesitate to challenge the mortality of the soul, and Miss Eve, the violinist, said with that slight vibration her voice had caught from her fiddle-strings that she believed one was born doubting everything, and that *she* even doubted sometimes whether death meant extinction at all. Survival—

"Survival," said Bellingham, the man in the low chair beside Lois, who had up to now been talking about Greece, "simply isn't a matter of fitness, I consider; it's a matter of tenacity."

Lois, who was getting sleepy, nodded at the fire like a mandarin, and after a pause said weightily, "I should think that is very true"; but the young man with the horn-rimmed glasses challenged this remark of Bellingham's, sitting bolt upright and staring inexorably at him like an owl. He said in a deep drawl: "Surely the two are synonymous?"

Bellingham was less well in hand than the rest of Mrs Henneker's pack; he did not want to discuss the larger abstractions, he wanted to talk about Greece, which he had lately visited, and Greece itself, in its actuality, not, as Mrs Henneker would have directed, Hellenism. Now he saw her leaning back and drawing herself up and narrowing her eyes for utterance, and he realised that if he took any notice of that young man they two would be left skirmishing in a back alley while the talk swept by without them. However brilliant his repartee, however remarkable his agility, it would be unnoticed by Lois, who even now hung passionately on the lips of Mrs Henneker.

So he repeated generally, with an inclusive glance challenging the semicircle, that survival was a matter of tenacity. Now in Greece—

"Tenacity to what?" Lois asked the fire.

"*Ah*..." said somebody. "Yes—"

"Well," he hesitated, "it depends what plane we're on. On the purely physical—"

The word attracted two young women in the corner, who leant forward, suddenly illuminated, thinking he was going to talk about sex. Of course, the word had not always this connotation, but having read widely they knew it to be a word of possibilities.

"—On the purely physical alone," said Mrs Henneker, "there's always, isn't there, a slackening of the grip?" She illustrated this with her hands. "Fitness and unfitness is such a purely objective way of pigeon-holing. Besides, all that is *circular*, isn't it? Fitness for what? To survive. But to survive what? What is one fit for?"

They all wondered. She swept a glance round them smilingly, to glean up any wandering attention. The little fair, plump man did not even look up at her; he did not seem to realise who she was. He sat with his legs crossed, his hands clasped on his knee, looking around him modestly and unintelligently, with an air of not having realised anybody. Somebody who came in late had brought him, with an apology, and had whispered an explanation into somebody else's ear. They had seated him, and he sat, looking propped-up and a little dejected, like an umbrella that an absent-minded caller has brought into the drawing-room. Once or twice, when the conversation prior to the entrance of Mrs Henneker had veered dangerously near the comprehensible, he had volunteered remarks—oh, quite intelligent—quoting a friend, a banker who sometimes wrote to him from Modern Athens. He obviously belonged to one type of club, read the confessions of eminent diplomats' wives, and lunched with friends who considered him an entertaining fellow. Now he submitted, looking up at Mrs Henneker with his little, perplexed blue eyes: "It's extraordinary, isn't it, what one does survive..."

"After death," said Mrs Henneker, hanging poised for a moment, then sweeping forward over him, "the only criteria of our reality for those who have not passed over are the senses—*their* senses, or perhaps what I always think of as that finer internal fabric of the senses: I mean the soul."

"But surely," said the young man with the horn rims, deferentially, but as one having authority, "the soul doesn't exist."

"That's just the point of it," said Lois, a little too bluntly; "*does* it?"

"Exist *when?*" said Bellingham crossly. "Now, or when we're dead? I don't quite see what we're getting at."

Mrs Henneker looked at him sideways like a wounded dove. "The survival of the soul after death," she said gently, "the survival of the *us*—oh, surely, Mr Bellingham, of the *you* and of the *me*, is a matter, it always seems to me, that we are unable to consider, to weigh up for ourselves clearly, because in considering it we can only represent the thing to ourselves in terms of the *physical*. We stand aloof from the after life of the spirits of our friends, from that persisting essence of them which we call the spirit, in *giant ignorance*. It is like shutting out, if such a thing were possible to imagine, the sensuous appeal of music because we have not the score under our eyes to analyse—"

"Analysis?" said the young man with the horn rims, holding her up politely: "ah, there you interest me very much, Mrs Henneker. Now, you contend that there does exist in us a consciousness, an apprehension of the—er—people in the after state which will permit of quite definite analysis, like our power of apprehending music, or our sense of smell? A consciousness quite apart from the sensory manifestations of the spiritualist—table-rapping, gramophone-horns, planchette?"

"Oh, Spiritualism!" said Mrs Henneker, shrinking into herself. "Oh, that's horrible, I think, that is so horrible! No, Mr Mennister, that way of approach, if it could or did ever mean anything, is vulgarised. Besides, have we need of verbal communication? No, I think we attain our consciousness of *them* as one attains that finer intercourse, if you like, *telepathic*, of two people, any two of us here, maybe, who are closely knit together, emotionally, or by unity of interest."

"Ah," said several people, rustling; "yes…" Lois leant sideways and fingered a fold of Mrs Henneker's dress.

"By a prolongation," she continued, "by an ever-increasing frequency of this intercourse, in presence and in absence, we possess within us and have access to a more and more complete personality, grafted on to our own. When that personality has emerged wholly from the muddle of our unperceptiveness, like Galatea out of the marble, a given relationship is complete."

Her voice dropped beautifully from sentence to sentence, lingered over the peroration and was still.

"I don't quite see," said Bellingham, and the young man with the horn rims looked at him in despair. Lois let a sharp little sigh escape her, and the little man beyond the fire brightened visibly.

Mrs Henneker was infinitely patient, "I mean," she said, speaking very slowly, "that such a complete cognisance of one being by another must give the one *known* a second distinct vitality apart from that either of the known or of the knower. You know how during those rather terrible séances a face or body sometime takes form out of the psychic fluid generated by the medium. This face or body may become detached from her, liberated, and has then its own vitality and is definitely *objective*…" She leant forward, spreading out her hands.

"Objective," said Mennister. "Ye-es. You contend that imagination, memory, cognisance, have the power of carrying themselves over from the *sub*jective into the *ob*jective?"

"Because you remember a thing," said Lois diffidently, "or even imagine it, or from loving it very much really know it, it *exists* apart from itself and from you, even though you don't remember it, imagine it, or know it any more?"

"Yes," said Mrs Henneker simply, "that is what I meant. I grope. I don't express myself very clearly, I'm afraid."

They dissented murmuringly.

"That," Mennister informed them, leaning back and putting the tips of his fingers together, "is very interesting. Though we're not, of course, covering new ground. What it all comes down to ultimately is: a question of the visibility or—er—perceptibility of thought-forms. What Mrs Henneker contends for is: their indefinite or their even infinite survival. Mr Bellingham finds that survival is a matter of tenacity—though he hasn't yet distinguished tenacity, in this particular sense, from fitness, or given us any reason why we should oppose them. If we are to go all the way with Mrs Henneker"—he pulled out a stop in his voice and it became richly humorous—"we accept that we may only hope for immortality in so far as we have attracted favourable attention, and become somebody else's thought-form. We then survive, not by our own tenacity, but by somebody else's. We—"

"In so much of Hardy's poetry—"

"Quite," said Mr Mennister, suppressing the young woman who had contributed this remark. "The idea is not a new one; it becomes increasingly popular, doesn't it? In fiction—"

"Popular fiction is not my line, of course," said Bellingham swiftly. "I know very little about it, but"—Mennister's glasses blazed at him, he looked up blandly at the ceiling—"but, getting down to the ghost story, the ghost story pure and simple: well, I remember saying to a man only a few weeks ago, as we walked in the streets of Athens—"

Something stirred beyond the fire; the little man came alive from his torpor, uncrossed his legs and sat up, clearing his throat. "Ah," he said, "ghosts! Yes. What a fascinating theme for speculation!"

Everybody turned to look at him; it was as though the umbrella had spoken.

"Very," said Mennister dryly.

Mrs Henneker turned her mournful eyes full upon him and inquired, "It *does* interest you?"

"Oh, Mrs *Hen*neker!" said one of the young women, sobbing with laughter.

"One cannot fail to be interested," said the little man earnestly, looking from Mrs Henneker to Lois, as though they were of equal importance, and even including Miss Eve and the two young women in the opposite corner—"one cannot fail to be interested if one has *experienced...*"

He was getting out of hand, quite suddenly. Mennister hummed softly and raised his eyebrows, and Lois slid to the floor from her chair and sat at Mrs Henneker's feet, leaning up against her friend's knee protectively. Only Bellingham secretly and cynically grinned.

"Because I *have* had experience," said the little man, looking at them in surprise. "I can't, I really cannot account..."

Lois said "Hell!" under her breath. "Bring in the Yule log, this is a Dickens Christmas. We're going to tell ghost stories." Mrs Henneker laid a hand on her shoulder and said, "Hush, Lois!" and Miss Eve, who had been waiting for some time to catch Bellingham's eye, smiled at him with an air of secret understanding. Back and behind the artist, the woman in her was enchanting: this was what Miss Eve liked to convey.

There was something very guileless about the little man; he thought they were all so clever. "I expect some of *you*'d make it fit in at once," he said trustfully. "I think it would fit in with some of that you've just been saying: about memory, or perhaps about love. May I tell you what occurred? It was very curious.

"A cousin of mine has property in Ireland. He is a sporting man; we have little in common, though I think all the world of him, he is a very nice fellow; and I have the greatest admiration for his wife—she is one of the few people I know who really makes her poultry pay, or she did so, at least, until these civic disturbances began. I have seen very little of them lately; they were worried about the place, and had several times been raided. Lately, since things in their part of the country began to improve, my cousin began writing again to say, 'Do come over.' My previous (and only other) visit there had been very pleasant; there was a good deal of croquet in the neighbourhood, and I am an enthusiastic player. I bicycle a good deal, too, and when my cousin wrote to say the roads, those pretty roads round there, were really safe again (not *good*, they are never good),

I was greatly tempted to accept his invitation, and at length did so—that was last year. So I went over to Ireland."

"Ireland," said Mrs Henneker, "unforgettably and almost terribly afflicted me. The contact was so intimate as to be almost intolerable. Those gulls about the piers of Kingstown, crying, crying: they are an overture to Ireland. One lives in a dream there, a dream oppressed and shifting, such as one dreams in a house with trees about it, on a sultry night."

"Now *that*," said Bellingham, "just illustrates what I said about tenacity. Compared with Greece—"

"Quite," said Mennister. "A beastly country, I thought. Of course, their plays—"

The little man, having looked wistfully from one to another of them, at last raised his voice and continued:

"I went to Ireland, and found my cousins much as ever, and the place looking very well. Several dozen of her chickens had been stolen, but it turned out to be a case of an ill wind—she had since introduced a new strain of Leghorns, which were doing very well indeed. My cousin was as busy as usual, but he had arranged for me to borrow a bicycle belonging to the cook's brother: a new bicycle, which was supposed to be very good.

"The first day after my arrival I went out for a ride. We had not had time to talk very much the night before, but they had told me a certain amount of what had happened in the neighbourhood, and warned me that I should find the country around them dilapidated and rather depressing. And it did look indeed very sad. Sad, I should say, when one passed ruined cottages along the roadside, and a poor police-barrack like a box with its lid off, with the sky staring through the windows. When I got clear of these, however, my depression forsook me. I am always sensitive, I believe, to the beauty of landscape, and the country did that day look very beautiful in a pale-coloured, early-autumn way which is, I think, peculiar to Ireland. It was a very smooth, clear day, quite windless; with a pale grey sky, and no lights or shadows anywhere. The only accents in the landscape were the mountains; these were dark and grew darker—a bad sign, almost invariably portending rain. My bicycle went well for some hours, and I went easily along, free-wheeling a good deal, and perhaps a trifle absent-minded. I must have been absent-minded, for I rode right over a patch of sharp stones which had been put down (but not rolled) to mend the road. I am seldom so careless, and I acknowledged myself punished for it as with sinking heart I felt my back tyre go completely flat."

"Quite," said Mennister. "You should write your cycling experiences—er, er—'Potters on a Push-bike.' It is not impossible that they might be published, even read." The others acknowledged by involuntary glances that Mennister had spoken with unnecessary sharpness; but the little man took correction with humility.

"I do perhaps linger," he admitted, "over the not quite necessary preface to my story. I will now proceed to the point of it, which is very curious. Well, my tyre, you must understand, went really flat, and after having tried to ride, and descended to re-pump it every two or three minutes, I began to feel that my plight was a miserable one. I am not a good walker, and I was a very considerable distance from my cousin's house. Though I could have retraced my way, I had no idea of my whereabouts; I was in strange country where I had never been before. To increase my embarrassment, the sky was growing perceptibly darker, and I had that uncomfortable feeling of being overtaken and closed in upon, which I—and I find several of my friends also—often experience in open country when heavy rain is imminent. I was greatly cheered, therefore, to gather from certain indications—hewn-stone walls along the roadside, good though dilapidated iron gates into the fields, and two avenue-like rows of beech trees making a tunnel over the road—that I was skirting the boundary of a gentleman's demesne, and that it was not impossible that I should pass the gate. I walked quickly, wheeling my bicycle, and heard now and then a big drop of rain fall—plop—into the leaves above my head. Soon, sure enough, I did come to the gates: they stood wide open with an expression of real Irish hospitality—it is whimsical of me, but I do always feel that people's gates and door-posts have expressions—and I walked in, after a glance at the lodge: there was a trickle of smoke coming out of the chimneys, but the door was barred across and the windows shuttered. I remember thinking this curious.

"Along the avenue the trees were planted closer together, and it was as dusky as evening. It was overgrown with moss, too, so that I could scarcely hear my own footsteps, only the rattle-rattle of my bicycle. Judging from the width of the avenue, it must be a big place I was coming to; and how I did hope somebody in it would understand repairs, or perhaps lend me a bicycle, or even offer to drive me home in a trap or a motor! In England, of course, one would not think of this, but the Irish, I find, are always unconventionality itself."

"Quite," said Mennister.

"*I* entirely agree," said Bellingham.

"From now on," said the little man, looking at Bellingham, Lois, and Mrs Henneker, "I would like you to believe that all my impressions were distinct, quite distinct, but perhaps a little isolated from one another. In the intervals of these distinct impressions my mind was a little blurred; things slipped past it rather; as they do when one is tired, worried, or put out. I felt—"

"Oh, forgive me," Miss Eve vibrated, releasing Bellingham momentarily from her eyes, "but I *do* know how you felt, I *can* imagine! You felt an extraordinary sense of foreboding as you came up to that house with its great dark windows. You longed to fly, and something held you, gripped you, drew you in. You looked along the front of the house, expecting, expecting..."

"You had a sense of immanence," said Mrs Henneker authoritatively. "Something was overtaking you, challenging you, embracing yet repelling you. Something was coming up from the earth, down from the skies, in from the mountains, that was stranger than the gathered rain. Deep from out of the depths of those dark windows, something beckoned."

"Like in that poem of De la Mare's—"

"Exactly," said Mennister, again suppressing the young woman who had spoken. "It has been often described. Let Mr—Mr… er… proceed to the point of his story." His voice regretted that there was one.

"Well, no, do you know," said the little man politely, with the reluctance of a Washington, "I cannot say that I experienced, that I remember to have experienced, what you have described, though of course I possibly may have. I walked very quickly down the avenue and across the gravel sweep to the steps of the house, and I remember thinking humorously, as I hunted for the bell, that if the bell *were* out of order (as bells in Irish houses often are—the Irish don't mind, they are the soul of unconventionality)—that the noise my poor bicycle made coming across the gravel would quite sufficiently advertise our arrival."

"And what was the house like?" asked Lois. "Was it very obviously haunted? *Weren't* there any dark windows?"

"I don't quite understand you. Dark windows? I cannot remember that the windows looked any darker than windows seen from the outside, in daylight, usually do. I did not look in, of course. The house seemed very large and high. I heard a dog running on a polished floor and skidding, the way dogs do. The hall door was open, and I could swear I did hear the bell tinkle, somewhere down below, but still nobody came. I felt no more raindrops; the rain held off, but the air was cold and heavy with it, and the trees were very quiet. The place was completely and very closely encircled with trees, and it was all so quiet I could hear myself breathe. Only, now and then I heard the ping-pong of tennis-balls, somewhere beyond the trees, and people calling to one another in the game. Sometimes this sounded very clearly, sometimes as though a long way away. I guessed that they must be having a tennis-party, and I felt a little shy of presenting myself—unconventional as I knew they would all be—all dusty and in my cycling knickerbockers. So I propped my bicycle up at the foot of the steps, and presently, as no one came, I walked into the house. I had never walked into anybody's house like this before."

"And the hall?" they cried.

"Hall?" he repeated, looking at them mystified. "It was a very ordinary hall, like in other country houses. There was a window on the staircase, which sent down a little light; otherwise the place was dark."

"And the *smell?*"

"And the *sound?* Didn't you hear an echo. Hadn't you a queer foreboding? Didn't you want to go but yet have to go on?"

"Well, no," he hesitated, carefully considering. "I do remember that I felt a little awkward, coming in like that—well, even in Ireland people might have wondered. And the misapprehensions… these bad times, you know. Why, anybody seeing me suddenly might have shot me, in their impulsive, simple way. I was really worried, and I'm afraid I don't remember that I noticed anything particular. Well, the smell, yes. People evidently hung their mackintoshes there, and there were dogs in the house. I imagine, too, that they didn't throw away their old tennis-balls, but kept them somewhere on a tray, possibly for the dogs. I stood in the hall and coughed a little and rapped with my foot—like in a village shop, you know, when it is empty. I was very much ashamed of myself and felt very nervous, but I was really desperately worried about my poor bicycle and how I was going to get home. So I stood there, tapping with my foot."

"Yes," said Mennister, "exactly. But, my dear fellow, you're an expert in the finer forms of torture. Don't you see, we're…? tell us about the ghost. Something gripped you, rattled at you, made itself unpleasantly visible. For one who does not profess the modern manner—well, *mes compliments*—you've hit something quite distinctive for your *décor*. But all ghost stories have one of three possible climaxes, A, B, or C, and every climax has its complementary explanation. Get on to the climax, and I'll guarantee you the explanation pat—"

"Or is it possible he might care to finish his own story for himself?" suggested Bellingham, with detachment. "One never knows."

"Quite."

"Oh, *hush,*" appealed Mrs Henneker. "Won't both of you hush? We are so *intrigued*. And then?"

"Well, I just stood there, tapping with my foot. No one came. Then a door at the back of the hall opened, somebody looked out. It was a lady's figure, standing right against the light, so that I could only see her outline, which was tall and pretty. I said something, began an explanation, but without speaking she turned and went in again, leaving the door open. I—I don't know what came over me. I—I followed her in."

"Ah," said Bellingham, with appreciation. "Yes?"

"I followed her into a drawing-room, a back drawing-room, with an arch with a curtain over it, and a window looking out into some trees. It was nicely furnished, I thought, but a little sombre, because of the trees outside the window."

"And smells? And sounds?" cried Lois and Miss Eve, while the others peered curiously, as though through bars, at the little man who sat perplexed and baffled, knowing nothing of atmosphere.

He said at length: "It smelt chiefly of geraniums. I remember then, some fine tall plants in pots, standing on a table by the window. And the wallpaper smelt a little musty; I remember thinking as I stood there (among many other things) what an improvement central heating would have been. I looked round and could see nobody; then I heard sobbing, really a pitiful sound. Well, you may imagine—here was I, unintroduced, in a back drawing-room, really quite an intimate room, where I believe only favoured visitors are usually admitted, with a lady sobbing on the sofa. I saw her head move where I thought there was just a pile of cushions; it made me jump. The room received less and less light from the windows, probably because of the rain, which was now coming down heavily, and partly because of the thick lace curtains—really thicker than one cares for nowadays. I do not know for how long I listened; then I said (I remember saying it), 'My dear lady,' I said; 'really, my dear lady!' I felt so terribly sorry for her, do you know, I couldn't go away, though I had no right to be there, of course. I may say that I am not an impulsive person even for an Englishman, and that I am as a rule quite singularly loth to intrude. When she looked up I was quite startled—"

"—As though you had not known she had a face—"

"Why, ye-es, as though I had not known she had a face. She looked up at me, and her expression was—was like…"

"Drowning?"

"Drowning," he accepted, with a grateful side-glance. "Drowning, and I could do nothing for her. Do you know, it quite appalled me. I don't know whether drowning people are frightened: I submit that they are—I know I should be. I don't think that if my life did pass before me then, I should glance at it. I should be too much afraid, looking forward to all that was going to happen to me."

"No, to the world," amended Mrs Henneker, "to the whole of a world, your world. Because it is the quenching of a world in horror and destruction that happens with a violent death; just as one knows a whole world is darkened when one sees a child crying its heart out. Even a good death means a world quenched, but beautifully, like a sunset. So she looked at you like that—with fear?"

"Yes, fear. It was terrible. She had not a young face; the way she was crying was not young either. I am not a *nervous* man; I tell you that up to now I felt nothing but embarrassment. But I could not look away from her eyes. I did not wonder what she thought of me; it did not seem as though there were room for her to think. And she was looking at where I was, not at me."

"She was menaced…"

"Yes. It was terrible, more than distressing. It would have been no more than that if I had remained outside it, but I didn't. I make no bones about it—I was terrified. She made me feel the end of the world was coming, and I felt myself beginning to perspire all over, as I had not done the whole summer. I couldn't speak to her again; she—she…"

"Beat it back."

"Beat it back. I stood there, and she put down her face again, all wet, among the cushions that were crumpled and faded and smelt musty from even where I stood. So I went back into the hall, thinking only of one thing, to get away quickly before something had actually happened. Every step seemed dangerous—"

"—Like the House of Usher—"

"—Terribly dangerous. The hall was as empty-sounding as ever, and I rushed down the steps, seized my bicycle, and wheeled it as fast as ever I could down the avenue again, simply not caring if they did think I was a burglar or a Republican, and fired at me from the bushes. Once I paused for just a second to listen, and the tennis-balls had stopped, and the voices too. There was nothing to say where they had all gone. It was quite quiet."

"Except for the rain?"

"Yes, I heard the rain in the trees. The lodge was still shut up when I passed it; I was relieved at that—didn't want them to see me. Well, I just turned up my collar and trudged it. Nothing passed me, no conveyance, scarcely even a soul, except an old woman driving two cows—she looked at me queerly. Not a walk I should care to do again, wheeling a bicycle. Mercifully, the days were still longish; I got back to my cousin's before it was quite dark, and even so they were worried—I met them walking about on the avenue. They said (I remember), 'Well, you have been keeping up a pace, anyway!' and I was surprised to find myself panting, till I found I had done that big distance in under the two hours.

"I had a hot whisky at dinner, and told them where I'd been. I told them exactly, and my cousin seemed puzzled, kept on contradicting. 'No, no, you couldn't have been *there*. No houses along that road.' That irritated me; I made him get his motor map, and I traced where I'd been, every turn. Just where I expected there was a place marked Kilbarran, and I put my thumb on it at once and said, 'That's the house!' He laughed and said, 'That's impossible, there isn't a house there.' I said, 'Why?' and he said there hadn't been one for two years. 'Oh, there *was* one,' he said, 'and this marks it; this is an old map.' I can't tell you how angry I felt—for no reason. He said, 'There was a place, you see, until two years ago—very fine it was; then they came one night and burnt it, the winter before last. We had expected it would have gone sooner, and the Barrans—the people themselves—did too, though they never said a word. Those women went about looking green.'

"Well, he didn't say much more, and of course I didn't; but his wife sighed, then started off talking. She started talking about the people at Kilbarran—an old gentleman with two daughters, not young, and a gay, pretty niece who had been often there. She spoke as though they were dead; I rather assumed it, but asked. She said, 'Oh no; they're in Dublin, I think, or England.' I couldn't help saying she seemed to have rather lost interest in her old friends, and she looked at me (quite strangely, for such a practical woman) and said, 'Well, how can one feel they're alive? How can they be, any more than plants one's pulled up? They've nothing to grow in, or hold on to.' I said, 'Yes, like plants,' and she nodded. Then it was time for her to go and shut up the chickens."

"That illustrates exactly—"

"Quite."

But Mrs Henneker was silent, staring at the fire. She did not raise her lids when Lois rose, and only held her hand out, offering it vaguely in perfunctory valediction as others rose to go. Some one collected the little man and took him away quietly—in the confusion he protested, but was overruled. He lingered, looking round the room, and even escaped once and got half-way back to Mrs Henneker, his lips wide for further speech. But she was petulantly blind to him, and he was led away. When the rustle of departure had subsided and the street door down below had faintly slammed, the broken semi-circle drew closer together, intimately. They asked each other with raised eyebrows, "Whose importation?" And this remained unanswered; no one knew.

"Dunno," said Lois to the last inquirer. They all looked up expectantly at Mrs Henneker, but Mrs Henneker was silent. And the silence lasted, because Mennister was gone.

1977

THE RAISING OF ELVIRA TREMLETT

William Trevor

William Trevor (1928–2016) was born in Co. Cork and lived a great part of his life in the province. His works of fiction are highly acclaimed; he became a member of the Irish Academy of Letters and was appointed as Commander of the British Empire due to his literary talents, while he was the recipient of several awards and nominations for his accomplishments in the field of literature. Among his most notable works are *Two Lives* (1991), *Felicia's Journey* (1994), *After Rain* (1996) and *Death in Summer* (1998).

He was the author of more than eighty short stories, which were gathered in *The Collected Stories* (1992), among which are a few supernatural tales of fine literary artistry. In this respect, "The Raising of Elvira Tremlett" is a modern ghostly tale that takes place within the harsh life of a dysfunctional family harbouring secrets; this is an unsettling sorrowful narrative endowed with deep psychological insight about coping mechanisms, reality and delusion.

My mother preferred English goods to Irish, claiming that the quality was better. In particular she had a preference for English socks and vests, and would not be denied in her point of view. Irish motor-car assemblers made a rough-and-ready job of it, my father used to say, the Austins and Morrises and Vauxhalls that came direct from British factories were twice the cars. And my father was an expert in his way, being the town's single garage-owner. *Devlin Bros.* it said on a length of painted wood, black letters on peeling white. The sign was crooked on the red corrugated iron of the garage, falling down a bit on the left-hand side.

In all other ways my parents were intensely of the country that had borne them, of the province of Munster and of the town they had always known. When she left the convent my mother had immediately been found employment in the meat factory, working a machine that stuck labels on to tins. My father and his brother Jack, finishing at the Christian Brothers', had automatically passed into the family business. In those days the only sign on the corrugated façade had said *Raleigh Cycles*, for the business, founded by my grandfather, had once been a bicycle one. "I think we'll make a change in that," my father announced one day in 1933, when I was five, and six months or so later the rusty tin sheet that advertised bicycles was removed, leaving behind an island of grey in the corrugated red. "Ah, that's grand," my mother approved from the middle of the street, wiping her chapped hands on her apron. The new sign must have had a freshness and a gleam to it, but I don't recall that. In my memory there is only the peeling white behind the letters and the drooping down at the left-hand side where a rivet had fallen out. "We'll paint that in and we'll be dandy," my Uncle Jack said, referring to the island that remained, the contours of Sir Walter Raleigh's head and shoulders. But the job was never done.

We lived in a house next door to the garage, two storeys of cement that had a damp look, with green window-sashes and a green hall door. Inside, a wealth of polished brown linoleum, its pattern faded to nothing, was cheered here and there by the rugs my mother bought in Roche's Stores in Cork. The votive light of a crimson Sacred Heart gleamed day and night in the hall. Christ blessed us half-way up the stairs; on the landing the Virgin Mary was coy in garish robes. On either side of a narrow trodden carpet the staircase had been grained to make it seem like oak. In the dining-room, never used, there was a square table with six rexine-seated chairs around it, and over the mantelpiece a mirror with chromium decoration. The sitting-room smelt of must and had a picture of the Pope.

The kitchen was where everything happened. My father and Uncle Jack read the newspaper there. The old battery wireless, the only one in the house, stood on one of the window-sills. Our two nameless cats used to crouch by the door into the scullery because one of them had once caught a mouse there. Our terrier, Tom, mooched about under my mother's feet when she was cooking at the range. There was a big scrubbed table in the middle of the kitchen, and wooden chairs, and a huge clock, like the top bit of a grandfather clock, hanging between the two windows. The dresser had keys and bits of wire and labels hanging all over it. The china it contained was never used, being hidden behind bric-à-brac: broken ornaments left there in order to be repaired with Seccotine, worn-out parts from the engines of cars which my father and uncle had brought into the kitchen to examine at their leisure, bills on spikes, letters and Christmas cards. The kitchen was always rather dusky, even in the middle of the day: it was partially a basement, light penetrating from outside only through the upper panes of its two long windows. Its concrete floor had been reddened with Cardinal polish, which was renewed once a year, in spring. Its walls and ceiling were a sooty white.

The kitchen was where we did our homework, my two sisters and two brothers and myself. I was the youngest, my brother Brian the oldest. Brian and Liam were destined for the garage when they finished at the Christian Brothers', as my father and Uncle Jack had been. My sister Effie was good at arithmetic and the nuns had once or twice mentioned accountancy. There was a commercial college in Cork she could go to, the nuns said, the same place that Miss Callan, who did the books for Bolger's Medical Hall, had attended. Everyone said my sister Kitty was pretty: my father used to take her on his knee and tell her she'd break some fellow's heart, or a dozen hearts or maybe more. She didn't know what he was talking about at first, but later she understood and used to go red in the face. My father was like that with Kitty. He embarrassed her without meaning to, hauling her on to his knee when she was much too old for it, fondling her because he liked her best. On the other hand, he was quite harsh with my brothers, constantly suspicious that they were up to no good. Every evening he asked them if they'd been to school that day, suspecting that they might have tricked the Christian Brothers and would the next day present them with a note they had written themselves, saying they'd had stomach trouble after eating bad sausages. He and my Uncle Jack had often engaged in such ploys themselves, spending a whole day in the field behind the meat factory.

My father's attitude to my sister Effie was coloured by Effie's plainness. "Ah, poor old Effie," he used to say, and my mother would reprimand him. He took comfort from the fact that if the garage continued to thrive it would be necessary to have someone doing the increased book-work instead of himself and Uncle Jack trying to do it. For this reason he was in favour of Effie taking a commercial course: he saw a future in which she and my two brothers would live in the house and run the business between them. One or other of my brothers would marry and maybe move out of the house, leaving Effie and whichever one would still be a bachelor: it was my father's way of coming to terms with Effie's plainness. "I wonder if Kitty'll end up with young Lacy?" I once heard him inquiring of my mother, the Lacy he referred to being the only child of another business in the town—Geo. Lacy and Sons, High-Class Drapers—who was about eight at the time. Kitty would do well, she'd marry whom she wanted to, and somehow or other she'd marry money: he really believed that.

For my part I fitted nowhere into my father's vision of the family's future. My performance at school was poor and there would be no place for me in the garage. I used to sit with the others at the kitchen table trying to understand algebra and Irish grammar, trying without any hope to learn verses from "Ode to the West Wind" and to improve my handwriting by copying from a headline book. "Slow," Brother Cahey had reported. "Slow as a dying snail, that boy is."

That was the family we were. My father was bulky in his grey overalls, always with marks of grease or dirt on him, his fingernails rimmed with black, like fingers in mourning, I used to think. Uncle Jack wore similar overalls but he was thin and much smaller than my father, a ferrety little man who had a way of looking at the ground when he spoke to you. He, too, was marked with grime and had the same rimmed fingernails, even at weekends. They both brought the smell of the garage into the kitchen, an oily smell that mingled with the fumes of my uncle's pipe and my father's cigarettes.

My mother was red-cheeked and stout, with waxy dark hair and big arms and legs. She ruled the house, and was often cross: with my brothers when they behaved obstreperously, with my sisters and myself when her patience failed her. Sometimes my father would spend a long time on a Saturday night in Macklin's, which was the public house he favoured, and she would be cross with him also, noisily shouting in their bedroom, telling him to take off his clothes before he got into bed, telling him he was a fool. Uncle Jack was a teetotaller, a member of the Pioneer movement. He was a great help to Father Kiberd in the rectory and in the Church of the Holy Assumption, performing chores and repairing the electric light. Twice a year he spent a Saturday night in Cork in order to go to greyhound racing, but there was more than met the eye to these visits, for on his return there was always a great silence in the house, a fog of disapproval emanating from my father.

The first memories I have are of the garage, of watching my father and Uncle Jack at work, sparks flying from the welding apparatus, the dismantling of oil-caked engines. A car would be driven over the pit and my father or uncle would work underneath it, lit by an electric bulb in a wire casing on the end of a flex. Often, when he wasn't in the pit, my father would drift into conversation with a customer. He'd lean on the bonnet of a car, smoking continuously, talking about a hurling match that had taken place or about the dishonesties of the Government. He would also talk about his children, saying that Brian and Liam would fit easily into the business and referring to Effie's plans to study commerce, and Kitty's prettiness. "And your man here?" the customer might remark, inclining his head in my direction. To this question my father always replied in the same way. The Lord, he said, would look after me.

As I grew up I became aware that I made both my father and my mother uneasy. I assumed that this was due to my slowness at school, an opinion that was justified by a conversation I once overheard coming from their bedroom: they appeared to regard me as mentally deficient. My father repeated twice that the Lord would look after me. It was something she prayed for, my mother replied, and I imagined her praying after she'd said it, kneeling down by their bed, as she'd taught all of us to kneel by ours. I stood with my bare feet on the linoleum of the landing, believing that a plea from my mother was rising from the house at that very moment, up into the sky, where God was. I had been on my way to the kitchen for a drink of water, but I returned to the bedroom I shared with Brian and Liam and lay awake thinking of the big brown-brick mansion on the Mallow road. Once it had been owned and lived in by a local family. Now it was the town's asylum.

The town itself was small and ordinary. Part of it was on a hill, the part where the slum cottages were, where three or four shops had nothing in their windows except pasteboard advertisements for tea and Bisto. The rest of the town was flat, a single street with one or two narrow streets running off it. Where they met there was a square of a kind, with a statue of Daniel O'Connell. The Munster and Leinster Bank was here, and the Bank of Ireland, and Lacy and Sons, and Bolger's Medical Hall, and the Home and Colonial. Our garage was at one end of the main street, opposite Corrigan's Hotel. The Vista cinema was at the other, a stark white façade not far from the Church of the Holy Assumption. The Protestant church was at the top of the hill, beyond the slums.

When I think of the town now I can see it very clearly: cattle and pigs on a fair-day, always a Monday; Mrs Driscoll's vegetable shop, Vickery's hardware, McPadden's the barber's, Kilmartin's the turf accountant's, the convent and the Christian Brothers', twenty-nine public houses. The streets are empty on a sunny afternoon, there's a smell of bread. Brass plates gleam on the way home from school: Dr Thos. Garvey M.D., R.C.S.; Regan and Broe, Commissioners for Oaths; W. Drennan, Dental Surgeon.

But in my memory our house and our garage close in on everything else, shadowing and diminishing the town. The bedroom I shared with Brian and Liam had the same nondescript linoleum as the hall and the landing had. There was a dressing-table with a wash-stand in white-painted wood, and a wardrobe that matched. There was a flowery wallpaper on the walls, but the flowers had all faded to a uniform brown, except behind the bedroom's single picture, of an ox pulling a cart. Our three iron bedsteads were lined against one wall. Above the mantelpiece Christ on his cross had already given up the ghost.

I didn't in any way object to this bedroom and, familiar with no alternative, I didn't mind sharing it with my brothers. The house itself was somewhere I was used to also, accepted and taken for granted. But the garage was different. The garage was a kind of hell, its awful earth floor made black with sump oil, its huge indelicate vices, the chill of cast iron, the grunting of my father and my uncle as they heaved an engine out of a tractor, the astringent smell of petrol. It was there that my silence, my dumbness almost, must have begun. I sense that now, without being able accurately to remember. Looking back, I see myself silent in a classroom, taught first by nuns and later by Christian Brothers. In the kitchen, while the others chattered at mealtimes, I was silent too. I could take no interest in what my father and uncle reported about the difficulties they were having in getting spare parts or about some fault in a farmer's carburettor. My brothers listened to all that, and clearly found it easy to. Or they would talk about sport, or tease Uncle Jack about the money he lost on greyhounds and horses. My mother would repeat what she had heard in the shops, and Uncle Jack would listen intently because although he never himself indulged in gossip he loved to hear it. My sisters would retail news from the convent, the decline in the health of an elderly nun, or the inability of some family to buy Lacy's more expensive First Communion dresses. I often felt, listening at mealtimes, that I was scarcely there. I didn't belong and I sensed it was my fault; I felt I was a burden, being unpromising at school, unable to hold out hopes for the future. I felt I was a disgrace to them and might even become a person who was only fit to lift cans of paraffin about in the garage. I thought I could see that in my father's eyes, and in my uncle's sometimes, and in my mother's. A kind of shame it was, peering back at me.

I turned to Elvira Tremlett because everything about her was quiet. "You great damn clown," my mother would shout angrily at my father. He'd smile in the kitchen, smelling like a brewery, as she used to say. "Mind that bloody tongue of yours," he'd retort, and then he'd eye my uncle in a belligerent manner. "Jeez, will you look at the cut of him?" he'd roar, laughing and throwing his head about. My uncle would usually be sitting in front of the range, a little to one side so as not to be in the way of my mother while she cooked. He'd been reading the *Independent* or *Ireland's Own*, or trying to mend something. "You're the right eejit," my father would say to him. "And the right bloody hypocrite."

It was always like that when he'd been in Macklin's on a Saturday evening and returned in time for his meal. My mother would slap the plates on to the table, my father would sing in order to annoy her. I used to feel that my uncle and my mother were allied on these occasions, just as she and my father were allied when my uncle spent a Saturday night in Cork after the greyhound racing. I much preferred it when my father didn't come back until some time in the middle of the night. "Will you look at His Nibs?" he'd say in the kitchen, drawing attention to me. "Haven't you a word in you, boy? Bedad, that fellow'll never make a lawyer." He'd explode with laughter and then he'd tell Kitty that she was looking great and could marry the crowned King of England if she wanted to. He'd say to Effie she was getting fat with the toffees she ate; he'd tell my brothers they were lazy.

They didn't mind his talk the way I did; even Kitty's embarrassment used to evaporate quite quickly because for some reason she was fond of him. Effie was fond of my uncle, and my brothers of my mother. Yet in spite of all this family feeling, whenever there was quarrelling between our parents, or an atmosphere after my uncle had spent a night away, my brothers used to say the three of them would drive you mad. "Wouldn't it make you sick, listening to it?" Brian would say in our bedroom, saying it to Liam. Then they'd laugh because they couldn't be bothered to concern themselves too much with other people's quarrels, or with atmospheres.

The fact was, my brothers and sisters were all part of it, whatever it was—the house, the garage, the family we were—and they could take everything in their stride. They were the same as our parents and our uncle, and Elvira Tremlett was different. She was a bit like Myrna Loy, whom I had seen in the Vista, in *Test Pilot* and *Too Hot to Handle* and *The Thin Man*. Only she was more beautiful than Myrna Loy, and her voice was nicer. Her voice, I still consider, was the nicest thing about Elvira Tremlett, next to her quietness.

*

"What do you want?" the sexton of the Protestant church said to me one Saturday afternoon. "What're you doing here?"

He was an old, hunched man in black clothes. He had rheumy eyes, very red and bloody at the rims. It was said in the town that he gave his wife an awful time.

"It isn't your church," he said.

I nodded, not wanting to speak to him. He said:

"It's a sin for you to be coming into a Protestant church. Are you wanting to be a Protestant, is that it?" He was laughing at me, even though his lips weren't smiling. He looked as if he'd never smiled in his life.

I shook my head at him, hoping he might think I was dumb.

"Stay if you want to," he said, surprising me, even though I'd seen him coming to the conclusion that I wasn't going to commit some act of vandalism. I think he might even have decided to be pleased because a Catholic boy had chosen to wander among the pews and brasses of his church. He hobbled away to the vestry, breathing noisily because of his bent condition.

Several months before that Saturday I had wandered into the church for the first time. It was different from the Church of the Holy Assumption. It had a different smell, a smell that might have come from mothballs or from the tidy stacks of hymn-books and prayer-books, whereas the Church of the Holy Assumption smelt of people and candles. It was cosier, much smaller, with dark-coloured panelling and pews, and stained-glass windows that seemed old, and no cross on the altar. There were flags and banners that were covered with dust, all faded and in shreds, and a Bible spread out on the wings of an eagle.

The old sexton came back. I could feel him watching me as I read the tablets on the walls, moving from one to the next, pretending that each of them interested me. I might have asked him: I might have smiled at him and timidly inquired about Elvira Tremlett because I knew he was old enough to remember. But I didn't. I walked slowly up a side-aisle, away from the altar, to the back of the church. I wanted to linger there in the shadows, but I could feel his rheumy eyes on my back, wondering about me. As I slipped away from the church, down the short path that led through black iron gates to the street at the top of the hill, I knew that I would never return to the place.

"Well, it doesn't matter," she said. "You don't have to go back. There's nothing to go back for."

I knew that was true. It was silly to keep on calling in at the Protestant church.

"It's curiosity that sends you there," she said. "You're much too curious,"

I knew I was: she had made me understand that. I was curious and my family weren't.

She smiled her slow smile, and her eyes filled with it. Her eyes were brown, the same colour as her long hair. I loved it when she smiled. I loved watching her fingers playing with the daisies in her lap, I loved her old-fashioned clothes, and her shoes and her two elaborate earrings. She laughed once when I asked her if they were gold. She'd never been rich, she said.

There was a place, a small field with boulders in it, hidden on the edge of a wood. I had gone there the first time, after I'd been in the Protestant church. What had happened was that in the church I had noticed the tablet on the wall, the left wall as you faced the altar, the last tablet on it, in dull grey marble.

Near by this Stone
Lies Interred the Body
of Miss Elvira Tremlett
Daughter of Wm. Tremlett
of Tremlett Hall
in the County of Dorset.
She Departed this Life
30 August 1873
Aged 18.

Why should an English girl die in our town? Had she been passing through? Had she died of poisoning? Had someone shot her? Eighteen was young to die.

On that day, the first day I read her tablet, I had walked from the Protestant church to the field beside the wood. I often went there because it was a lonely place, away from the town and from people. I sat on a boulder and felt hot sun on my face and head, and on my neck and the backs of my hands. I began to imagine her, Elvira Tremlett of Tremlett Hall in the county of Dorset, England. I gave her her long hair and her smile and her elaborate earrings, and I felt I was giving her gifts. I gave her her clothes, wondering if I had got them right. Her fingers were delicate as straws, lacing together the first of her daisy-chains. Her voice hadn't the edge that Myrna Loy's had, her neck was more elegant.

"Oh, love," she said on the Saturday after the sexton had spoken to me. "The tablet's only a stone. It's silly to go gazing at it."

I knew it was and yet it was hard to prevent myself. The more I gazed at it the more I felt I might learn about her: I didn't know if I was getting her right. I was afraid even to begin to imagine her death because I thought I might be doing wrong to have her dying from some cause that wasn't the correct one. It seemed insulting to her memory not to get that perfectly correct.

"You mustn't want too much," she said to me on that Saturday afternoon. "It's as well you've finished with the tablet on the wall. Death doesn't matter, you know."

I never went back to the Protestant church. I remember what my mother had said about the quality of English goods, and how cars assembled in England were twice the ones assembled in Dublin. I looked at the map of England in my atlas and there was Dorset. She'd been travelling, maybe staying in a house near by, and had died somehow: she was right, it didn't matter.

Tremlett Hall was by a river in the country, with Virginia creeper all over it, with long corridors and suits of armour in the hall, and a fireplace in the hall also. In *David Copperfield*, which I had seen in the Vista, there might have been a house like Tremlett Hall, or in *A Yank at Oxford*: I couldn't quite remember. The gardens were beautiful: you walked from one garden to another, to a special rose-garden with a sundial, to a vegetable garden with high walls around it. In the house someone was always playing a piano. "Me," Elvira said.

My brothers went to work in the garage, first Brian and then Liam. Effie went to Cork, to the commercial college. The boys at the Christian Brothers' began to whistle at Kitty and sometimes would give me notes to pass on to her. Even when other people were there I could feel Elvira's nearness, even her breath sometimes, and certainly the warmth of her hands. When Brother Cahey hit me one day she cheered me up. When my father came back from Macklin's in time for his Saturday tea her presence made it easier. The garage I hated, where I was certain now I would one day lift paraffin cans from one corner to another, was lightened by her. She was in Mrs Driscoll's vegetable shop when I bought cabbage and potatoes for my mother. She was there while I waited for the Vista to open, and when I walked through the animals on a fair-day. In the stony field the sunshine made her earrings glitter. It danced over a brooch she had not had when first I imagined her, a brooch with a scarlet jewel, in the shape of a spider. Mist caught in her hair, wind ruffled the skirts of her old-fashioned dress. She wore gloves when it was cold, and a green cloak that wrapped itself all around her. In spring she often carried daffodils, and once—one Sunday in June—she carried a little dog, a grey cairn that afterwards became part of her, like her earrings and her brooch.

I grew up but she was always eighteen, as petrified as her tablet on the wall. In the bedroom which I shared with Brian and Liam I came, in time, to take her dragon's brooch from her throat and to take her earrings from her pale ears and to lift her dress from her body. Her limbs were warm, and her smile was always there. Her slender fingers traced caresses on my cheeks. I told her that I loved her, as the people told one another in the Vista.

"You know why they're afraid of you?" she said one day in the field by the wood. "You know why they hope that God will look after you?"

I had to think about it but I could come to no conclusion on my own, without her prompting. I think I wouldn't have dared; I'd have been frightened of whatever there was.

"You know what happens," she said, "when your uncle stays in Cork on a Saturday night? You know what happened once when your father came back from Macklin's too late for his meal, in the middle of the night?"

I knew before she told me. I guessed, but I wouldn't have if she hadn't been there. I made her tell me, listening to her quiet voice. My Uncle Jack went after women as well as greyhounds in Cork. It was his weakness, like going to Macklin's was my father's. And the two weaknesses had once combined, one Saturday night a long time ago, when my uncle hadn't gone to Cork and my father was a long time in Macklin's. I was the child of my Uncle Jack and my mother, born of his weakness and my mother's anger as she waited for the red bleariness of my father to return, footless in the middle of the night. It was why my father called my uncle a hypocrite. It was maybe why my uncle was always looking at the ground, and why he assisted Father Kiberd in the rectory and in the Church of the Holy Assumption. I was their sin, growing in front of them, for God to look after.

"They have made you," Elvira said. "The three of them have made you what you are."

I imagined my father returning that night from Macklin's, stumbling on the stairs, and haste being made by my uncle to hide himself. In these images it was always my uncle who was anxious and in a hurry: my mother kept saying it didn't matter, pressing him back on to the pillows, wanting him to be found there.

My father was like a madman in the bedroom then, wild in his crumpled Saturday clothes. He struck at both of them, his befuddled eyes tormented while my mother screamed. She went back through all the years of their marriage, accusing him of cruelty and neglect. My uncle wept. "I'm no more than an animal to you," my mother screamed, half-naked between the two of them. "I cook and clean and have children for you. You give me thanks by going out to Macklin's." Brian was in the room, attracted by the noise. He stood by the open door, five years old, telling them to be quiet because they were waking the others.

"Don't ever tell a soul," Brian would have said, years afterwards, retailing that scene for Liam and Effie and Kitty, letting them guess the truth. He had been sent back to bed, and my uncle had gone to his own bed, and in the morning there had begun the pretending that none of it had happened. There was confession and penance, and extra hours spent in Macklin's. There were my mother's prayers that I would not be born, and my uncle's prayers, and my father's bitterness when the prayers weren't answered.

On the evening of the day that Elvira shared all that with me I watched them as we ate in the kitchen, my father's hands still smeared with oil, his fingernails in mourning, my uncle's eyes bent over his fried eggs. My brothers and sisters talked about events that had taken place in the town; my mother listened without interest, her large round face seeming stupid to me now. It was a cause for celebration that I was outside the family circle. I was glad not to be part of the house and the garage, and not to be part of the town with its statue and its shops and its twenty-nine public houses. I belonged with a figment of my imagination: an English ghost who had acquired a dog, whose lips were soft, whose limbs were warm, Elvira Tremlett, who lay beneath the Protestant church.

"Oh, love," I said in the kitchen, "thank you."

The conversation ceased, my father's head turned sharply. Brian and Liam looked at me, so did Effie and Kitty. My mother had a piece of fried bread on a fork, on the way to her mouth. She returned it to her plate. There was grease at the corner of her lips, a little shiny stream from some previous mouthful, running down to her chin. My uncle pushed his knife and fork together and stared at them.

I felt them believing with finality now, with proof, that I was not sane. I was fifteen years old, a boy who was backward in his ways, who was all of a sudden addressing someone who wasn't in the room.

My father cut himself a slice of bread, moving the bread-saw slowly through the loaf. My brothers were as valuable in the garage now as he or my uncle; Effie kept the books and sent out bills. My father took things easy, spending more time talking to his older customers. My uncle pursued the racing pages; my mother had had an operation for varicose veins, which she should have had years ago.

I could disgrace them in the town, in all the shops and public houses, in Bolger's Medical Hall, in the convent and the Christian Brothers' and the Church of the Holy Assumption. How could Brian and Liam carry on the business if they couldn't hold their heads up? How could Effie help with the petrol pumps at a busy time, standing in her wellington boots on a wet day, for all the town to see? Who would marry Kitty now?

I had spoken by mistake, and I didn't speak again. It was the first time I had said anything at a meal in the kitchen for as long as I could remember, for years and years. I had suddenly felt that she might grow tired of coming into my mind and want to be left alone, buried beneath the Protestant church. I had wanted to reassure her.

"They're afraid of you," she said that night. "All of them."

She said it again when I walked in the sunshine to our field. She kept on saying it, as if to warn me, as if to tell me to be on the look-out. "They have made you," she repeated. "You're the child of all of them."

I wanted to go away, to escape from the truth we had both instinctively felt and had shared. I walked with her through the house called Tremlett Hall, haunting other people with our footsteps. We stood and watched while guests at a party laughed among the suits of armour in the hall, while there was waltzing in a ballroom. In the gardens dahlias bloomed, and sweet-pea clung to wires against a high stone wall. Low hedges of fuchsia bounded the paths among the flower-beds, the little dog ran on in front of us. She held my hand and said she loved me; she smiled at me in the sunshine. And then, just for a moment, she seemed to be different; she wasn't wearing the right clothes; she was wearing a tennis dress and had a racquet in her hand. She was standing in a conservatory, one foot on a cane chair. She looked like another girl, Susan Peters in *Random Harvest*.

I didn't like that. It was the same kind of thing as feeling I had to speak to her even though other people were in the kitchen. It was a muddle, and somewhere in it I could sense an unhappiness I didn't understand. I couldn't tell if it was hers or mine. I tried to say I was sorry, but I didn't know what I was sorry for.

In the middle of one night I woke up screaming. Brian and Liam were standing by my bed, cross with me for waking them. My mother came, and then my father. I was still screaming, unable to stop. "He's had some type of nightmare," Brian said.

It wasn't a nightmare because it continued when I was awake. She was there, Elvira Tremlett, born 1855. She didn't talk or smile: I couldn't make her. Something was failing in me: it was the same as Susan Peters suddenly appearing with a tennis racquet, the same as my desperation in wanting to show gratitude when we weren't in private.

My mother sat beside my bed. My brothers returned to theirs. The light remained on. I must have whispered, I must have talked about her because I remember my mother's nodding head and her voice assuring me that it was all a dream. I slept, and when I woke up it was light in the room and my mother had gone; my brothers were getting up. Elvira Tremlett was still there, one eye half-closed in blindness, the fingers that had been delicate misshapen now. When my brothers left the room she was more vivid, a figure by the window, turning her head to look at me, a gleam of fury in her face. She did not speak but I knew what she was saying. I had used her for purposes of my own, to bring solace. What right, for God's sake, had I to blow life into her decaying bones? Born 1855, eighty-nine years of age.

I closed my eyes, trying to imagine her as I had before, willing her young girl's voice and her face and hair. But even with my eyes closed the old woman moved about the room, from the window to the foot of Liam's bed, to the wardrobe, into a corner, where she stood still.

She was on the landing with me, and on the stairs and in the kitchen. She was in the stony field by the wood, accusing me of disturbing her and yet still not speaking. She was in pain from her eye and her arthritic hands: I had brought about that. Yet she was no ghost, I knew she was no ghost. She was a figment of my imagination, drawn from her dull grey tablet by my interest. She existed within me, I told myself, but it wasn't a help.

Every night I woke up screaming. The sheets of my bed were sodden with my sweat. I would shout at my brothers and my mother, begging them to take her away from me. It wasn't I who had committed the sin, I shouted, it wasn't I who deserved the punishment. All I had done was to talk to a figment. All I'd done was to pretend, as they had.

Father Kiberd talked to me in the kitchen. His voice came and went, and my mother's voice spoke of the sodden sheets every morning, and my father's voice said there was terror in my eyes. All I wanted to say was that I hadn't meant any harm in raising Elvira Tremlett from the dead in order to have an imaginary friend, or in travelling with her to the house with Virginia creeper on it. She hadn't been real, she'd been no more than a flicker on the screen of the Vista cinema: I wanted to say all that. I wanted to be listened to, to be released of the shame that I felt like a shroud around me. I knew that if I could speak my imagination would be free of the woman who haunted it now. I tried, but they were afraid of me. They were afraid of what I was going to say and between them they somehow stopped me. "Our Father," said Father Kiberd, "Who art in heaven, hallowed be Thy name..."

Dr Garvey came and looked at me: in Cork another man looked at me. The man in Cork tried to talk to me, telling me to lie down, to take my shoes off if I wanted to. It wasn't any good, and it wasn't fair on them, having me there in the house, a person in some kind of nightmare. I quite see now that it wasn't fair on them, I quite see that.

Because of the unfairness I was brought, one Friday morning in a Ford car my father borrowed from a customer, to this brown-brick mansion, once the property of a local family. I have been here for thirty-four years. The clothes I wear are rough, but I have ceased to be visited by the woman who Elvira Tremlett became in my failing imagination. I ceased to be visited by her the moment I arrived here, for when that moment came I knew that this was the house she had been staying in when she died. She brought me here so that I could live in peace, even in the room that had been hers. I had disturbed her own peace so that we might come here together.

I have not told this story myself. It has been told by my weekly visitor, who has placed me at the centre of it because that, of course, is where I belong. Here, in the brown-red mansion, I have spoken without difficulty. I have spoken in the garden where I work in the daytime; I have spoken at all meals; I have spoken to my weekly visitor. I am different here. I do not need an imaginary friend, I could never again feel curious about a girl who died.

I have asked my visitor what they say in the town, and what the family say. He replies that in the bar of Corrigan's Hotel commercial travellers are told of a boy who was haunted, as a place or a house is. They are drawn across the bar to a window: Devlin Bros., the garage across the street, is pointed out to them. They listen in pleasurable astonishment to the story of nightmares, and hear the name of an English girl who died in the town in 1873, whose tablet is on the wall of the Protestant church. They are told of the final madness of the boy, which came about through his visions of this girl, Elvira Tremlett.

The story is famous in the town, the only story of its kind the town possesses. It is told as a mystery, and the strangers who hear it sometimes visit the Protestant church to look up at the tablet that commemorates a death in 1873. They leave the church in bewilderment, wondering why an uneasy spirit should have lighted on a boy so many years later. They never guess, not one of them, that the story as it happened wasn't a mystery in the least.

1935

ENCOUNTER AT NIGHT

Mary Frances McHugh

There is not much information on the life of Mary Frances McHugh (1899–1955) except the fact that she was the daughter of the writer Martin J. McHugh (?–1951). To the lovers of Irish literature she is mainly known for her novel *Thalassa: A Story of Childhood by the Western Wave* (1931), whereas her tales of mystery and the macabre can be found in anthologies that were published in the 1930s.

"Encounter by Night" was included in *Thrills, Crimes and Mysteries* published by Associated Newspapers in 1935, but it was also reprinted in the 1995 anthology *Great Irish Tales of Horror: A Treasury of Fear* edited by Peter Haining (Souvenir Press, 1995). Noteworthy for its masterful storytelling, "Encounter by Night" is a little gem of horror and suspense in a modern setting. As the story escalates, the reader, just like the main character, is navigating an unknown realm of terror within the borders of an enclosed space, right up to a shocking denouement.

DUBLIN was growing deserted; only an odd car slid by in the dark, rainy night, for the second of its passing throwing a dazzle on the shiny pavements and lighting up the shuttered shops. Figures would pass, hurrying by with hunched shoulders—but less and less frequently.

Tom Donovan and his three friends scarcely felt the rain. They were hot and happy and bemused. All that each of them wanted was somehow to continue talking and drinking and smoking in genial company... But Jim, the red-haired barman at Flynn's, had bolted the doors against them. There was nothing for it but to go home.

"Take care of yourself, Joe!"

"Well, good-night, boys!"

"Take care—see you tomorrow!"

The milk of human kindness flowed in them, and they patted one another's backs affectionately again and again before each went his separate way. Donovan, the shiftless poet, was left standing on the pavement, last and lonely. Slowly there faded from his face its smile of convivial bliss, and into his sobering mind crept back those thoughts which now, with the fleeting years, possessed him more and more in his solitary moments.

Wretched, killing thoughts. No, not thoughts—not thoughts, but feelings—or one feeling only, corroding unhappiness. A sense that life was vain and empty, with comfort nowhere—not even in drinking, in friendship, or in love. If even he knew friendship or love! A certainty that never, during all his existence, even when he had been young and gay and roystering, had he known ease: always a shadow had been lurking at his elbow. And it whispered to him that he was a fool to go on with the sham from day to day, that there was only one solution to everything: a knife or a rope for his throat.

Cruel memories came thronging. He saw a miserable, beaten peasant child: himself. All that child had really known was suffering, though the man had made sweet lilting songs of a boy, barefooted, in the West, birds'-nesting or tickling for trout in a mountain stream. The boy had been there, the sun, the stream, the idyllic sky, the irrational light-heartedness of childhood. These were the stuff of his verse—but not the harsh home, the pain and puzzled grief, the cold and hunger which had been more true and near. These things had made him!—they were with him even now.

Later, there was the man. A poet he was now, praised and wondered at for the clear innocency of his songs, toys fashioned for the cultured mind by a queer bohemian fellow. That he was so different from his poetry merely gave it zest. He knew this, and cultivated his oddity; and it was partly to curry favour with his admirers that he drank and sang his way through Europe without a word of any language but his own.—Here, standing on a Dublin pavement in the night, he recalled the troubadour adventure and shivered—not because the steely rain was stinging his face and sending cold arrows through his clothing. No; but because from those wanderings from which he had so triumphantly returned he could now remember only a haunting horror. He evoked without willing it a night in Russia, when he lay in a country tavern with his familiar spirit beside him. There, in a big common room, several poor travellers slept about the stove. The air was humid with their breath and the odorous damp of their clothing, and the windows were sealed to blindness by the snow outside. In the yard there suddenly arose the commotion of a sledge being unharnessed; a bulky figure stepped into the room and looked stealthily around at the sleepers and fixedly at him, Donovan, before flinging itself likewise down in a corner. Donovan through half-closed eyes saw the stranger's Mongolian face, and as though he were a child it smote him with its mystery of a locked mind, of a race other than and alien to his own. There was no reason for his sudden panic of fear, or for the anguish of loneliness which overcame him then. It was simply part of the encompassing oppression of the world to his soul, driving him whither he knew not.

He tossed his head, heedless to the rain, appealing to the sky above him to protect and save. There must be rest somewhere, a cooling of this fever: why should he, more than other men, be so tormented? Why could he not be like little Terry Shaughnessy, caring nothing for anyone, whether drunk or sober, in funds or out of them?—Now, there was an idea! Why go back, in this mood and in this weather, to his cold room and unwelcoming bed, when Terry would be glad enough for him to drop in for a smoke and a talk? He'd be there, sure enough, in his attic in Eustace Street. He wouldn't be in bed. Who ever heard of little Terry being in bed? He'd have a warm fire, and maybe a taste of something—"one for the worms", as he called it... Donovan turned towards Eustace Street.

He trotted along mechanically, now thinking cheerfully of himself and Terry. They were the only bachelors among the boys—and taking it all in all, he'd swear they were as well off like that. He thought of Ned Buckley's wife, and grinned to himself. A nice exhibition she made of the poor man, running to his newspaper office or writing to the editor when she wanted money. Ned was a good sort—but what kind of man was he to put up with that? Now, if any woman tried to manage *him*—! Or Terry: he'd swear Terry would know how to deal with her, too. Keep a firm hand. That was it.

Yet, maybe—Terry as well as himself—in their hearts they'd like to have a home, and a woman waiting for them, and children. Maybe they'd die in the workhouse, no one caring enough for them to follow them to the grave... At these sad thoughts Donovan's mouth turned down again behind his coat collar, and he felt nearly dismal enough to cry. But resolutely he clung to the advantages of his state. He was his own master, anyway. He could drop in on Terry like this, tonight, and Terry be welcome to drop in on him, any hour he liked.

The rain beat on his face, stood in tears on his eyelashes till the street lamps carried a halo, each of them. Then he blinked and shook his head, and the long, deserted street shone straight before him again. A clock struck twelve. Ah, here was Terry's door. God, it was good to get in out of the rain!

The door stood ajar. That saved ringing the bell. Probably someone had left it like that on purpose—goodness knew how many lived in the old rookery. Not a glimmer of light. But Donovan felt his way to the banisters, gripped them, and mounted, cautiously counting the stairs.

Terry's door was opposite the fourth turn. Two... three... The next one... *Mother of God, what was that?*

Someone, coming out of the darkness, had struck him softly. A blow of a doubled-up fist in the face. Like a joke, by the Lord! But where had the fellow got to?

"Who's that?" called out Donovan, his voice a little startled in the night. "Who's there? What the blazes are you doing?"

There was no answer. Donovan crouched a moment in the darkness, very still, then changed his walking-stick to the other hand. But he must have been flustered, for his fingers didn't catch on it, and down it went clattering again, staying finally where it was. He stopped and groped, but thought better of going back for it. He stared about him and in the blackness thought he saw a solider patch, a man facing him a couple of steps up. That was the man who had struck him. But why on earth didn't he say something?

"Who's there?" he shouted again. "Speak up, whoever you are!"

There was no answer, so he stepped forward boldly. But again someone pushed him—pushed him so plainly, as though with a playful gentleness, that he could feel the woollen jacket of the shoulder thrust against him. As in indignant alarm he tried to grasp it, it silently eluded him, moving soundlessly, eerily, out of reach.

Donovan's blood crept in his veins, and his heart seemed to lunge downwards in his body. Suddenly he wished he felt steadier, that he hadn't had so many drinks. Then he thought instinctively how another good stiff whiskey would hearten him—yes, give him fire to tell this sly fellow, whoever the hell he was, what he thought of him.

He paused and gasped, listening with all his ears. Not a sound could he catch; and swiftly changing mood, convinced that it was only some silly trick being played on him, he became wildly angry.

"Come on!" he shouted, his excited voice falling back to the cadence of his native West. "Come on, you puppy! Come on, you coward you, if you're a man at all, and I'll wrastle you in the Connemara fashion!"

He bent down over his right knee in an attitude of defence. "I'll fight you! I'll wrastle you!" he repeated belligerently.

For a few seconds he held up his fists, awaiting his assailant. But the latter did not move. Then, like a bull, Donovan made to rush up the stairs. *Ah!*—With a soft thud he struck his head into the stomach of the lurking enemy. The invisible man, silent and unshocked, moved stealthily away.

But Donovan followed him, and as he did so was surprised to find the other coming towards him. He flung away caution and grasped his man about the body. Something rigid but yielding, human yet cold, lay unprotestingly within his arms. He released it and stepped back, weak and shuddering.

It swung—it hung... Ah, God!

Donovan recoiled, as sober as at morning. For a full minute he waited where he stood, overwhelmed with a nameless dread. Then he struck a match and, peering up, saw above him the blackened face of little Terry Shaughnessy, hanging from his attic banisters...

1990

A GHOST STORY

Mary Beckett

Mary Beckett (1926–2013) was a Northern Irish author born in a Catholic family in Belfast. Her first notable literary success was her winning a BBC short story competition in 1949. She contributed tales to several literary magazines while working as a teacher, but in 1956 she got married and moved to Dublin and the demands of her new family life as well as her having entered a totally new environment did not enable her to continue pursuing a writing career at that point in her life. However, in 1979 she resumed her writing and she published the short story collections *A Belfast Woman* (1980) and *A Literary Woman* (1990), along with the novel *Give Them Stones* (1987). Her works were distinguished by subtle feminist and political concerns while she has been ingeniously described by her fellow Northern Irish author Brian Moore as "an extraordinary miniaturist of ordinary lives".

"A Ghost Story", included in the collection *A Literary Woman*, is a domestic horror tale in which the supernatural agent disrupts the ostensibly safe environment of a young couple, mirroring the discrepancies in their relationship; while at the same time it demonstrates the author's ability to merge the ordinary with the extraordinary and the mundane with the uncanny.

THE house was a cause of dissension between them from the first. Fiona said her father would buy them a house for their wedding present, as he had done for her three sisters. He was a builder, of the kind who drove round in a polished Rover and wore gloves while he inspected his sites. He not only had money now, but his people had been rich for generations which was a source of wonder to Fintan. It was one of the things that attracted him to Fiona. She appeared to him as some aureate butterfly that he hoped to pin down. But he was not going to sponge on his father-in-law. He insisted they must buy their own house.

"Don't be ridiculous," Fiona said. "All your money will go on paying for the house and mine will go on housekeeping and we'll have nothing to spend. I thought we'd have a lovely life together, but not if you insist on this."

"We have to pay our way first if I'm to have any self-respect," Fintan said, surprising himself.

"Such a peasant attitude," she teased.

"Oh well you can take the man out of the bog but not the bog out of the man," Fintan quoted his father, a big handsome school-inspector who was given to such dicta.

"I'm not discussing turbary rights," Fiona laughed, and he laughed back, but the problem remained, holding up their wedding until an agent told him one day that he could sell him a house for twenty-five thousand pounds. It had been on his hands for several years—he just wanted rid of it. He'd settle for twenty-five thousand. It was a modest detached house built in the sixties and never lived in for more than a few months at a time because it was said to be haunted. But since Fintan was a modern young man who wouldn't heed such womanish nonsense he could pick up a bargain. Fintan said he'd have to consult Fiona and the agent raised his eyebrows and turned down the corners of his mouth.

Fiona thought the house was cute in a way but the rooms were smaller and the ceiling lower than anything she'd been used to. Besides, the kitchen was just a small square with a sink unit and the main bedroom had doors across one alcove by way of a built-in wardrobe. Fintan thought she was using these complaints as excuses, that she was really worried about the ghosts. He pointed out that if the house had been old he could have understood ghosts, but since the house the two old ladies were supposed to have lived in had been completely razed and this one built on the site he didn't see how ghosts could have survived. If it would make Fiona any easier in her mind they could get a priest, he was sure, to come and bless the place. Fiona scoffed at him, "You know I don't go along with all that mumbo-jumbo."

"I'm never too sure about you," Fintan said. "You roll out with your family every Sunday like a dutiful daughter."

Fintan himself lived in a flat, having been asked by his father to leave home because he wouldn't go to Mass. "I'm not criticising your religion or the lack of it," his father had said. "It is your own affair. And as far as the Almighty is concerned I'm sure you are just one of the flies flattened on the wind-screen. But your mother sees things differently and I'm not going to have you worrying her Sunday after Sunday."

"I can't be dishonest," Fintan protested. "I've got to make my own statement. I can't pretend, just to please my mother."

"There's many a better man than yourself did just that all his life and maybe got to heaven at the heel of the hunt. But if you won't, just take yourself off quietly to a flat of your own. Say it's to leave more room at home for your brothers. But leave her in peace and don't have her saying Rosaries night after night in bed when she thinks I'm asleep."

"She was always religious. It's not just for me."

"Until you began troubling her she never said Rosaries when I was in the bed," his father stated, and Fintan had moved out with no recriminations anywhere.

He found the wedding awkward from that angle—a huge number of guests, a plethora of priests, and Fintan had to explain beforehand that he would not receive Holy Communion. Fiona did, devoutly to all appearances, but during the honeymoon she neglected Mass, not mentioning it at all. It was their economic approach to life that provided a series of surprises for both of them. Even though they earned similar salaries, prices meant entirely different things to each. Fintan looked forward to coming back to his own house where he was sure their lives would blend better.

He had had no objection to presents of carpets and furniture from his rich in-laws, but his tastes were different and he saw no reason to keep quiet about that. Fiona wanted him to accept gifts quietly, whether the suites were too big or the patterns too striking. He complained that he had to live with them and she'd have to adjust herself to smaller rooms. He went round auction rooms and bought small pieces of old furniture. One he had especially loved was a walnut desk with moss-green leather on the writing place, and little drawers with wooden handles all delicately turned and never a nail or a rough edge to be seen. He gave it to Fiona for a present but her offhand acceptance hurt him. He borrowed a spade from a brother-in-law and tackled the front garden. It was stony and grey. A neighbour stopped in passing and advised him that he'd never grow anything in that barren patch unless he got a few loads of topsoil and manure as everyone else had done. "What is topsoil?" Fintan wondered, but assured the neighbour that he'd see about it and stood the spade in the garage with relief.

When the house was more or less painted and furnished they decided to have a house-warming. They agreed that a brunch party some Sunday would suit and they'd have their own friends, leaving out all the middle-aged people who were at the wedding. On the Friday before the party they got an anonymous letter in the post telling them they ought to know that their house was haunted by the two old ladies knitting. They laughed, passed the letter to each other across the table, relishing it, and argued over who should bring it into work to share the joke there. In the end Fintan took it, with Fiona agreeing to wait until Monday.

The brunch was not really a success. They had thought that the party would begin around noon and end about four in the afternoon, but nobody went home until all the wine had been drunk and by then it was nearly eleven o'clock at night. Fintan enjoyed that, but Fiona was annoyed because things didn't turn out as she had expected. Besides, a close friend of Fintan's, whom she was meeting for the first time, disliked her and took every opportunity to sneer at her cooking, her decorating, her wealth and her father's wealth. Fiona laughed it off so that nobody else felt uncomfortable and to divert them she produced the anonymous letter and handed it around. People started talking about haunted houses they had heard of, at a distance. They all agreed a new house could not possibly be haunted, although somebody said, "How about the air waves?" One girl had heard her grandfather tell of a cottage in the bog. The man who lived alone there brought in his friend to visit after they left the pub. They drew up their chairs to the fire and a third chair drew up from the far wall on its own accord.

"I see, James, you have company tonight," the friend said.

"That, John," said the owner of the house, "is company that I am seldom without."

Fiona, watching Fintan listening intently, was resentful that he should seem so detached from her, and when at last the guests took themselves off she attacked him. "How could you let him insult me all day? You could easily have made him stop. Anyway, I don't know how you could even have liked such an ill-mannered creature." Fintan shrugged and rubbed his cheek with his hand. Glaring at him, Fiona could feel, as his fingers did, the warm dry skin of his face. She wanted to put her cheek against the broad plane of his forehead. "You don't love me at all," she complained, and went into the sitting-room to collect more glasses. Fintan looked, a bit helplessly, at the mess of dirty serving plates on the kitchen table. He was annoyed that Philip hadn't liked Fiona but he hadn't blamed Philip. Fiona was his wife; therefore she should have been in herself pleasing to his friend. It was awkward that they didn't like each other. He supposed they were jealous since they were both attached to him. What, after all, was love? His mother loved him, of course. That was natural. Mothers love their children. And, he assumed, his father loved his mother—all that business of protecting her from worry about him. He didn't feel like protecting Fiona. She was a big girl, clever, rich. It might be the way he felt after making love successfully, but then when she found him inadequate he felt like slitting her throat. She came into the kitchen, clattering glasses. "We'll have to knock down that wall between those two rooms," she said. "I can't bear that little poky room. It gives me claustrophobia."

Fintan protested. "We've just painted the whole place white to give you space. We're not going to start knocking down walls. Anyway, it's a supporting wall."

"Come in and I'll show you what we could do," she said, putting her two hands on his arm and feeling him tense against her.

"What idiot turned on the television?" she exclaimed when they were at the sitting-room door. The sound had gone wrong. On the screen was an old-fashioned room with a coal fire in a black iron fireplace and an old lady sitting in a rocking chair knitting and talking vigorously, but it was impossible to make out a word she was saying. "Somebody's been fooling with the buttons," Fiona said. "Turn it off."

"It's not on," Fintan said exultantly. "The plug's out."

She gripped his arm then but he didn't notice; he was concentrating hard on the picture and on the strange light old voice. She was a fine-looking old lady with white straight hair brushed back into a bun at the nape of her neck. She wore little gold-rimmed glasses and a black skirt and blouse with a jet rectangular brooch at the throat. She put down her knitting and took up a hank of wool, spreading it round her knees to wind it into a ball. She had a black shiny apron with a black frill all the way round. The rocking chair moved as she wound the wool. Above the rockers the wooden frame was composed of little carved pillars and the seat was like a deckchair seat, only made from some kind of carpet material. Gaslight came from two globes on curved arms from the wall above the fireplace. The fire itself was only slightly red, not blazing, not reflected in the brass fire irons on the black iron fender. Opposite the rocking chair was a wing chair and a figure in it practically hidden and silent, perhaps sleeping.

They stood watching, transfixed, until the picture faded. Fiona whispered, "The two old ladies knitting," and then they both corrected that, "But it was a man. In the big chair it was a man." They were quite sure, although when the picture was there it had been impossible to see. Fiona was trembling. Fintan was nervous but exuberant, wanting to telephone their friends and tell them, unable to stay still. Fiona suggested that they continue clearing up, that maybe it hadn't happened, she didn't really believe it had happened. It was the wine they had drunk during the day. It was late when they went to bed, Fiona reluctantly, as if there was thunder in the air. They lay stiffly on their backs, not touching.

For several nights after that they stayed out of the house until late and hurried to bed without looking into the sitting-room, but everything seemed quiet and gradually, without mentioning it to each other or to anyone else, they pushed it to the back of their minds. Fiona even brought up the idea again of knocking down the wall between the two rooms. Fintan said no. Fiona thought her father could be consulted before they scotched the idea out of hand. Fintan said no, it was his house and nothing at all to do with her father. He had bought a haunted house so as to owe nothing to her father and he wasn't going to backtrack now over a silly notion of hers. "That wall stays up," he shouted, thumping against it.

The television screen flickered and bright horizontal lines ran from the bottom to the top. The unintelligible commentary began before the picture settled. This time the woman was on her knees at the rocking chair which had come unstuck and had lurched to the side away from the fire. The little pillars that held the top part of the chair to the rockers were out of their sockets and she was trying to fix them in. When she got one in another hopped out. The man still sat silent in his big solid chair. After a time she began to cry, a childish cry which increased in volume until it was a terrible wail, on and on. "God," Fiona breathed, but Fintan gripped her arm and she put her hands over her mouth. Eventually it all faded, the crying persisting for some seconds after the picture went.

"I can't stand this," Fiona said. "I can't live here."

Fintan was too shaken to hear what she said. During the next month they saw the quiet scene several times, so that Fintan said he was growing quite fond of the old lady. Fiona didn't answer him. Then one night the kneeling woman appeared again, and the broken chair and the same crying. Fiona said, "Do something, can't you. Don't just stand there." Fintan spread his hands helplessly and she rushed into the kitchen and came back carrying a stool. He grabbed at her arm and said, "Don't, you can't," but she whirled the stool at the television set, smashing it through the screen and dealing it blow after blow. Fintan felt outrage at the ugly look on Fiona's face and at the wrong use of the sturdy little pine stool with "Made in Poland" printed in black under the seat. When she turned triumphantly to him, still brandishing the stool, he felt frightened for a moment that she meant to attack him. Instead she said, "There! That's settled it. How long would you have stood there before you realised some action was called for? The active sex! God Almighty!"

"The set was rented. How are we going to pay the company?" Fintan said.

"Money again. I'll pay if you're so upset."

"You just may. You broke it." He put the broken set out with the dustbin the following Friday and they had no more television and no more ghostly films.

Fiona was careful to be gentle, having frightened herself with her demonstration of violence. She acquiesced in whatever Fintan wanted, even when he suggested that it would be better if they went out separately now and again to avoid feeling suffocated. They didn't talk about their experiences, but as the weeks went by they relaxed and settled amicably enough together. Then they were invited to a party given by Fintan's friend Philip. Fiona said she wouldn't go; Fintan could make what excuse he liked but she would spend the evening in comfort at home in her parents' house. They wanted her to stay the night in her own old room, all aired and beautiful with its white carpet and mirrored wardrobes and old mahogany bed. They didn't like her driving home to an empty house, probably cold. Fiona laughed, said she did it quite often, and drove off before they persuaded her otherwise. The house *was* cold. It looked cramped and ordinary, just cheap. The bed hadn't softened yet into any degree of cosiness, and she lay reading for an hour before trying to sleep. A full moon shone in on her face when she turned to the window, so she curled up with her back to it. She was restless, missing Fintan, and she told herself resentfully that she'd probably be just asleep when he would come in and waken her. Then she heard the childish crying downstairs and listened in horror until it reached a crescendo of that frightful wailing. She started to cry herself, "God, God," huddling under the quilt. As soon as the noise downstairs died away she got up and dressed, gabbling to herself, grabbed her bag and car keys and drove back to her parents' house. Fintan, coming back at four o'clock and seeing the empty tossed bed, felt only relief that he wouldn't have to justify the lateness of the hour or the fact that he was not sober.

Fiona insisted that the house be sold and every stick of furniture in it. She had no wish to break up their marriage. She would live with him in a flat or wherever he liked, but not with anything out of that house. In the meantime she stayed with her parents and Fintan was lucky enough to get the loan of a flat from a friend who was in America on a training course. Selling the furniture they had got from her family gave him no trouble and he forced himself to part with the pieces he had bought, but not with the walnut desk. He told Fiona it was hers, but she exclaimed in horror that she couldn't even look at its little carved pillars and knobs without seeing the rocking chair, that she'd never live in any house it stood in. He brought it to the flat and polished it lovingly.

They met for lunch or parties or concerts. They were still married, just temporarily without living quarters, only celibate for the moment. When a possibility came up of a job in Saudi Arabia he asked her would she come if he got it and she, tired of the ambiguity of her position, agreed, providing he brought nothing pertaining to the house. He called to explain his plans to his parents and found his father alone.

"There aren't any ghosts in the desert," Fintan laughed.

"What?" his father said. "With all those mutilations and executions? You amaze me."

Fintan mentioned his attachment to the desk.

"Give it to your mother," he was told.

Fintan laughed. "What on earth would she want with it?"

"She is not illiterate, you know," his father retorted, and Fintan hurried to apologise that he had not meant to imply that.

"She will care for it because you gave it to her. God knows none of you have given her much, with all your fine jobs."

"You didn't give her much yourself," Fintan said, rattled. "Nothing but the daily paper when you have done with it."

His father tapped him on the shoulder. "Your mother and I understand each other. Don't take it on yourself to worry about us."

"Such arrogance," Fintan thought, but he took his father's advice about the desk and was rewarded by his mother's obvious delight. He even managed to sell the house at a small profit to an American who was interested in ghosts.

"You don't realise how very lucky you are," his mother-in-law told him one day when he called for Fiona before she was ready. She was an elegant woman, partly due to expensive clothes and hair, partly to her very slim figure. He found himself hoping that Fiona would fine down eventually and look like her.

"You have both been given a new chance," she went on. "One fright does nobody any harm and you have lost nothing at all. You must have had somebody's prayers," she finished with an ironic lift to one eyebrow.

"You don't like me," he said. "You never thought me good enough for Fiona. Just because I'm not rich."

"My dear Fintan, there are none of us as rich as people think. Fiona has had a good salary up to now—she didn't need a rich husband. But you are not a kind person. I always wished for my daughters that they would marry kind men. Kindness lasts even if the couple are no longer in love." Fintan smiled that she should use such a term, and she accused him, "You are not kind to Fiona."

"She is not always kind to me," Fintan answered back childishly. "Her voice has a very unkind edge to it at times." His mother-in-law shrugged, and when Fiona came into the room he glared at her so that the happy look on her face slid away. Later on in the evening she asked if it was worthwhile her going out to Saudi Arabia with him at all if he didn't really want her. He said, "Oh please do, Fiona. I couldn't bear it if you didn't."

One evening before they left he paid a visit to the house. He had already given up the keys but the American had said it wasn't sensible to move in before the fall. The house didn't look a bit sinister, just slightly pathetic, even though all their curtains had been sold in the deal and still hung at the windows but a little stiffly because no one had touched them for weeks. Fintan regretted the loss of the house, the loss of his status as a citizen and resident with responsibilities in the community. He would even have tackled the garden, he thought, standing and looking at the stony soil with starving ragwort and a couple of frail poppies as its crop. The limestone rock was only two feet down, a neighbour had said, but on this patch it seemed to be breaking through. At least in the desert the sand would cover the bones. He didn't really mind the poor old ghosts. He could have lived with them, even though the crying was hard to take. But then all crying was hard to take. He thought of Fiona and the brightness gone so rapidly from their life. The sadness shook him so that his legs trembled and wouldn't move out of the garden. Sweat broke out on his neck and head even though it was a cool evening for early September with a bank of mist along the foot of the mountains. He reached out to steady himself and held on to the iron railing he'd painted black after they moved in. The spasm passed and he let go, but when he saw a black stain on the palm of his hand he scrubbed at it in panic. Once he had shut himself into the security of his car he wondered had Fiona felt like this during previous emanations while he didn't, and if so was she in this way and, who knows, perhaps in other ways a protection to him. He could manage to be kind, he was sure, if he practised, if that would please her and keep her with him, especially in a strange country with no friends and no position other than as his wife. The street lamp glowed red, suggesting dusk, and he switched on his own lights and drove away from the house, only very slightly shaken now, to meet Fiona in town.